Raggedy Panties

Raggedy Panties

By

Lawanda Howard

Cover photo by Charlie Pizzarello

ISBN 1-58500-336-0

About the Book

"*Raggedy Panties*" is the story about one woman's journey to self-realization.   It's centered around the life of a young, upwardly mobile, nubile female, Carmen Layfield.   It tells the story of her obsession with the relationship with the man of her dreams, Kyle Sealy, and the showdown between her and "the other woman", her arch nemesis, Robbi Gant.   It goes on to depict how she deals with the constant pressures of her roller coaster relationship.   She is enlightened when she is challenged to admit truthfully to herself about her own behavior in her relationships of romance.   She discovers an innovative method for helping herself deal with the high expectations and pressures of society with regard to the relationships between men and women.

Many books have been published that focus on male bashing and what the male's contribution is to a demised relationship with a woman.   What makes "*Raggedy Panties*" unique is that it candidly addresses the *female* and her undeniable contribution to a man's behavior and the outcome of her relationship with him.   It exposes what females do from the outset, and beyond, to lay a foundation for disappointment in the quest for happiness with a man.   In addition, "*Raggedy Panties*" offers an innovative *solution* for women for identifying and solving ones own emotional problems associated with a relationship of love or obsession...*especially when you're just too ashamed to tell anyone else!*

Katherine, nice meeting you.
It was really a wonderful person!
You are truly the nice.
I hope you enjoy the Occasion!

Dream and Rise to the Occasion!

Lamar
5/1/08

PH: 770-987-7999
LAWANDA S LAMAR GOLAR

Acknowledgements

I would like to start by giving God all the praise and the glory! For without Him, nothing would be possible. With Him, *all* things are possible. Because of Him, I am.

I would also like to thank my extremely loving and supportive family. The Lord blessed me with the greatest parents, Jasper and Henrietta Howard, the most wonderful brothers, Gerald and Kent, and my best friend, my beautiful sister, Vertrina. I would be remiss if I did not give much love and thanks to my awesome grandmother, Carrie Bell Callier. Thank you all for your unconditional love, for believing in me and encouraging me to follow my heart and my dreams. I love you all so much!

Much love and gratitude is extended to all my friends. I would like to make special mention of the following comrades: Logan Holt, we have been friends since forever. You know me like the back of your hand. You know how so very valuable your friendship has always been and will always be to me. Thank you for being such a cheerleader and making me believe. Cynthia Bowles, you are truly my dear friend. Thank you for *always* being there for me for whatever. I don't know what I would have done or would do without you. Kelvin Walker, thank you for listening to me complain about my problems and for helping me to see that I could make lemonade out of lemons. I would also like to extend very special thanks to Michelle Price, Michelle Holley, Mary Turner, Katrina Rolle, Cathy Goings, Jewell Smith, Andre' Staten, Leila and Leon Grant, and Zane Tankel... thank you all for all the encouragement and never giving up on me. And finally, I would like to say thank you to my dear friend, Felicia "Star" Gardner, who is no longer with us. Thank you for sharing your dreams with me and giving me the courage and encouragement to complete this project. I can still hear you saying, "Damn, La, you *actually* did it!"

Chapter 1

"I'm always late! Nicolette Vaughn is going to kill me. She told me two weeks ago what time her flight was going to get in. I should have prepared better. But oh well, she just needs to be happy her butt doesn't have to spend forty dollars on a taxi. That's it, I feel better already about being late. I just hope her plane is a little late so I don't have to feel *so* bad. Come on light, *change!* OK, OK, five minutes, I'll be at the curb. I'll only be, let me see...thirty-five minutes late! Lord, I'm dead meat."

Carmen was racing through traffic to get to the Philadelphia airport. She was slightly stressed as she was trying to make up some time because she unable to leave work when she had originally planned. Nevertheless, she was ecstatic that it was Friday and that the workweek was over. She was about to enjoy the weekend to the fullest with her best friend, Nikki, who was arriving from Chicago to hang out with her for the next couple of days to relax and to just enjoy the wonders of life. She smiled to herself and took a deep breath as he reached over to turn up the volume on her radio. The sound of the upbeat music was a great mood setter.

"Look at that loud outfit. That must be Nikki," Carmen thought to herself as she swerved her freshly washed Green Silver, turbo charged, convertible SAAB alongside the curb where her best friend of ten years was standing.

With suitcases at her side, hands on her size-eight hips, shades on top of her head, and the I'm-gonna-kill-you stance, Nikki walked to the edge of the curb to meet Carmen as she got out of the car. "Carmen Layfield, you are the sorriest excuse for a friend I've ever seen," Nikki said as she smiled and reached out to embrace a smiling and excuse-giving Carmen.

"Hey, Girl! I'm sorry I'm late, but traffic was heavy. I didn't get a chance to leave work until late. You know how it is on Fridays," Carmen offered as she began to help Nikki put her bags into the trunk of her car.

"So Carmen, do you rehearse your excuses for being late or is that the same one you use all the time?" Nikki joked.

"Hold up, Missy, I was trying to be late on purpose to give you a chance to change that neon outfit you're wearing before I take you to happy hour," Carmen retorted with laughter.

"What's wrong with my outfit? You liked it when I first bought it. Don't you recognize it? Remember?...It's the lime green pantsuit outfit I bought last year at *Harrods* when you and I went to London on a shopping spree. Remember how we convinced ourselves that we needed instant therapy and that shopping was the only cure for our so-called depression."

"Yes, I do remember. We had a *great* time getting un-depressed. Girl, we came home broke!" Carmen said as she shut the truck. "That outfit sure *brightened* your day," Carmen said with a chuckle.

"I like my outfit. You're just jealous. Anyway, you can't talk...You look like a walking fruit basket with that multi-colored sundress that I'm praying you did not wear to work today. And I was just about to ask you if those were shoes you were wearing or if you recently had orthopedic surgery," said Nikki in her usual sassy tone, while laughing at her own humor. "You like my new hair cut?" she continued as she gestured her head forward smoothing the hair down to her neck with her fingers.

"Your new haircut? You mean Halle Berry's haircut. Yes girl, I like that "new" one-in-a mil'.., I mean, million-in-a-million look. I'm just kidding. It's cute. Now, get your behind into this car and let's go. Since it's hot, you want me to put the top down?" Nikki looked at Carmen like she had to be kidding, given she had just talked about her hairdo. But then Nikki thought about it for a second. "Hey, it is the summer. It is the weekend... Drop the top!"

———————

Carmen and Nikki were anxious to get back downtown to attend happy hour at the new jazz club, Jazz-matazz. It was supposed to be the new hot spot in town for young professional singles. They both were professional women in their late 20s.

Carmen worked for an advertising firm, Atkins and Darmas as an Artistic Designer. Although she had a degree in Mathematics, she discovered very early on that while she was extremely analytical, she favored her right-brain dominance. She was very creative, had an eye for detail and also had excellent interpersonal skills. She was well respected at the firm. Many of her projects had generated significant revenue for the organization. While she did not mind her ideas contributing to the success of the agency, she knew she would eventually like to experience the gratification of seeing *her* own name associated with *her* talent rather than Atkins and Darmas.

Nikki was a Certified Public Accountant and loved her job. She just knew someday she would land a rich husband and her money management talents would make them even wealthier.

"It's only 7:30p.m. It's still light out here," Carmen said as she pulled into the parking lot of Jazz-matazz.

"Well, that gives me time. Give me a comb," said Nikki. "My hair is whipped. I can't go in there looking all raggedy. There might be some fine rich man inside waiting to meet me," she said as she began to fix her hair while looking into the rear view mirror.

"It doesn't matter. If you find a man, you don't live here. So you would just be his part time woman. You'd be "Nik, the Chick... on-the-side," Carmen said laughing.

"Please! Once that man meets me, I'll have him dealing pink slips to these locals and he'd be buying me a one-way ticket to come here to be with him."

"In your dreams, Nik. Hurry up with the mirror."

After about thirty minutes of primping, Carmen and Nikki

proceeded to enter the club.

The crowd was thick. Because people were standing around mingling, seats were a little easier to find. People, men and women, were noticing them as they walked across the room. They were both very attractive and visibly well kept.

"OK, OK, pinch me. Did I die and go to heaven? Carmen, this place is a gold mine," whispered Nikki. "So tell me one more time, why don't you have a man?"

"Waiting for the right one," Carmen answered.

"Take your pick. Look at these fine bodies…in suits! Ooh, ooh, Carmen, look over there by the band. Now he's gorgeous. Girl, is the air on in here? Is it hot or is it me?"

"Settle down, Nik. We just got here. Let's order you something cold to drink to cool your hot butt down," Carmen said as she signaled for the waiter who was headed in their direction.

"May I take your orders?" the waiter asked as he approached their table.

"I'll have a Tom Collins with grenadine," Carmen replied. Nikki leaned over to the waiter. "What's that gentleman's name standing by the band? The tall one with the dark suit and red tie, and no ring on his finger?"

"That's Stephen Bradshaw. He's part owner of this club."

"Part owner! OK, you can take my order now. I'll have a Stephen Bradshaw with grenadine," Nikki joked. "I'm just kidding. I'll have a Strawberry Daiquiri."

"Thank you ladies, I'll be right back with your drinks," said the waiter as he left their table.

"Carmen, how does this sound...Nikki Bradshaw?"

For a moment, Carmen was confused about what Nikki was asking until she remembered the name of the gentleman Nikki had recently inquired about. "Sounds like you have lost your mind. You've married the man before you've met him, or before he has met you for that matter. Why are we women like that?" Carmen chuckled. "We see a man who looks good, appears to be single, appears to have money, appears to be straight, appears not to be on parole, appears not to be an axe murderer...and then

4

we do a sound check on his last name with our first name, and mentally have and name our kids before we know the first thing about him."

Nikki gave Carmen a look like, "what *else* are you supposed to do?" She looked around the room as if she were sizing up the selection of men. Then she replied, "Sad, but true. But, I tell you, Carmen, if I find a man where I can check all of these things on the list, then call me Mrs. Right for Mr. Right."

"You won't get any arguments from me. I'm looking for Mr. Right, too. We have a lot to offer, so we deserve to be happy. I just think that it's hard to find a man with everything. I'm only twenty-seven. I want to be married before I turn thirty, so I need to find someone quick, fast, and in a hurry!"

Nikki gestured her hands as if she were waving a wand around the room. "Well, Carmen, you seem to be living in the land of plenty. I'm sure you won't have any problems. Since I will only be here for another couple of days, I need to work a little faster. If I get lucky, I might have to come and visit you a little more often.

"Whatever happened to Kevin?" Carmen asked remembering that Kevin was Nikki's last relationship project.

"Kevin is just too slow. I need more excitement. I mean he's a *really* nice guy, but he's boring with a capital 'B'. I need drama. Girl, can we talk about something else?…The thought of him makes me sleepy." Nikki mimicked yawning as she patted her hand against her opened mouth. "Let's enjoy the weekend."

--- *Chapter 2*

It was 7:30a.m., Monday morning. Carmen was almost dressed for work. She was sort of dragging because of her busy weekend with Nikki. They covered every inch of Philadelphia, it seemed. Carmen had to be in the office by 9:00a.m. She had showered and bumped her shoulder-length hair with the hot curlers. She continued her Monday morning ritual by putting on a Gospel CD.   It was her way of up-lifting her spirits and strengthening her mind in preparation for another workweek. This morning she was in the mood for some Kirk Franklin. She adjusted the volume so that she could hear the music from her bedroom where she continued to get dressed.

Standing in her closet in her underwear and pantyhose, Carmen began to sort through her suits in an effort to select something that fit her mood for the day. Today she felt kind of sassy and confident. She usually felt this way on Mondays since she had the responsibility of leading the Monday-morning roundtable meetings at the agency.   She wanted to create a persona of leadership to her superiors.   She knew she was intelligent and talented, but wanted to make sure she got the recognition she felt she deserved in the form of a title and compensation.

Carmen gave "Blue Monday" a new meaning. She ended up selecting her periwinkle blue suit with the tapered, above-the-knee length skirt. The jacket was tailored to fit. It had four buttons down the front with the top button starting a couple of inches above her cleavage. She accessorized with silver jewelry. A sleek pair of accenting Anne Klein sling back pumps completed her ensemble. She finished her makeup as she sang along with the Gospel music. She decided to tone down her lipstick, it was a bit too bright. She wanted a promotion, not a proposition.

Carmen completed her ritual by giving her completely

7

dressed, size-six, 5'6" stature one last glance in the full length mirror on her closet door. She examined herself from all angles for the final approval. With a wink and a smile at herself, Carmen grabbed her Coach bag and matching Coach briefcase and proceeded to leave her house for work at 8:35a.m.

"Darn it, I'm going to be five minutes late if I don't rush. I'm always late," Carmen thought to herself as she weaved in and out of Monday-morning traffic to get to her downtown office. She only lived twenty minutes from work, but her office suite was on the 15th floor, so she had the elevator traffic to contend with as well. She had taken this assignment in Philadelphia only a little over a month ago. Coming from New York City, she thought she could master the routine in Philly with no problem. However, she had not yet perfected her routine. She instantly began thinking of excuses and rehearsing them in her head in case she arrived late.

Carmen checked her watch as she parked her SAAB in her favorite spot. It was 8:55a.m. She grabbed her briefcase and purse from the back seat and began her sprint. Her meeting was not going to really get started until 9:30, but she wanted to be at her desk at 9:00 to do last minute preparation. As she made a mad dash for her last hope for a timely elevator, she noticed the doors reopening as if someone had seen her coming and pressed the OPEN button in the elevator to allow her to get on. She leaped into the elevator dropping her keys. The doors closed behind her and there he was. In front of her very eyes was Mr. Drop-dead Gorgeous!

"Good Morning," Carmen said in a breathless voice. "Thanks for holding the door for me."

"It was my pleasure, Miss...?" the man said as he kneeled down to pick her keys up off the floor.

"Carmen. I mean Layfield. I mean my name is Carmen Layfield," she said nervously as she gazed at what she swore to be a gift from heaven. "And you are...?"

"I'm Kyle. Kyle Sealy. It's very nice to meet you."

Carmen remembered she had not pressed the button to her floor. As she reached for the panel to press floor number 15, she noticed that floor number 8 was lit.

"Let me get that for you," Kyle suggested. "What floor?"

"15 please," Carmen answered trying not to sound like this was information she wanted him to remember although she wanted him to lock it on the brain. Kyle reached around her to press 15. She got a sniff of his cologne. She recognized the scent. It was Issey Miyake, one of her favorite fragrances! She then thought to herself, "This man *smells* good and he *looks* good. The dark suit, white shirt and power tie are definitely in order. But now I have to make sure he passes the ultimate test before I decide I want to be interested." The elevator made a couple of stops on the way up allowing her a little more time to make her assessment. She glanced down to get a look at Kyle's shoes. To Carmen, this would tell the story. "Whew! Praise the Lord," she thought. "The man has some taste." Kyle had passed the all-important shoe test!

The elevator had reached the 8th floor before Carmen could start any more conversation. She could tell that Kyle found her attractive. She didn't want to come across too anxious, but she knew she wanted to find out more about "Mr. Right". She felt like she had something to work with...she knew what floor he worked on. As the doors began to open, Carmen thought to herself, "I don't *know* if this man works on the 8th floor or that he works here *at all*."

"It was nice to meet you, Carmen. Perhaps we can do lunch soon," Kyle said as he stepped off the elevator, holding the doors open.

"I'd like that, Kyle. It was very nice meeting you also."

Carmen watched him as he walked to his office before the doors closed in front of her. She was on cloud 99. Soon she had reached her floor. She reached in her purse searching for her security badge when she got off the elevator. She was so nervous, the receptionist buzzed her in before she located it.

"Hi, Phyllis. Thanks for letting me in," Carmen said panting.

9

"Did you have a good weekend?" Phyllis asked.

"I had a great weekend. My girlfriend, Nikki, was in town. We had a blast! I was feeling a little tired driving in, but for some reason, I feel rejuvenated now," Carmen said as she continued to her desk. "See ya' later, Phyllis."

Carmen rushed to her desk. She threw her purse into her desk drawer and began to pull out the overhead slides for her meeting from her briefcase. She began checking her voicemail while she gathered her material. There was a message from Nikki. She was just calling to thank Carmen for a great weekend and asked that she call her once she got a chance.

Carmen quickly skimmed through her notes for the meeting. She felt prepared. She went through her checklist one final time. As Carmen glanced at her watch, she noticed it was 9:15. She was dying to call Nikki to tell her about Kyle, but she knew she couldn't tell her everything in fifteen minutes. Although she had met Kyle for only two minutes, she knew talking to Nikki would, at least, be a thirty-minute conversation. Details, she would have to tell Nikki all the details. Carmen was bubbling, but she knew she had to stay focused on work.

At 9:25, Carmen dashed off to her meeting.

After her meeting, Carmen checked her calendar for appointments. She was happy to see that she didn't have any meetings or customer calls until the afternoon. She was dying to call Nikki. She wanted to wait until lunch hour, but was about to burst in doing so. She checked her watch. It was now 11:15a.m. She got up from her desk to try to locate a vacant conference room so that she could have some privacy since her cubical was surrounded by people. She realized how she knew everyone else's personal business just by listening over the walls. She didn't want to generate any Monday morning scoop about her personal life for the listening ears around her. She was a relatively private person around the office.

She quickly located a conference room. She checked the sign-up sheet to make sure no one had the room reserved.

"Great. This room is vacant until 1:00," Carmen thought to herself. She took a deep breath and quickly began to dial Nikki's work number.

Nikki answered her phone. "Good Morning... Nikki Vaughn."

"Hey Nik. Ya' got a minute to talk?"

"Yeah, What's up?"

"Girl, sit down."

"What? What?" begged Nikki.

"I met him!" exclaimed Carmen.

"You met who?"

"My Husband!"

"What!"

"Nik, I met the man I'm going to marry," said Carmen with confidence.

"Stop the madness....what did you spike your orange juice with this morning?"

"Nik, listen," Carmen said ecstatically. "This man is tall, gorgeous and *FINE*. Whew! I can't stop panting."

"Hold up, is this Carmen Layfield I'm talking to?" Nikki said sarcastically. "Given that you didn't mention this man this past weekend when I was there, I take it that you've only met him since I left. And given your state of mind at the present, I would say that you just met him *real* recently. Now, is this the same woman who sat up in Jazz-matazz and preached about how we meet a man and marry him without knowing squat about him?...OK, I'm through preaching...gim'me the scoop!... What about the visual?" asked Nikki with a sense of urgency.

"Well, he's tall, handsome, well dressed, well-groomed, wears nice shoes, has pretty teeth, masculine...nice ass..., and *no* ring!" said Carmen.

"Hold up. He's that fine and not married. He must be gay. Did he look like he was losing weight?"

"I don't think so. He didn't seem real muscular, but he's not a stick man either. I also watched him kneel down to pick up my keys when I dropped them. It was a masculine kneel. I checked out his walk when he got off the elevator. It's very masculine, too. Besides, he's too fine. He was making eyes at me," said Carmen. "Gay men don't make eyes at women ...unless they are trying to pick up a few beauty tips," she joked.

"OK, OK, what about the audio?" asked Nikki begging for more details.

"Yes, he can articulate the English language. I didn't hear any *had dids*, *had wents and had cames*. And his voice sounded masculine, smooth and sexy!"

"So far, so good. Well, break it to me gently, is he working?...You know, like employed and making a lot of money?"

"Nikki, you are such a gold digger," Carmen said playfully. "I think he is an attorney. He got off the elevator onto the floor where the legal offices are."

"You *think*! How do you know he's not the receptionist?" joked Nikki. "Men do get hired for those positions, ya' know."

"You are so crazy," Carmen said laughing.

"I need to do a little more digging. When I find out everything, you will be the first to know. Welp ... gotta go. I'll call ya' later."

"OK, Dick Tracy," joked Nikki. "Talk to you later." Click.

Carmen now felt like she was on a mission. She was determined to find out everything she needed to know about Kyle. She was nubile, he appeared available. She was certain she had found Mr. Right. She had already mentally given birth to and named their two children. She returned to her desk. It was now 11:30. Her message light on her phone was blinking. She had two new messages. Her first message was regarding her afternoon appointment. She was informed that the deadline for one of her projects had been moved up and needed to be completed by the end of the day. She immediately removed herself from the euphoria she was experiencing surrounding Kyle. She was now in work mode. She began to plan in her head how she could juggle her schedule to ensure that the project was completed as requested and also in a quality fashion. She loved being challenged at work. She viewed it as an opportunity to showcase her professionalism and dedication. It was her goal to do well and advance quickly in the firm. She listened to her second message. It was a message from Kyle. He wanted to know if she was available for lunch today at noon. He requested a call back. Carmen gasped. She was extremely flattered that Kyle had taken the time to locate her and her number. This was confirmation that he was interested. She began to debate with herself about playing hard-to-get versus accepting the lunch offer. She also knew she had an afternoon deadline to meet at work. Although, she began thinking that her deadline would give her an excuse to rush lunch with Kyle if he turned out to be uninteresting. "But what if I like him?" Carmen thought. After a couple of minutes of debating with herself, she elected to call him to ask for a rain check.

Reluctantly, Carmen dialed his number to give him the "bad" news about her unavailability for lunch. His voicemail picked up. 'Hello, you've reached the voicemail of Kyle Sealy. I'm not available at the moment. Please leave a message and I'll return your call by the end of the business day.'

Carmen sighed as she listened to his voice. She thought his voice was sexy and very masculine. "Hello, Kyle. This is Carmen. I just got your message. I was calling to tell you I won't be able to make lunch today. Perhaps you've left already. Please call me and let me know if tomorrow is good for you. Let's say around noon. Hope to talk to you soon. Bye."

She began to fantasize about her anticipated lunch date with Kyle. She imagined what he would look like. She could envision him gazing at her and smiling with approval. She smiled to herself. She felt confident Kyle would call her back and accept her lunch proposal. She immediately began to plan her attire.

The ringing of the phone snapped Carmen out of her daze. "Hello, this is Carmen," she answered. It was her manager. "Carmen. Glad I caught you before you headed out to lunch. Listen, I need to meet with you to discuss the deadline for this afternoon. I'd like to meet with you this afternoon around 1:30."

"Sure, Jim. I'll be there," she said. Carmen was now glad she had declined lunch with Kyle. She would now have to use her lunch hour to work on meeting the deadlinefor her account. She decided to just grab something to eat from the vending machines on her floor.

At almost 1:30, Carmen was successfully rapping up meeting her end-of-day deadline. She felt productive and promotable.

Her phone began to ring. She purposely didn't answer it because she didn't want to get tied up before her 1:30 meeting. She waited for the message light to began blinking so that she could check the message. She privately wished it was Kyle returning her phone call. As she began to input her password, she took a deep breath. It was Kyle. "Hi Carmen, this is Kyle. Sorry I missed your call. I missed your company for lunch today. I would love to have lunch with you tomorrow, but I already have plans. However, I'm available for dinner tomorrow. Let's say around 7:30 if you are available. I can pick you up at your place if that's not a problem. Just call me back and let me know."

Carmen melted from the phone message. She didn't have much time to savor the moment because she had to make her meeting on time and in the right frame of mind. Besides, she would have the entire evening to think about Kyle and all day tomorrow before their date. She made a note to herself to call him back to confirm and to provide directions to her apartment.

--- Chapter 3

It was now the next day. Carmen fantasized about Kyle during her commute to work.

She was very interested in Kyle. She felt like yesterday was her lucky day. She hardly got a wink of sleep last night... She was on the phone all night with Nikki and with her mother telling them how she knew it was only a matter of time before she would be married. She was convinced that fate had brought her from New York to Philadelphia and fate had put her on the elevator at just the right time to meet Kyle.

With no time to waste, Carmen put her things down shortly after arriving to work and walked up to Phyllis's desk. She began to ask questions about Kyle.

"OK, Phyllis, I need the scoop. What's the deal on this guy in the building? His name is Kyle Sealy." Phyllis began to smile as she recognized Carmen's interest in getting closer to him. Phyllis knew who Kyle was because he was handsome and popular. "Why are you smiling?" Carmen asked.

"No reason, I don't like to get into other people's business."

"Come on Phyllis! What, What? Is he married?" begged Carmen.

"No, he's not."

"*And...*" said Carmen with frustration.

"And nothing."

"Phyllis, I got it, he's an axe murderer, right?" Carmen joked.

Phyllis laughed at Carmen's humor, but was still reluctant to supply any information. It was obvious to Carmen that she wanted to. Phyllis was the typical receptionist type...full of information, but careful about whom they gave it up to. Carmen knew that Phyllis wasn't withholding information about Kyle because she was interested in him for herself. Phyllis was middle-aged with gray streaks in her hair. She was also slightly overweight. She was attractive, neat and well manicured. She did, however, do serious overload with her jewelry. Her jewelry seemed somewhat ostentatious. Carmen looked at Phyllis sort of like the mother type who was also one of your best girls. "I thought I was your girl, Phyllis. You're always asking why I don't have a man. I'm trying to get one and you won't help me."

"Carmen, you're so young and so pretty. You have a lot going for you. I have no doubt you will have the man who's right for you someday."

Phyllis' response was very little consolation to Carmen. "Uh huh. Well I think I found the man who is right for me just yesterday."

"Why do you think so?" asked Phyllis.

"I can just look at him and tell," replied Carmen.

"Really?" said Phyllis. "How do you know that there aren't other women who have just *looked* at him and thought they had found their Mr. Wonderful as well? He must be wonderful if all he has to do is get women to *look* at him and be considered the man of their dreams. Is that why women fall head over heels for him?"

Suddenly, another possibility hit Carmen. "He has a girlfriend?"

"Well, all I know is he's not hurting for attention," said Phyllis.

"So does he have a girlfriend?"

"Why don't you ask him?"

"I will when I get a chance, but I need some heads-up information now. Please, Phyllis, tell me."

"OK girl, you didn't hear this from me. He used to date this girl in his office named Robbi. I know they were engaged at one time. I'm not sure what happened ... I don't think they're engaged any longer, but I see them talking to each other from time to time on the deck. She does seem to be hot on his trail. She doesn't let too many women get close to him. I can already tell you…she is not going to like you…you look like the kind of woman Kyle would like.

"What's the deck?" asked Carmen.

"It's just a place off the building's cafeteria where people go to take breaks and socialize."

"OK, so what else?"

"That's all I know. Since she still loves him, you're going to have a hard time getting around her without his help."

"Why do you think that?" probed Carmen.

"I don't know, just intuition I guess. You know how women can tell when a woman is sick over a man. We've all been there."

"So, this Robbi woman isn't dating anyone else?" asked Carmen hoping for the answer to be yes.

"Not to my knowledge. She may be hoping that she and Kyle can work things out."

"OK, one more question. Does Kyle still love her?"

"Child, who knows what goes on inside a man's head. That really may be a question you ought to ask him. Good luck on getting the truth."

Phyllis' response made Carmen even more curious about Kyle and Robbi. As she was gearing up to ask more questions, Phyllis' phone rang. "Good morning, Atkins and Darmas Advertising Agency, how may I direct your call?"

Acknowledging that Phyllis couldn't talk any longer, Carmen mouthed, "Thank you", as she began to walk back to her desk.

Carmen sat at her desk processing the information Phyllis shared about Kyle. Although she had obtained many answers, she had so many other questions like, What does Robbi look like? How old is she? How tall is she? What's she like? The only thing Carmen could imagine was a woman who was as beautiful as Kyle was fine. Never mind what was in the woman's heart, Carmen wanted to know immediately what the woman looked like. Wanting desperately to go back to Phyllis to get more information, Carmen elected not to. She didn't want to appear childish and desperate. She decided to concentrate on the information she did have ... a woman named Robbi who worked in Kyle's office and who can be seen occasionally talking with him on the deck. Carmen looked at her Day-

Planner; she had a lot of work to do. Even still, she felt like she had to make time to run downstairs to scope out the deck. She grabbed some money from her purse so that she could be prepared to buy something from the cafeteria in order not to look suspicious.

As Carmen began to leave her desk, her phone rang. It was Phyllis. "Robbi is usually on the deck at 10:30 with her friends."

Chapter 4

Like a scene from *Columbo*, Carmen approached the deck with wondering, yet inconspicuous, eyes. The collection of accurate clues was key to her investigation. She knew her face would be the focus of attention to onlookers. New faces always attract attention. Therefore, she had to be smooth and her motive for being on the deck could not be easily detected. Ignorance would be her excuse in the case of a slip-up. After all, she was new in the building.

Upon entry onto the deck, Carmen noticed the crowd was sparse. She looked around for a group of women. There was a huddle of women standing around and two older men. Carmen figured she was early. It was only 10:20a.m. She decided she should probably buy something *now* so that she could blend in with the others. She decided on a bagel and tea.

"So, how are you today?" Carmen asked the gentleman behind the checkout counter as she gazed out over the deck.

"I'm fine. That'll be $1.50, and how are you? You must be new here. I haven't seen your pretty face around here before."

"This is my first time on the deck. I've only been in this building for about two weeks. It's pretty nice here actually."

Trying not to be rude, Carmen rushed to pay the cashier so that she could cut the conversation short and proceed to seat herself where she could have a clear view of all the women who came in.

It was now 10:30. Carmen couldn't really stay at the deck too much longer, she did have a job that paid her to be a designer, not a detective. Growing slightly impatient, she started to gather up the remains of her bagel she had torn into several pieces as she waited nervously for "Miss America". Suddenly, Carmen heard laughter and there were three women entering the deck. Her heart rate began to increase. Which one of these women, if either, was Robbi? So far so good, neither one of them seemed to be anything like she had envisioned. One of them was 5'2" and weighed about 250 pounds. "Strike one," Carmen thought to herself. The second one was an older lady who looked to be in her 40s. "Strike two," she thought. The third one was very thin and looked rather matronly. "This couldn't be her either," Carmen thought. "If this is her, then I should have no problem."

Although Carmen had ruled out any competition among the three women she had seen, she still needed confirmation. This wasn't as easy as she thought. She took a mental picture of each of the women thinking she could get a positive identification from Phyllis when she got back upstairs. As she began to exit the deck, she noticed a woman entering with a man. This woman didn't seem to be the catch of the day either. She was wearing a tight blue suit that showed off her figure. She seemed to have a nice body even though she didn't appear to be the most stylish woman in the world. She had a hairdo which looked to be the product of a close encounter with pink sponge rollers…With a little moisture it could have been a "gerry curl". Nevertheless, the woman did appear somewhat professional in her demeanor. Carmen thought the woman was one of those people who liked to kiss-up to get ahead. Yet, the woman exuded confidence. Carmen could imagine that this woman thought she was fine enough to have a man as fine as Kyle. Although not certain, Carmen felt this woman was probably Robbi. Even though Carmen wasn't particularly impressed with the woman, she did find her somewhat threatening. Noticing the time, Carmen thought she'd better head back up to her office. The woman seemed to notice her as she began to leave. She caught the woman checking her out from head to toe. In case the woman was Robbi, Carmen added a little more strut to her walk to show off her confidence, as well.

As the day progressed, Carmen grew anxious to have her highly anticipated date with Kyle. She had many questions. She hoped that Kyle wouldn't cancel. It was almost time for Carmen to leave when her phone rang. It was Kyle calling to confirm their date. Kyle agreed to pick Carmen up at her apartment like they had planned, at 7:30p.m.

It was now about 6:30p.m. Carmen had showered and put on most of her make-up. She had on her short silk robe with her hair pinned on top of her head. She stood in her closet sifting through several outfits as she tried to decide what to wear. She wanted to be impressive. One of her choices would show off her figure, but seemed a little suggestive. Another outfit was nice and conservative, but seemed too boring. Decisions, decisions. Carmen wasn't panicking yet. Since they were only going to a Bar and Grill type restaurant, she settled on her black Calvin's and blouse she could tuck inside to show off her butt. She accessorized with a nice black belt and her black Via Spiga sandals. When she removed the pins from her hair, it fell nicely into place. Her hair was bouncy and full. Staring at herself in the mirror, Carmen decided to add her final accessory, her diamond stud earrings. She felt these added the elegance she needed to go with her casual attire.

Carmen was nervous as she waited for Kyle to buzz her door. It was now 7:25. Carmen got this sudden urge to pee. She wanted to quickly go, but she didn't want to have to undo her carefully assembled attire and risk being in the bathroom should Kyle show in the next couple of minutes. She paced the floor constantly. Nature was winning. She decided to take her chances and sure enough as she began to release, the door buzzed. "Damn!" Carmen cried. She tried to hurry because she didn't want Kyle to get concerned about what was taking so long. Quickly pulling herself together and freshening up, Carmen rushed to let Kyle in. She peeped through the keyhole to make sure it was him. She gasped as she saw what she thought to be the finest man alive. She opened the door. "Hi, Kyle. Sorry for the delay, I was on the phone with my mother…"

The service was good, the food was good, and the company was outstanding. Carmen was in heaven. Kyle talked about work a lot. He loved being an attorney. He talked about his college days. He also talked about his hobbies and interests. He told Carmen he liked boating and basketball. He told her he also participated in the local Big Brother program. Kyle seemed to be a very busy man. He couldn't seem to find his way to talk about ex-girlfriends or relationships. He asked Carmen a lot about her profession, where she matriculated, and what she liked to do in her spare time. He thought it was interesting that she drove a convertible turbo SAAB. He told her it was kind of sexy. Yet, he skillfully avoided initiating any dialog about relationships.

Being the creative person she was, Carmen thought she could maneuver this conversation. When Kyle made another comment about her car, she quickly began talking about how expensive maintenance was and how she wished she had mechanical skills to do the work herself. This would be the cue for Kyle to ask why she didn't get her man to do some of the work. Like a good fish, Kyle took the bait. "Why is your man letting you pay for all the maintenance?" Kyle asked.

Beaming at the opportunity to let him know she was available, Carmen quickly replied, "Well, I can't say that I have a man to take care of those things for me."

"Are you saying you don't have a man who can take care of these things or that you don't have a man. I'm sure a beautiful woman like you has a man," Kyle inquired.

Trying not to sound like she couldn't get a man or that she was desperate, Carmen carefully answered. "Well, I can always get a man, but I'd rather have a man with substance and if he has the skills of a technician, that's gravy. I'd rather pay for a technician and hold out for the right man."

"I see," said Kyle.

Carmen waited for him to continue, but he just smiled and stared at her. "So, do you have a special someone?" Carmen probed.

"No," he replied.

Echoing Kyle's inquiry of her, Carmen suggested. "I'm sure a handsome man like you has a special lady". Kyle went on to explain to Carmen how he had dated, but found women to be jaded, cold hearted and reserved. He explained that he is often misunderstood because he's very nice and that women don't want men who treat them nice – that they would rather have a man who dogs them out because that's what women have come to expect. He offered his thoughts that women think that nice men have hidden agendas. He also said that women thought that nice guys who had never been married and had no kids, like himself, must be gay.

Carmen listened patiently and took mental notes. She had no concerns whatsoever about Kyle being gay. She wanted to know about Robbi, but Kyle never got around to talking in specifics. So she thought she would ask some lead-in questions. "Have you dated anyone recently?"

Kyle admitted to Carmen that he dated someone recently, but insisted that he was glad the relationship was over. When Carmen inquired about why he had broken up with the woman, Kyle offered that the woman was too snooty and thought she was better than everyone else. He said she was cold hearted and liked to bitch all the time. Kyle went on to tell Carmen how if this woman ever saw her, she would go out of her mind with jealousy. When she asked him how this woman could or would ever see her, he began to supply her with the information she had been fishing for.

"You may have seen her in the building. Her name is Robbi Gant. I'm telling you, if she ever saw you, she would go crazy."

"Why?" Carmen asked with a puzzled look on her face.

"Because you're very pretty and she can't stand anyone who she thinks looks better than she does. You have pretty hair and a very nice figure and you're obviously professional and carry yourself well. She thinks she's better than all the other women in the office just because she rubs elbows with the executives in the company. I'm sure you'll meet her someday. But I'm warning you, don't pay attention to anything she says. She'll say anything to make herself appear to be on top."

23

As Carmen listened, she pictured this Robbi person to be the woman she had seen on the deck. She also remembered how the woman stared her up and down as she was leaving the area. This had to be her. She then asked Kyle about Robbi's hair. Kyle told her that Robbi wore her hair in a curly style. She took this information as confirmation of Robbi's identity.

"Why do you want to know about her hair? It's not as long and pretty as yours," Kyle said flirtatiously.

"No reason," Carmen replied. "So, how long did you guys date?"

"About a year or so, off and on."

"A year or so? Did you guys ever consider marriage?"

"Yes, but that's a whole 'nother story. It was forced. I mean I cared for her, but it was a proposal under duress."

"Was she pregnant?"

"No, just pushy. I was young and foolish and didn't know what I really wanted. I'm glad we didn't get married. I would've had to come home to her bitchin' everyday. On top of that, she couldn't cook. I'm from the south and you know that it is unheard of for a woman not to know how to cook."

"How old is this woman and why can't she cook?" Carmen asked.

"She's one year younger than I am. She grew up with maids and servants. Her family was kind of well off. They were rather recherché."

"Really? Even if I had grown up in a well todo family, I would have learned how to cook at some point," said Carmen in an effort to be all that Robbi was not.

"Can you cook?" asked Kyle.

"I can cook almost as well as my mother, " Carmen lied. She thought she had better quickly change the subject before he started to ask her for recipes. "How old are you?" she asked.

"I'm thirty-two, and yourself?"

"I'm twenty-seven. I'll be twenty-eight in November. November 15th, actually," Carmen offered making sure she communicated her actual birth date.

"November 15th ...a Scorpio!" Kyle salivated.

Carmen could feel that Kyle was immediately assessing and fantasizing about her sexual prowess because of the stereotypes of Scorpios. She didn't care. She figured that was just one more thing she had going for her. "So tell me, Mr. Sealy, when is your special day?"

"If you mean my birthday, it's September 25th. I don't make a big deal out of birthdays. It's just another day."

To be sure Kyle understood that she didn't share his sentiment about birthdays, particularly hers, she thought she'd better make herself perfectly clear. "Well, I don't happen to feel that way. I mean, your birthday is *your* day. All the other holidays are days you share with millions of other people, but your birthday is a day to celebrate your life. Carmen insisted that her birthday was very important to her. She was making sure Kyle knew to acknowledge November 15th as a special day for her with nice gifts and plenty of romance.

Their evening progressed nicely. Carmen had done as much information gathering as she could. After all, she was on a mission to become Mrs. Kyle Sealy.

Kyle dropped Carmen back at her apartment at around 11:30p.m. He was the perfect gentleman. He walked her to her door and expressed what a lovely evening he had and how it was especially nice to be in the company of such an enchanting lady. Carmen didn't know if she should invite Kyle in. Heaven knows she wanted to, but she settled for a soft wet kiss on the cheek accompanied by a tickle from Kyle's dark groomed mustache. "When can I see you again?" Kyle asked as he pulled back from the kiss. Elated that he wanted to see her again, Carmen wanted to tell him to go gather up his things, move in and he could therefore see her everyday. "How about tomorrow? I can order pizza and we can have a quiet evening in, " she said.

"That sounds nice. Let's plan on it then. What time shall I be here?"

"How about 7:30?"

"7:30 it is. Goodnight beautiful."

Carmen said goodnight and floated into her apartment. She was falling in love.

No sooner than Carmen had been home for fifteen minutes, her phone rang. She answered thinking it might be Kyle calling to ask if he could come back over and spend more time with her. It was Nikki. "Do you have company?" Nikki inquired.

"No... Girl, I can't believe you are calling me."

"I'm sorry. I couldn't wait. I figured if you were busy, you wouldn't pick up the phone. So why *are* you answering your phone?... He must have made you pick up the tab for dinner."

"No. My man is the perfect gentlemen."

"*Your man?*" Are you guys going out now?"

"Not yet, but that's the plan. Nikki, I can feel it. Kyle was meant to be my husband. It was destiny for us to meet. Girl, I am in love..."

"Uh huh. Have you done all your research? What kind of car does he drive?"

"What?" Carmen reacted, caught off guard.

"You heard me. What kind of car does he drive? You're stalling. He must drive a Pinto."

"No. He drives a Ford Probe."

"A *Probe!* Nikki shouted in ridicule. "Homeboy couldn't find a nice European car? I thought you said he was an attorney."

"He is. Nik, you are so shallow, not to mention materialistic."

"So what, I don't care. Somehow, Ford Probe and attorney just don't sound right in the same sentence. Are you sure the Probe isn't just a rental car he is using while his BMW, Porsche or Benz is in the shop?"

Carmen couldn't help but laugh at Nikki because she had to admit to herself that the same thing had crossed her mind. She wouldn't, however, admit this to Nikki or anyone else for that matter. "Nikki, I don't care if this man drives a horse and buggy, he is *"fwine"*. Besides, if women decide not to date him because of the car he drives, then that's less competition for me to deal with. Anyway, he will get a Mercedes Station Wagon when we get married so that we will have enough room for our kids," Carmen joked.

"A *Station Wagon*? OK, since it would be a Benz, I guess that's acceptable," said Nikki.

"Guess what? He's been engaged before, so that means he's the marrying kind."

"Or he might be just the engaging kind. So why didn't he get married?" inquired Nikki.

"He said it was forced and that she wasn't really the right one for him."

Nikki sighed. "Well, you know what my next question is. How big was the diamond?"

"Ya' know, I forgot to ask. Or maybe I assumed it was a nice size."

"Hold up. Homeboy drives a Probe, a wannabe sports car, and you assumed he gave his ex-girlfriend a nice ring? Maybe that's why they didn't get married, because she felt insulted when he proposed to her with a diamond chip...a wannabe diamond."

Carmen burst into laughter. "See, that's why yo' ass don't have no man."

"That's all right, I'd rather be by myself than with a cheap man," proclaimed Nikki.

"Who said Kyle was cheap? You just wait. Kyle is going to be everything I think he is. Kyle is a God-send. You just keep calling the 1-900 Psychic hotline looking for your Mr. Right."

Nikki and Carmen laughed at each other's humor. Although Carmen felt slightly offended by some of Nikki's remarks, she knew that Nikki was only looking out for her in her own shallow way. Nevertheless, Carmen was convinced she had found the man of her dreams.

Chapter 5

It was a beautiful Saturday morning.   Carmen gazed at the splendor of the outdoors from the balcony of her apartment. She had just awakened moments earlier with fantasies and visions of Kyle in her head. It had almost been a week since they met, but she felt like she had known him forever. She had not seen him since the previous Wednesday when they managed to have lunch since Kyle had to cancel their original plans to get together for their second dinner date.   They had, however, talked on the phone on a couple of occasions. Kyle had mentioned that he might give her a call on the weekend if he got a free moment. He had explained to her that he was part owner of an apartment complex in a small town called Bentford, about sixty miles away from Philadelphia. It was almost 10:00. Carmen had thought of calling Kyle, but didn't want to appear overly anxious. Unable to resist, she picked up the phone and began to dial the numbers. When his answering machine picked up on the first ring, she figured he had already left for Bentford. She didn't bother to leave a message.   She thought to herself, "Wow, what a wonderful man. Not only is he a successful attorney, he is an entrepreneur as well!"   She couldn't help but to think about Kyle's financial stability. She became very excited that Kyle was probably stable enough to provide for the family they would have. She fantasized about the kind of luxury home they would live in. She loved her SAAB, but embraced the idea of Kyle upgrading from the Ford Probe to something more suitable for their dual incomes. Carmen expected that she would be getting a promotion in the near future as well as a few bonuses. She decided she would use her bonus money to establish a savings account to pay for the elaborate wedding she wanted to have. Suddenly, Carmen's phone rang snapping her back to reality. She answered it quickly hoping it was Kyle. It turned out to be a telemarketer instead. Carmen chuckled at herself for planning so far in advance for a man she had known for less that a week. Nevertheless, she found it fun and if things turned out the way she planned, she would only have to execute what she had already so carefully thought out.

Feeling hungry, she popped two *Eggo* waffles into the toaster and put on a fresh pot of gourmet blend coffee. Carmen felt like hanging out, but didn't know many people since she had only been in the city for a little under two months. She had one girlfriend who was usually inaccessible because she spent most of her time with her boyfriend. Carmen had considered going into the office to get a jump on work, but that idea quickly dissipated.

Carmen loved to paint. She was in a particularly good mood and felt like painting something cheery. She was running low on art supplies, but figured she could run out and do some quick shopping at the arts and crafts store and return to her peaceful balcony and just paint until her heart was content. She loved to paint images of strong and inspiring women. Some of her idols were Oprah, Lena Horn, and Princess Diana. One of her favorite creations was an image of Diana Ross singing *Ain't No Mountain High Enough*. She liked to capture the expressions of women singing a favorite song or playing an instrument and creating rhythms from their souls. She found a sense of peace while capturing these images on canvas. The art of taking a blank surface and turning it into an expression of life and inner spirit was most gratifying and fulfilling.

Soon Carmen was dressed and out of the house. She put the top down on the SAAB. Her hair was pulled back into a bouncy ponytail. She loved the way her turbo engine sounded when she was in a free-spirited mood. She loved the way her sunglasses gave the world a smooth and even tone. All of the rough edges of life just seemed to mellow out. Cruising through the city, Carmen scoped out a few open markets where she could possibly showcase and sell her art on weekends. She had always considered her talent a gift from God. The old people in her hometown used to always tell her that God will take away the talents he has given to you if don't use them. She had always shared her talents very casually. She had never really considered making money off her gift until her very close gay friend, Lewis, shared his perspective. He told her that many people were talented in many different things, not necessarily with artsy things like singing, dancing or drawing. For instance, he told her that some people were talented salespeople and lived very elaborate lifestyles as a result. He reminded her that just because you make it big doesn't mean you have to forget where you came from and never give back. He added that God loves a cheerful giver.

Carmen often wondered how Lewis could always interject God into every conversation, yet be gay. She never really pressed the issue because it was no different than straight people interjecting God into every conversation, yet be fornicators. She never held the fact that Lewis was gay against him because she loved him for who he was, which she thought was a deeply caring and loving individual. Besides, there were many people who were straight whose hearts and souls would pale in comparison to Lewis'.

She began to reminisce about the day when she first learned Lewis was gay. She always found it strange that Lewis could be so fine and never had a girlfriend. He always escorted beautiful women to social functions and would always comment on their voluptuous body parts such as breast and buttocks, which he referred to affectionately as titties and ass. He was particularly fond of women with long legs - long hairy legs, actually. At the end of an evening out with a woman, Lewis would always take her home and never try anything. It was funny how women would view that behavior as rather gentlemanly. But after the third date, the women would think perhaps they needed to try something. Because Lewis was very good looking and not visibly feminine, most women thought they were being brushed off because Lewis couldn't manage one more horse on the carousel. Nevertheless, women always pursued him...because in the minds of those who didn't know he was gay, he was a challenge. And in the minds of those who suspected he might be, they felt that he hadn't experienced a *real* woman yet and was probably sitting on the fence of sexuality and that once he stepped foot into their pasture, he would tread the meadows of ecstasy for all eternity.

Carmen remembered the time she had gone over to Lewis' apartment to watch a baseball game on television. By this time, she had accepted her relationship with Lewis as strictly platonic. She didn't have visions of Lewis lusting for her between innings. The home team was winning and it was the bottom of the seventh. Lewis said he needed to run out and get his clothes out of the cleaners before it closed and that he would be right back since it was just around the corner. Carmen just said OK and continued to watch the game. During one of the commercials, Carmen thought she'd quickly excuse herself to the bathroom. She didn't bother to shut the door since no one was home except her. Then she heard Lewis' phone ring twice before his answering machine picked up. She was washing her hands when she heard the voice of a gentleman began to speak. She quickly shut off the faucet so that she could hear the message just in case it was Lewis calling. What Carmen heard next astonished her – to put it mildly.

"Hey, pick up the phone. I know you're there. Pick up the phone ... are you watching the baseball game? Well, I just called to tell you that the fine motherfucker who just hit that home run is going to be hitting this ass if you don't get your shit together. I'm tired of you thinking you can just strut your ass over here and climb into my bed whenever you feel like it and then not call me for days at a time. I know you can hear me. I'm not going to keep putting up with your shit, Lewis!" The caller hung up.

Carmen was stunned. She stood in the bathroom doorway with her mouth open and eyes glued to the answering machine as if it were the person who had just called. "My God, Lewis is gay!" she hissed. "Oh my God!" Carmen tried to compose herself before Lewis returned. She felt tears come to her eyes. "How can this be?" Carmen questioned herself. "How could I have not known? My God, Lewis is gay. But he's so fine. My

God, what a waste. Why? Thank God, I never slept with him ... not that he ever wanted to sleep with me anyway." Carmen took a deep breath and sat on the living room couch. She was limp as she felt despair. She noticed the baseball game was still on. She began to look at every man on the set as a potential homosexual. She listened for the announcers to identify who had hit home runs in an effort to identify who the gentleman caller referenced as his potential lover. There didn't seem to be any mention of any home runs other than the two she had witnessed in the second and fourth innings. She began flipping through the channels only to find out that there were several games going on at the same time in various cities throughout the country. The caller never identified who he was or which game he was watching. Also, there was nothing to say that the caller wasn't just fantasizing about being with the player he was attracted to. Carmen didn't have a lot of details. All she knew is that she heard a man express his annoyance with Lewis' behavior with regard to their sexual relationship. Suddenly, she heard Lewis putting his key in the door returning from the cleaners. She tried to act as natural as possible. Lewis and Carmen were pretty close friends; when he looked at her, he instantly knew she was trying to cover up something. She had thought to lie and insist that everything was OK. As hard as she tried, she couldn't. "Your friend called while you were out," Carmen said expressing shame for having listened to Lewis' message.

"What friend?" Lewis probed as he wondered why Carmen would answer his phone. "I heard them leaving you a message on your machine... you didn't have the volume turned down." Carmen dropped her head.

"What did they say?" Lewis asked.

Carmen lifted her head. "What did *they* say? --- You mean *he* don't you?"

Lewis stared at Carmen with submitting eyes because he knew she knew his secret. He didn't bother to listen to the message. He conceded by dropping his head and maintaining a roaring silence that she would never forget. Carmen watched Lewis while her judgmental attitude dwindled. Despite anything and everything, this man was her friend. She couldn't feel betrayed because Lewis never tried to engage her in any relationship other than friendship. She finally broke the silence. She walked over to Lewis and began hugging him. "You are my friend and I love you. No matter what, you are my friend."

Carmen suddenly spotted a parking space. The day was absolutely beautiful. The nice weather had obviously drawn many people to the outdoors. As she parked her freshly washed SAAB, she became very excited about meandering through the crowd at the market.

She watched kids dance and old men play tattered instruments with the hopes of enticing the onlookers to drop money into the receptacles. As she continued through the crowd, she noticed several artists displaying a variety of artworks. Some of the paintings were abstract, some of the paintings were depictions of scenes of the city. There were many pieces of art characterizing various jazz artists, mostly of men. Carmen loved jazz. One piece of art in particular captured her attentions. It was a picture of a man playing a trumpet. His face wore an expression of will that seemed to resound the note he was playing at that instant. For Carmen, this picture represented a commitment to excellence that she wanted to manifest in herself. She decided to purchase the artwork. She was able to negotiate a price that allowed her to have additional money to spend while she entertained herself with browsing and shopping. She spent the remainder of the afternoon accessing the merchandise and buying decorative items for her apartment. She wasn't quite sure yet what her product would be to sell at the market, but all she knew was that she did have comparable talent to many of the merchants and she was enjoying the day.

Carmen returned to her apartment at around 3:00p.m. hoping to find a message from Kyle waiting for her. She had stopped by the grocery store on her way home to pick up some things to cook for the evening. She had every intention of preparing a meal to impress Kyle with her culinary skills, of which she had none. She had heard that the way to a man's heart was through his stomach. She didn't want her inability to cook to be a reason for losing the opportunity to win over the man of her dreams. She remembered how Kyle had made reference to Robbi's shortcomings in the kitchen. Carmen had picked up a couple of cookbooks while she was at the supermarket to aid in her efforts to prepare a meal fit for a king… her king she thought.

Carmen began listening to her messages. She had a message from Kyle indicating that he would be over at 7:30 as previously planned. She was ecstatic. Then she felt anxiety. She couldn't cook! She knew Kyle had southern roots and wouldn't be particularly impressed with a peanut butter and jelly sandwich. Heck, it was Saturday – he wouldn't expect anything heavy like collard greens and fried chicken. Carmen looked at the groceries she had picked up. She couldn't believe she had spent money on stuff with no plan. It would have seemed more logical for her to have planned a menu and selected ingredients accordingly. She had packages of chicken, ground beef and ocean perch. She also had bags of frozen vegetables and several spices of which she had never heard. Many of the spices she had purchased were probably in the spice rack on her kitchen counter that she, of course, never used. In fact, most of the things she had purchased were already stocked in her refrigerator or pantry. There was, however, one item Carmen felt was essential for the evening, a bottle of wine with an excellent vintage.

Feeling frantic, Carmen picked up her phone to call Nikki. They both laughed at the situation Carmen had gotten herself into. Nikki was able to calm Carmen by suggesting that she not try to cook like the Soul Food queen so soon. She suggested that she prepare something a little more romantic for a Saturday evening. Carmen joked that chilidogs might not be a bad idea. Nikki convinced her that spaghetti and a garden salad along with French bread would be suitable. Carmen looked through one of her cookbooks and found a spaghetti recipe, however, she and Nikki agreed that she would botch it. Carmen insisted that she had most of the ingredients and could probably doctor up her

Ragu to taste like homemade sauce. After much debate, they settled on Carmen adding a little seasoning salt, a few chunky cut onions and green peppers and a large bay leaf for homemade authentication.

"So, are you giving up the nooky tonight?" Nikki inquired jokingly.

"No, I'm not giving up the nooky. Kyle is practically a stranger. Besides, I'm sure Kyle is a respectable gentleman and would not try to take advantage of me just because I have prepared a romantic dinner, with wine, soft music and candlelight," Carmen answered semi-sarcastically.

"What are you going to wear?"

"I haven't decided. Probably a soft sundress. I have this sleeveless turquoise blue dress I could wear. It fits pretty nicely. It's kind of long with a slit up one knee. It's cool and comfortable and sexy, yet conservative. I think I'll just wear that. Anyway, I need to run and get this show on the road."

"OK, call me tomorrow and let me know how it went," Nikki requested with the suggestion that Carmen's date could progress through the night.

"I'll call you tonight after he leaves, thank you very much," Carmen insisted. She then noticed that the time for Kyle's arrival was getting closer. She had a lot to do. She wanted the evening to be perfect. She began the preparation of dinner while she made a checklist in her head of all the things she needed to take care of.

Kyle arrived on time. When the doorbell rang, Carmen felt her heart. Her heart pace grew very rapid. She did a quick check in the mirror before she answered the door. There he was…tall, handsome, neatly groomed, and a smile that could melt a glacier.

"Come in," Carmen summoned. Kyle greeted Carmen with a hug and a kiss on the cheek along with a bouquet of red long stem roses and a bottle of wine. "What a classy gentleman," she thought to herself.

"Wow, something smells good," Kyle said as he looked around the apartment at the candlelit dining area.

"It's just a little something I threw together for a great Saturday evening," Carmen replied, trying to downplay her previously inflated proclamation of culinary talents.

"Everything looks lovely, including you," Kyle flirted. "Ahh… you made Spaghetti. That's my favorite."

After dinner, Carmen and Kyle cleared the table and cleaned the kitchen together.

Carmen was very impressed with Kyle not taking the position that it was the woman's job to do the cleaning. Later, they sat in her living room drinking wine and talking. Kyle seemed to admire Carmen's taste in furniture and art. She revealed to him that she had painted many of the pictures on her walls. Kyle commented on how talented he thought she was. They seemed to talk endlessly. They shared with each other many of their aspirations and fantasies. Carmen wished that she had discussed these things with Kyle during previous conversations instead of quizzing him about some woman named Robbi. Although, had Kyle not assured her that Robbi was not an issue, they might not be sharing this wonderful evening.

The music was soft and mellow. The mood was romantic. Carmen began to tell Kyle how amazing she thought he was. She told him she felt like she had known him forever. They obviously lusted for each other. Carmen was wondering when or if Kyle would make a move on her. Feeling more and more at ease as the evening matured, Carmen began to share stories with Kyle about her previous bad relationships with men. She told Kyle how she had given her heart to former boyfriends only to have it torn into shreds, how boyfriends had mistaken her kindness for weakness. She went on and on how men had dogged her out. She was trying to let Kyle know that she was afraid to enter into another relationship, assuming that Kyle would want one with her.

Kyle listened and waited patiently for Carmen to expose her

37

vulnerabilities. He offered her a look of condolence as he looked on. Before speaking, Kyle extended his arms to Carmen. Feeling sorry for herself, she graciously accepted his comforting embrace. "You just need someone to love you," Kyle said as he stroked her hair. Hearing these words from Kyle made her feel so protected, so appreciated, so trusting. Kyle pulled back from her and began to kiss her forehead, then her nose, and then her trembling lips. Suddenly, the passion between them was undeniable. Kyle wrapped his strong arms around hers as he covered her mouth with soft, but firm, wet kisses. His rhythm was smooth and erotic. His masculinity was stimulating. She could feel the wetness in the crotch of her panties. Kyle began to hold her upper body in a way that allowed him to caress her nipples with his thumbs while massaging the rest of her breast with his fingers. Then he began to kiss her neck. Carmen began to moan and pull herself closer to him. Kyle proceeded to pull down the strap to her dress as he fondled her shoulders with his tongue and lips. The split in her dress allowed her left thigh to be exposed. He caressed it with his strong and commanding hand. He began to reach for Carmen's left buttock by entering his hand through the elastic around the leg of her panties. Everything was feeling perfect, almost too perfect. Carmen was out of control. She wanted to make love with Kyle so badly, yet she knew this behavior was not decent.

"Kyle, we can't. We have to stop," Carmen begged as she continued to kiss him.

"Baby, I won't hurt you," moaned Kyle.

"I know, but we're moving too fast," Carmen said trying to control the situation.

"Just trust me, Carmen," Kyle said as he hugged her tightly and kissed her face.

Carmen continued to kiss Kyle. Meanwhile, the uncertainties of what Kyle would think of her flashed in her mind. She wondered if she would lose his interest if she didn't give in to him. She wondered if he would think she was not mature enough to handle someone five years her senior. She wondered if he would think she was "easy".

Kyle had begun to remove Carmen's panties as he kissed her commandingly. The touch of his hand, on her body and the motion of his tongue in her mouth were torrid and hypnotic. "Come on, baby. Let me make love to you the way you need to be loved," Kyle pleaded. "I'll take care of you, Carmen."

Carmen then seemed to yield to her resistance as Kyle personalized his plea for intimacy by calling her name and offering her the security she wanted. "You promise you won't hurt me?" she said begging for assurance.

"I would never hurt you," Kyle said as he pulled back looking directly into her eyes. "Carmen, we don't have to do this. I would understand, really."

"I want to, Kyle, but I would really like for us to know each other better." Kyle sat alongside Carmen with a visible erection and perspiration beading on his forehead.

"Tell you what, we'll get to know each other better and one day pick up where we left off," Kyle offered hoping that Carmen would change her mind.

"You mean that?" said Carmen.

"Of course I do," Kyle lied.

"That makes me happy," said Carmen. "I'm sure we'll end up really liking and loving each other."

--- Chapter 6

The fall had begun to reveal its presence. The foliage was spectacular even in the early stages. Carmen and Kyle had enjoyed a few movies and had dinners at exquisite restaurants by the cessation of the summer. On one occasion, Kyle had surprised Carmen with a picnic on the lake after they had completed a Sunday afternoon of sightseeing in the mountains. He had packed imported wine along with gourmet cheeses. He had also packed sandwiches from one of Carmen's favorite delicatessens. Kyle had brought along a portable cassette player to allow Carmen to listen to a tape he had made for her. The tape contained some of her favorite jazz artists and female vocalists. After the romantic picnic, they fed the ducks in the lake. They created a racing contest to see whose duck would get to the food faster. The afternoon was peaceful, playful and poetic.

"So what's the deal? Why haven't you given up the nooky to Kyle?" Nikki demanded of Carmen. "What's going on with you two?"

"I told you from the get-go that Kyle was a gentleman and a scholar. There is more to a relationship than giving up the nooky," said Carmen.

"Hasn't he earned it? I thought you told me he had taken you to nice restaurants and stuff like that."

"Earned it! Sorry, my stuff is not for sale. Besides, Kyle respects the fact that I have waited."

"Carmen, who are you trying to fool? We both know that you are just buying time so that you can appear decent. *I* know and *you* know that you had decided to give up the nooky the first time you met him. Now, I can't believe Kyle has gone without sex since you guys started dating. So, do you know where he sleeps at night?" said Nikki.

"I can tell you where he *doesn't* sleep at night, …with me... *yet*," Carmen joked.

"How do you know he's not still seeing that Robbi chick?" Nikki suggested.

"Girl please! Hey, I didn't tell you about what Kyle showed me while I was at his apartment the other day," said Carmen changing the course of the discussion.

"What?... a picture of Robbi?"

"No, her engagement ring. Well…what *used* to be her engagement ring."

"Her engagement ring? Why does *he* have it?" Nikki asked in a bewildered tone. "How big was it?…Was it a rock or a chip?"

"Nikki, you are so predictable. How did I know you were going to ask that question?"

"OK hussy. Now take me out of suspense. How big was it?"

"Well, it looked like a half carat marquise," answered Carmen.

"A half carat! That's it? Were there any baguettes?" Nikki ridiculed.

"No, just a single stone. It was cute."

"*Cute*? Girl, no woman should ever have to describe a ring from her man as cute. Now I bet I know why he has it…. Robbi probably threw it back at him," said Nikki with disgust.

"Believe it or not, you're almost right. He told me that Robbi had heard from one of her friends that they had seen him out one night at dinner with another woman that Robbi suspected he was having an affair with. She got angry, cussed him out and threw the ring at him."

"Was it true? Was he having and affair?" asked Nikki.

"He said he wasn't. He said that he was having dinner with a girl he had dated in college. Robbi thought the girl was scheming to get Kyle back and that Kyle couldn't resist her alleged advances."

"So if he wasn't guilty, why didn't he give the ring back?"

Nikki probed.

"He told me for two reasons ... one, he didn't want her to think she could control him by taking the ring off every time she got angry and two, because he really didn't want to marry her anyway. He said that he really did care for her but that the engagement was forced."

"So he didn't care for her enough to marry her?" Nikki continued to probe.

"Apparently not. He told me that she had a few shortcomings that he would like to have seen worked out before he popped the question. When she threatened to leave him, he agreed to marry her with the intention of giving their relationship the benefit of the doubt," explained Carmen.

"So, what's the deal now? Is she seeing someone else?"

"Phyllis, our receptionist, told me that she thought Robbi still had a thing for Kyle."

"How long has it been since they broke up?" asked Nikki.

"Kyle told me about a year."

"A year? Homegirl hasn't moved on yet? I assume she's still hoping they will get back together."

"I think so. They are still friends, so I think she is encouraged by the interaction. In a nutshell, I think Miss High-and-Mighty treated Kyle like one of the field hands when she had him and thought he should do all the worshipping. I think it was one of those cases where you don't know what you have until it's gone. So, I think it's safe to say she does want him back."

Nikki still wasn't satisfied that she had all the details. "So what's he going to do with the ring?" she asked.

"Actually, he said he would hold on to it and use it toward an upgrade for a much nicer ring for the woman he *really* wants to marry," said Carmen. To avoid more interrogation from Nikki, She decided to end the conversation abruptly. "On that note, I need to get off this phone and get ready for work tomorrow. You know how I hate Mondays."

43

Like a typical Monday when most people are dreading the reality of beginning another week of doing a job that is more rewarding for the bosses and owners than it is for oneself, the day showed up right on schedule. The bright side of life for Carmen was any opportunity she could seize to see Kyle. Maybe she would be able to steal a glimpse of him on the elevator or in the lobby between her dashing in and out of the building to visit her clients.

Carmen hardly ever got a chance to have lunch in the building because she was always out of the office; she traveled frequently to her headquarters office in New York City. Today would be different. When she arrived to work, she was informed by Phyllis that her main client had called to cancel the design review and that they would call later to reschedule. Carmen felt glad, because she didn't feel like she had designs reflective of her usual quality and creativity; her interest in Kyle had become a distraction to her work. Nevertheless, she was a perfectionist and always found a way to shine. It was always important to her to feel good about her work and her contributions to the agency. Carmen took advantage of the opportunity she was given to perfect her designs and the presentation. Even still, she felt she should also take the opportunity to make an attempt to have lunch with Kyle. When she called him to check his availability, he told her he was having a working lunch with a few of his co-workers. He also mentioned that they would be meeting in the cafeteria. Thus, she settled for the opportunity just to see him hard at work in the cafeteria instead. She loved to see him dressed in his nice suits and ties. It always reminded her of the first time she laid eyes on him.

As Carmen approached the cafeteria, she noticed Kyle and his colleagues, including Robbi, beginning to seat themselves at a table in the far corner. Robbi appeared to follow closely behind Kyle to insure a seat beside him. Carmen watched their interaction. Robbi seemed to laugh and bump shoulders with

Kyle. Carmen couldn't stand the less-than-businesslike behavior she interpreted. She tried not to stare, but she all of sudden felt threatened by Kyle and Robbi's relationship, be it past, present or possibly future. She then began to minimize the threat of Robbi in her mind by mentally cutting her down: "She looks just OK. Her hairdo looks tacky and outdated...like something from the '60s. Her outfit looks cheap and homely. And those granny pantyhose have to go. I suppose money just can't buy taste."

Carmen decided not to eat in the cafeteria. She grabbed a sandwich and retreated to the deck where she could regroup. Feeling territorial, she decided that it was time for Robbi to get a good look at her and Kyle together so that she could resign any thoughts she might have of a reunion with him.

Carmen waited patiently for the business luncheon to disperse. "Why is that woman walking so close to Kyle? If you didn't know better, you'd think they were a couple," Carmen thought as she reentered the cafeteria, making her way closer to Kyle.

"Hello, Kyle," Carmen said flirtatiously in Robbi's presence.

Kyle appeared to be caught off guard. "Oh, Hi Carmen," Kyle responded as he slowed down, but continued to walk to avoid the awkward situation.

"Did you have a good lunch?" Carmen asked, trying to make conversation and to generate an introduction of herself to Robbi from Kyle. She could see Robbi becoming agitated as she looked back and forth at Kyle. Robbi seemed to be awaiting an introduction or explanation as well.

"It wasn't much of a lunch," said Kyle. "Oh, Robbi, this is Carmen. Carmen, this is Robbi. Both Carmen and Robbi exchanged artificial hellos. Carmen didn't get the distinction she was after. She wanted to be introduced as his girlfriend. "'This is Carmen?"... Carmen who?...He would have been better off saying this is Wilma Flintstone...at least that would have generated *some* type of reaction," she thought.

"Kyle, I think we better get going, we have to get ready for the conference call at 2:00," Robbi summoned.

Carmen felt averted. She tried to play it off by pretending to have a pressing engagement of her own. "Speaking of getting going, I need to run myself. Hey, it was nice meeting you," she said glancing down at her watch to further convey a sense of urgency in her departure. Her heart was beating rapidly as she entered the elevator. She felt like a fool for creating a situation that seemed to backfire. The sequence of events was not at all how she imagined it would be.

Upon returning to her desk, she felt an urge to call Kyle, but remembered he had to prepare for a conference call and probably would not have time to talk. While she wanted very badly to dream up some way to recover from the embarrassing situation, she knew she was not afforded that luxury during work hours. Feeling even more distracted, Carmen knew she would have to assert herself even harder to work on her design review presentation. Concentrating on the job was proving to be more challenging than the job itself. This was not going to be easy.

———————

Carmen sat in the love seat in her apartment with her feet crossed in front of her. She still had on her clothes from work, including her pantyhose. She had only removed her shoes. They were in the middle of the floor as she had kicked them off when she got home just before she called Kyle's home to leave him a message. Unnerved by the day, Carmen had to force herself to eat the cheeseburger and fries she had picked up from Burger King on her way home. Between bites, she could hear Robbi's voice echoing in her head. The confidence Robbi had exuded was frightening. "Did Kyle find that attractive? Was Robbi able to make Kyle believe he would be missing out if he didn't choose her? Why did their encounter feel so strange?" Carmen thought to herself. Kyle couldn't provide answers quickly enough... "Why hasn't he returned my phone call?" she thought. She swirled her French fries around in the ketchup as she stared into space looking for answers. The phone rang. It was Kyle returning her call.

Without any hesitation, Carmen said hello and then launched into her interrogation. "So what's going on between you and Robbi? Why was she so friendly toward you today during lunch?"

Kyle answered her as if he called expecting a confrontation. "Carmen, I told you how she is. She knows that you and I have been going out and she's just jealous. She and I are friends, but I try to maintain my distance so that she won't think that she and I are getting back together."

"Oh yeah, right...I saw the way you were maintaining your distance today," Carmen said sarcastically. "You appeared to be keeping your distance from *me* rather than from *her*."

"Carmen, you don't know this woman. Had I made a big deal over you, she would have performed. I can't afford to have that kind of exposure in the workplace. Couldn't you see how jealous she was of you?"

"Did she ask you any questions about me?" asked Carmen in an attempt to gage Robbi's so-called jealously.

"She did, but I didn't give her a lot of information because she might start calling you trying to make trouble. You have to remember, she is a spoiled rich girl who is used to having her way. She would try to intimidate you if she knew how much we have been seeing each other. I'm telling you, don't pay attention to anything that woman says."

"I'm a little confused here, I thought you said you were friends, but you don't speak very highly of her," said Carmen.

"She doesn't have many friends because she comes off as being very arrogant. I just happen to know another side of her. She is a nice person, but not someone I could have a serious relationship with, even though I tried to in the past."

Carmen started to feel a little better. She had received the assurance she sought regarding Kyle and Robbi's relationship. "All I know is that one day she's going to have to get the hint that she needs to move on because you are no longer interested in her. I feel kind of sorry for her actually. I mean, she has to be broken up. She will never find another you." Carmen then changed the subject. "You have a big day coming up in a few weeks. What do you want for your birthday?"

Kyle insisted that his birthday was no big deal to him. He reminded Carmen that his birthday fell on a weekday this year and that they wouldn't have time to really celebrate anyway. Carmen didn't see this as an issue, but rather an opportunity to do something really special for him since he didn't have any expectations.

Carmen spent the following weeks planning for Kyle's birthday. She had been shopping in all the major department stores, but couldn't find anything she considered unique enough to make a statement of her love for him. She knew that despite Kyle's protest, many people would acknowledge his birthday anyway with cards and gifts. He seemed to have everything. She had thought about buying him apparel, but suits were too expensive, and ties and sweaters were too trite. Jewelry was not an option because he didn't wear much jewelry, just a watch and a gold necklace with a cross on it. He didn't have a gold bracelet, but somehow that seemed trite as well. Growing frustrated, Carmen suddenly remembered her own gift...she was a talented artist. She became excited about the idea of unveiling to Kyle a portrait of himself. This would be a gift from her heart that no one in this world could replicate. She had to get started right away.

Kyle's birthday was going to be on the upcoming Thursday. It was already Tuesday and Carmen was putting the final touches on the portrait. Since she was using acrylics, she didn't have to worry about the picture drying on time. She had planned to drop the picture off at a local frame shop on Wednesday so that they could assemble a frame around the canvas. The plan was to pick up the finished product from the frame shop on Wednesday night. She had been so busy with work and working on the portrait that she had not worked out the logistics for presenting the portrait to Kyle. Thus, she thought she had better

48

secure his time for that evening. When she called him, as always, she got his answering machine. She hated that. She decided to leave a message anyway. "Hi Kyle, this is Carmen. I know you've been working late hours lately, but I'd like to take you to dinner for your birthday. I know you probably just plan on working or staying home, but I'd like to see you. So call me when you get a chance. Smooches." She hung up the phone feeling joyful. She couldn't wait for him to call her back.

Kyle managed to get back with Carmen at 6:30 the following morning. He explained to her that he didn't return her call the night before because he had come home from a challenging day at work, drunk a couple of beers and had fallen asleep. He apologized and proceeded to tell Carmen that he had to go out of town on business and would be gone on Thursday, his birthday. He said he had to leave tonight and would not be back until Sunday. When Carmen inquired about where he was going, he explained that he was going out West. He said he had to be there for meetings on Thursday afternoon and Friday morning. He went on to explain that he had decided to stay through the weekend because this was an opportunity for him to take advantage of a free vacation. Carmen felt disappointment beyond belief. "How could this be?" she thought to herself. "Well, can I take you to the airport?" she offered to salvage any opportunity to present Kyle with his gift before he left. Kyle declined the offer, but said that he would drop by to see her on his way to the airport. "What time is your flight?" she asked.

"It's at 9:30 tonight. I'm trying to do some packing this morning so that I won't have to rush later. Don't worry, I'll come by tonight before I go to the airport, OK, Baby? I need to run, but I'll call you later. Give me a kiss."

Carmen felt her heart sink as he hung up the phone. It took everything she had to pull herself together to get ready for work now, let alone think about what she would do about Kyle's gift. One thing for certain, she didn't have time to get it framed.

Carmen left work early to make sure she was home in time for Kyle to stop by on his way to the airport. She had decided that she would present Kyle with the portrait when he came by. Nothing was working out the way she planned, but she would not let the day become a total waste; she stopped by the store on the way home to pick up a bottle of champagne to toast Kyle's birthday before unveiling her expression of love. She wanted to make the eve of his birthday as special as the day itself.

When Kyle arrived at her apartment, he appeared rushed. He explained to Carmen that he only had about thirty minutes and had to get going. Carmen followed her plan by popping the cork on the champagne and pouring Kyle and herself nice tall glasses of bubbly. Kyle seemed amused by the balloons and candles. Carmen gently removed the glass from Kyle's hand after he had taken a sip following the toast. She began to kiss him softly all over his face as she counted slowly to her destination of thirty-three kisses. When she had reached twenty, the kisses became more seductive. "Thirty-one, thirty-two..." Carmen prolonged thirty-two. She could feel Kyle becoming aroused. "Wait, I have something for you. It's a surprise," she said interrupting the moment.

She guided Kyle over to her easel. He had no clue what she was doing, he just followed her lead. "You can let me know if you like this by saying yea or nay to kiss number thirty-three," Carmen said as she unveiled the portrait with confidence and pride. Kyle was speechless. He stood in amazement with his mouth opened and his eyes aglow. "Carmen, this is incredible," he murmured. "Baby, you're very talented! No one else has ever done anything like this for me! Thank you! Thank you, Baby," Kyle said as he reached to hug her with extreme gratitude. "Hey, may I have my thirty-third kiss?"

Carmen was beaming. Kyle held her so tightly as they kissed and swayed. The kisses of gratitude soon began to mutate to heightened passion. Kyle picked her up while continuing to kiss her. His tongue was all over her face and neck. He proceeded to carry her into her bedroom and place her on the bed. He began to unbutton her blouse as he kissed her chest and neck. Quickly assessing the style of bra she was wearing, Kyle took advantage of the easily detachable front snap. Suddenly Carmen's breasts were exposed. Kyle massaged and kissed each nipple ever so gently, making his way down to her navel. He could hear her moans of approval. The motion of her body was the confirmation he needed to proceed. He then unzipped her side-zip skirt and removed it along with her panties and pantyhose all at once exposing her fully nude body. He began to move his hand along her body as if he were examining the contours of a sculpture. Carmen watched as he pulled off his Ralph Lauren polo shirt. Kyle had the silhouette of Adonis, she thought. He then ran his middle finger between her legs to collect the moisture of her vagina on the fingertip. Then he placed it in his mouth as if he were sampling the readiness of something delicious to eat. He had to have her. As he began to undo his belt, Carmen became slightly nervous. She didn't know whether she was nervous about what was about to happen or if she was about to be disappointed about the size of the penis on whom she thought was the perfect man. Suddenly, Kyle's fully nude body in full attention stood above her. There was no disappointment! Carmen's extended arms conveyed her inviting message... "Baby come to me." They made love repeatedly until they both fell asleep.

———————

"Kyle, wake up, you've missed your flight!" Carmen screamed when she awakened and noticed the time. To her surprise, Kyle calmly rolled over and said, " I can just catch the first flight out in the morning, since my meeting is not until the afternoon. I'll be able to gain time because of the difference in time zones."

"Are you sure?" Carmen said with a smirk of delight.

"Yeah, I'm sure. Being with you was worth missing my flight. What time is it anyway?" he asked.

"Uhh...it's now about 11:30," she replied.

"11:30? Baby, you wore me out. Damn, I slept right

through the night almost. I need to call the airlines to reschedule. I should get going because I need to finish packing. I came straight here from work," said Kyle as he began to get up and began dressing. "I'll just shower when I get home. I'll call you if I decide to come back early, OK?" He finished dressing. He then thanked Carmen for the evening and the portrait. He insisted that she not get up. Carmen agreed under one condition – that he stay until midnight; she wanted to be the first person to wish him Happy Birthday. He agreed. At 12:05 Kyle kissed Carmen goodnight and saw himself out, taking his gift with him.

Although the magical moment of intimacy with Kyle had not exactly followed the script Carmen would have liked, she felt satisfied nonetheless. The moment was spontaneous and fulfilling. As far as she was concerned, her relationship with Kyle was on course.

"*Carmen, you gave up the nooky?*" Nikki shouted in disbelief. "Well?"

"Well what?" Carmen hedged playfully.

"Girl, don't make me strangle you? Well, was Mr. Wonderful all that or was he Quick-Draw-McGraw? He had a little dick, didn't he?"

"You sure do ask a lot of personal questions." Carmen continued to tease. "But, for the record, Kyle Sealy has got it goin' on!" Carmen proclaimed with unwavering assurance. "And no, he is not Quick-Draw nor does he have a little dick.

Carmen was very giddy when she talked about Kyle to Nikki. Just like old times, they laughed and giggled about the possibilities of a love affair in the making. Because neither of them considered themselves promiscuous, a sexual encounter was an expression of commitment. Discussions of a wedding didn't seem at all premature.

She continued to share with Nikki how she felt Kyle was a God-send. She philosophized about how it must have been destiny that they met because she had initially shunned taking the assignment in Philadelphia. "Isn't life funny," she said.

"You never know who you're going to love. I think about all the times in the past when I settled for less than I wanted in a relationship. I mean, Kyle is everything I have ever wanted...all wrapped in one package. I feel like my life is now so complete."

Making love with Kyle had placed Carmen into another dimension. She felt like she was in love. She had perched Kyle on the pedestal of omnipotence.

It was now the Sunday following Kyle's birthday. Carmen had hoped Kyle would have called her while he was out West. But, thus far, she had not heard a word. She had called his answering machine occasionally just to hear his voice. She had also called his voicemail at work only to receive the impersonal system greeting: "The party you have called, Kyle Sealy, is not available." There was no indication of a return date. Carmen was annoyed even though she knew where he was. All she could do at this point was pray for Monday. Since she had a trip scheduled to visit her headquarters office in New York City on Tuesday through Thursday, Monday would be her only hope for seeing Kyle before she would have to leave. So she decided to leave him a message to help her secure this opportunity. "Hi Honey, I'm about to go to bed. I suppose you're taking the red-eye back. Hope you had good meetings and a good vacation and also I hope you're having a safe trip back. I miss you. Such a lover boy...You just love me and leave me," she joked. "I'll just plan on catching up with you at work tomorrow. Call me and let me know if you would like to do lunch. Oh...we can have lunch at my place, if you know what I mean. Hurry up and come home, baby. Miss you." Click.

Carmen had dressed especially nice in anticipation of impressing Kyle when they would finally catch up with each other. She wore a red figure-flattering suit. Kyle liked her hair down instead of up. So she had washed and set it so that it would have full volume and be as bouncy and shiny as possible.

He also liked her legs. So she made sure the hem line hit right above her knees. She had put on a fresh pair of panty hose to ensure no snags or sags. She was happy to hear a voice message from Kyle when she got to work accepting her lunch invitation. In his message, he went on to explain how his plane had not gotten in until 5:30 this morning suggesting that he had taken the red-eye as Carmen suspected. He also mentioned that he had a surprise for her when he saw her. She was elated.

"Girl, you know you get decked out on Mondays. I bet you have that boss of yours looking more at you than listening to your presentation," Phyllis said to Carmen.

"Actually, I have a lunch date today with my Honey," Carmen replied.

"Your honey? Who are you talking about, child?" Phyllis inquired suspiciously.

"Now Phyllis, don't play games, you know who stole my heart the first time I laid eyes on him."

"Kyle Sealy?"

"Who else?"

"Well, the last I heard, Kyle Sealy was your fantasy; now he's been promoted to "honey." What did he do to move up in the ranks?" asked Phyllis.

"Well, we've been going out a lot and getting to know each other. I like what I know and I think he does, too. I didn't want to mention anything to you until I was sure."

Phyllis studied Carmen for a couple of seconds. "So tell me, what are you sure about?" she asked.

"I'm sure that I trust this man and I want us to continue to grow closer and closer. Then we'll just have to see what happens," Carmen said suggestively as she waved her left hand wiggling her ring finger. "I'll keep you posted. I need to run."

"Be careful, Carmen. Make sure you know what you're doing. Take things slowly. You're a beautiful girl and you have all the time in the world," said Phyllis. Carmen smiled at Phyllis as she walked away ignoring her advice.

Carmen later joined Kyle for lunch as planned. She explained how much she had missed him while he was away. She was anxious to know how he felt about her since they had become intimate. To her liking, Kyle told her how much he thought about her and how he thought of coming home earlier but decided to spend time alone on the beaches to sort out his feelings. He told Carmen how he was experiencing feelings he had never felt before and wanted to sort out his priorities in life. He said his last birthday was a reminder that he wasn't getting any younger.

"I've always wanted to get married and have a family," he said. "I've never really thought that it would actually happen. I mean, the last few months have been great. What you did for me on my birthday really touched me. The picture will always remind me of just how sweet and thoughtful you are."

Carmen listened intensely for his comments on their intimacy. All indications suggested that he didn't think she was promiscuous, but she waited to hear him say it. She was interested in how he would reference their encounter. Would he say they had sex, made love, did it, screwed, or God forbid, fucked? Growing impatient, she asked, "So did you like being with me the night before you left?"

"Absolutely," Kyle replied. "It was great." Carmen thought to herself, "*It*...What the heck is *it*?". She cleared her throat. "What did you enjoy the most?" Carmen probed.

"I like the way we are together. You're very sexy. I like that. I like that a lot. You made me feel special." Kyle wasn't getting it, or so it seemed. He used the word 'special'. That seemed to be more in line with what Carmen was looking for, but not exactly. In an effort to coach him, Carmen asked, "So, would you like to make love to me again?"

"I'm really looking forward to spending more time with you. Like I said, I've never felt this way before. It's a good feeling. Who knows what could happen if things keep going as good as they are now." Although Carmen didn't get the exact descriptive she was looking for, she felt confident the relationship was on course. Kyle made no mention of the surprise he said he had for her. She didn't bother to remind him since she decided he would remember at some point and she could just receive it then.

When Carmen and Kyle returned to the building from lunch, they saw Robbi standing in the lobby with some of her friends. Robbi noticed them and was visibly fazed. She had a look of discomfort and insecurity. Carmen was loving every minute of it. She purposely walked closer to Kyle as they approached the elevators to get on. She could see Robbi continuing to stare. Kyle seemed a little uneasy. As the elevator doors shut, Kyle sighed.

"What's wrong?" Carmen asked.

"Nothing really," said Kyle. "I just know that woman is going to start up again because she saw me with you," he continued, referring to Robbi.

"What do you mean?"

"I told you. She's extremely jealous of any woman she thinks is prettier than her. Just remember what I told you. Stay clear of her…she's trouble. Let me know if she starts harassing you and I'll put an end to that foolishness," said Kyle. "Well, this is my floor. I'll call you later, OK? By the way, you look good enough to eat," continued Kyle as he stepped off the elevator. Carmen chuckled as she watched him disappear as the doors shut. She couldn't help but think about what Kyle said about Robbi. Was this women schizophrenic or what?

———————

It had been a long Monday. Carmen decided to leave work early to beat the traffic.

When she got on the elevator, it appeared that everyone else had the same idea. The elevator was filled near capacity. She wanted to stop on Kyle's floor to surprise him, but she wouldn't be able to do that since their offices were secured and required badge-ins when the receptionist was not present to announce visitors. Thus, her thoughts to relieve the elevator congestion dissipated. Suddenly, the elevator stopped on eight, which was Kyle's floor. Standing front and center waiting to get on was

Robbi Gant! Carmen quickly took a step backward to allow room for Robbi to board the elevator. She was anxious to know how she would be treated. To Carmen's surprise, Robbi seemed very anxious to get on the crowded elevator as if it were the last one for the afternoon. Neither Carmen nor Robbi said anything as the elevator moved downward stopping on every other floor, it seemed, before reaching the bottom. Everyone seemed to sigh relief as the doors opened on the lobby level. As everyone began to exit the elevator, Robbi turned to Carmen. "Hi, my name is Robbi. You and I met briefly in the cafeteria not too long ago. I believe your name is Carmen?"

"That's correct," Carmen replied trying to remain poised as she felt a cat fight coming on.

"I understand you to be a friend of Kyle Sealy's," said Robbi.

"That's also correct," Carmen said thinking to herself, "This hussy is about to perform."

"Well, as I'm sure Kyle has mentioned to you, he and I have been friends for *years*. Very *close* friends, I might add," said Robbi as if she were serving notice.

"I see," said Carmen. "Kyle is a very special person. I can certainly understand why anyone would want to be his friend. I'm sure that many people go to great lengths to be considered his friend," Carmen continued.

"You're absolutely right. Sometimes people just don't get the hint that friendship is all Kyle wants and *nothing* else," Robbi hinted to Carmen.

"I'm sure being as close to him as you are, you know this first hand," Carmen retorted.

"Of course," said Robbi, determined to win. "My, look at the time. I would love to chat longer, but I have a million and one things to do. Oh, I forgot to mention it... I saw that beautiful portrait you did of Kyle. You are so talented. Kyle is so vain for even asking you to do such a thing. But anyway, I'm going to be late for my aerobics class if I don't get going. Maybe we can do lunch sometimes," Robbi said hurriedly as she rushed away. Carmen stood paused for a moment. Then she thought, "Wait a minute. It's Monday. Kyle left last Thursday. When would Robbi have had an opportunity to see the portrait of Kyle?" Something wasn't right and Carmen knew she had to get to the bottom of it!

"Carmen, you believe anything," said Kyle responding defensively to Carmen's allegations. "I told you that woman was jealous and would say anything to confuse you." Carmen wasn't buying it. "I'm listening," she said. "Tell me *how* and *when* Robbi would have had an opportunity to see the portrait I gave you? You left for the West Coast on Thursday morning and didn't return until Monday morning. Unless of course you came back early and didn't tell me."

"What did she tell you?" asked Kyle trying to make sure he provided the right explanation.

"I told you. She said as she was about to walk away from me that she liked the picture I had done of you and that you were vain to ask me to do it for you. Where did she get the idea that you *asked* me to do the portrait of you?"

Kyle began to laugh. "That woman never ceases to amaze me. This is what happened," he began to explain. "Robbi was waiting for me when I walked into the office this morning. She began asking me all kinds of questions about where I had been and what I had done for my birthday. I mentioned to her that you had given me a very nice portrait of myself and that you were extremely talented. Robbi hasn't seen any picture you did for me. She's just jerking your chain. I can't believe she would tell you that. I told you not to believe a word that woman says."

"Oh. So then can I consider this harassment and expect you to handle her as you said you would?" said Carmen.

"Carmen, don't pay her any attention. Just be the bigger person. Don't play her petty games."

"How can you call this woman your friend?" asked Carmen. "I don't get it. To me, you're just as responsible for her behavior as she is. I mean, it's like you encourage her to be persistent with trying to mend things between you by being

58

cordial to her. And another thing ... what makes her think it's OK for her to go around telling lies on you and claiming to be your "very" good friend? Wait, let me answer. You allow her to, Kyle. You need to put that woman in check."

"Baby, please just chill out. Don't let Robbi Gant come between what we have. I want you and I to grow closer. These conversations about Robbi aren't going to do anything except pull us apart. Let's just move forward. Hey, guess what?" said Kyle changing the subject. "I told my mother and my favorite aunt all about you. They are convinced you are the type of woman I should marry. I told them they were right. They want to meet you. I told them to be patient...that you were worth the wait." Carmen accepted Kyle's version of the story. The last thing she wanted was to lose what ground she had made with him. She felt like she was "in" now that Kyle said he was talking about her to his family. She was determined not to let Robbi win Kyle's love back. Whatever Robbi did, it would be her mission to do it better.

For the next month, Carmen spent most of her time working and making herself available for Kyle. He had told her that his schedule at work had become very busy and that the tenants at the apartment complex he owned were running him ragged. It seemed as if Kyle was having less and less time to spend with her. Many nights he would come over to be with her and spend only about as much time it would take for her to give him great sex and for him to get a two-hour nap. He would always leave just before dawn claiming he needed to get home and get a head start on work. " I have a lot of cases to review and prepare for," he often said. Whenever she spent the night with him, he would set the clock for 4:30a.m. and proceed with his ritual of getting up, yawning loudly and profusely stretching, bending, moaning, and complaining about how much work he had to do... all before suggesting that she needed to get up and get going so that she wouldn't be late for work! At 4:30a.m. in the morning, there was a snowball's chance in hell that she would be late for work even if she had to walk to the airport and catch a plane to get there. Again, something was very wrong with this picture.

--- Chapter 7

The month of November had finally arrived. Things between Carmen and Kyle had not been so great. But Carmen didn't want to rock the boat for fear that Kyle would mend things with Robbi. Most importantly, she wanted her own relationship with him to be amicable since her birthday was on the horizon. Nevertheless, she found many of his actions questionable. Most of the time, she didn't know where he was. When he was with her, he seemed rushed. It was as if he rewarded her with his company if she didn't give him hell about his whereabouts. She remembered how he said he didn't like it when Robbi constantly argued with him about his whereabouts when most of the time he was working or just hanging out with the fellows.

Carmen's birthday would fall on a Saturday this year. She was extremely happy for the opportunity to be able to spend this time with Kyle and not have him be engaged in work activity. She only hoped he remembered how she felt about her special day. Saturday was approaching, but Kyle had yet to inquire about her availability. She tried not to be overly concerned because if he was planning a surprise, then asking her about her plans would give everything away.

Finally, on the Thursday prior to her birthday during a lunch time rendezvous at Kyle's apartment, he asked her about what she wanted for her birthday. She told him to surprise her. Not liking that answer, he asked her to be more specific. "Well, I really like surprises, but I'll try to help you out by telling you the kinds of things I like. Let's see, I like jewelry and uh ... let's see, romance. And uh, jewelry," Carmen responded even though she would have much preferred a romantic surprise.

"I have some running around to do on Saturday at the apartments in Bentford. A few of the tenants are delinquent on paying their rent, so I need to pay them, a visit, that is," said

61

Kyle.

"Oh come on, Honey. Can't you get someone else to do that. It's my birthday and I want to be with you," Carmen whined. "OK, OK, I know what I want for my birthday. Forget the jewelry request. I want to be with you all day on my birthday. Let me go to Bentford with you and then we can spend the rest of the day just enjoying each other's company," begged Carmen.

Kyle obviously didn't anticipate the request from Carmen to go to Bentford. He began to clear his throat and proceeded to stutter, "Baby, you wouldn't like the boring trip to Bentford to some 'ol dumpy apartments ... especially on your birthday. I just wouldn't feel right about subjecting you to that type of misery. Let me do something really special for you. I would really feel bad if I had to bear the memory of having my baby cooped up in a car for two hours on the road to Bentford on her birthday. Baby, please don't do that to me. Give me a chance to do something special for you," Kyle pleaded nervously. "Besides, I know what it's like to have someone do something special for you on your birthday, thanks to you. Let me make you feel as special as you made me feel." A reluctant Carmen consented to Kyle's offer. In the back of her mind she was hoping that Kyle was making up the entire story about Bentford and the tenants so that he would have more time to run last minute errands for her birthday. Maybe he was planning a surprise party, Carmen thought to herself.

Today was Carmen's special day. She had been awakened by a phone call from her parents, really her mother, wishing her a happy birthday. Several friends and relatives had called and sent cards to wish her happy birthday as well. Lewis had sent her a dozen yellow roses. Nikki had sent her two tickets to go see one of their favorite jazz singers, their long time college friend, Lark Devereau. Lark would be performing at the Civic Center in a couple of weeks. It was now 2:00p.m. There had been no sign of Kyle. Not even a phone call. The quiescence of her surroundings seemed unusual. Today was supposed to be festive. She was enjoying the thoughtfulness of all the people who recognized her birthday, but somehow Kyle's absence made her whole world seem to crumble. "Please God, don't let Kyle let me down," Carmen whispered and pleaded in desperation.

Carmen was so tempted to leave her apartment, but didn't want to risk missing a phone call from Kyle. She felt like a hostage, but quickly assessed that she would feel even worse if he called or came by and she was not there to receive him. It was now 2:30p.m. when her doorbell rang. It was a deliveryman. He was holding a vase with a dozen long stem roses. Carmen accepted the delivery and nervously checked the card. It was from Kyle! The card read "Today is a special day for a special lady - Happy Birthday...Love, Kyle." Surely this can't be what he calls special, Carmen thought to herself. She was happy to finally receive something from Kyle acknowledging her birthday, but she didn't know whether to smile or cry. "There has to be more. For starters, where the hell is he?...They have telephones in Bentford!" Carmen shouted to herself.

Kyle finally showed up at 7:45p.m. Carmen was furious when she answered the door.

She didn't bother to say anything initially because her frowned face told the story. Recognizing that she was probably angry, Kyle apologized profusely, offering every excuse in the world from having altercations with tenants to car trouble. Carmen began to retreat when Kyle kissed her and presented her with a box. The box was too large to contain jewelry, or so she thought. Kyle offered her another box that contained perfume. He asked her to put some on after she got dressed because he wanted to take her out to dinner. She didn't have the heart to tell him she had already eaten a Stouffer's Lean Cuisine chicken dinner almost two hours earlier. He seemed to be trying to redeem himself, so she allowed him to. Anxious to know what was inside the big box, Carmen began to tear away at the beautiful wrapping paper. She flipped off the box top. Inside she found a soft pink lamb's wool sweater with a gold toned 'C' pinned on the left chest area. She smiled despite her disappointment and said, "Oh, Thank you, Honey. It's nice."

––––––––––––––

"Wait a minute, Carmen, let me get this straight. Kyle Sealy, an attorney *and* an owner of apartment units, shows up on your birthday when it's almost *over*...I might add...with a sweater with a big ol' gold-plated *costume* jewelry broach pinned to the chest?" blasted Nikki. "And you're not pissed! Girl, I have heard it all. Didn't you tell him you liked jewelry? How about some pearls, some 14k or some 24k, and some precious stones? Has he never heard of diamonds! I bet you he got that shit in the costume jewelry section at Sears. I bet you think that 'C' stands for Carmen, don't you? I'll tell you what it ought to stand for ... something that represents him...like *Cheap* ... not to mention *Corny* and *Coulda* done a whole lot better. Carmen, tell me you didn't feel like choking his *Country* ass."

"I would have if I could have, Nikki," Carmen lamented. "But let's look on the bright side, at least the 'C' wasn't embroidered on the sweater."

"I'm not sure I get it," said Nikki. "How the hell is that cheap broach a brighter side than having the 'C' embroidered!

"Well, knowing you, your ass would have been calling me Lavern like that lady on Lavern & Shirley," Carmen joked to ease her disappointment. "At least I can unpin that shit he probably bought on clearance...embroidery would have been *permanent*."

"You have a point," said Nikki. She continued to express to Carmen how appalled she was with Kyle's behavior. "I tell you, Kyle's ass just takes the cake...I mean you can generally tell when you're about to receive cheap gifts. The warning sign is when the giver shows up with multiple boxes. The guilt about purchasing the first piece of cheap shit forces them to try to offset the cheapness with quantity...I know this from experience. But no...Kyle's ass shows up with *one* box with *all* the cheap shit in it. What a cheap ass. Just do me one favor, Carmen. Those two tickets I gave you to see Lark, don't invite Kyle's sorry ass as your guest. He's likely to be a no-show. I gave you those tickets with the thought of having my best friend spending a happy and joyful evening with a suitable companion, enjoying the vocals of someone she admires. Kyle Sealy will no doubt have you feeling exactly the opposite."

"We'll have to see. The show is two weeks away. Maybe we will see an improvement by then, or maybe not," said Carmen as she prepared to get off the phone. "Maybe you'll have to fly your ass over here to go with me if I don't have a date by then. Anyway I need to run, I'll talk to you later, OK. Thanks again for the tickets."

Standing before Carmen was the man of her dreams waiting to escort her to the concert with Alex Bugnon headlining and Lark Devereau performing the local opening act. Kyle was on time. He had taken the SAAB earlier to get it washed and waxed for the evening event. He had returned from getting dressed. He looked like a sheik prince in his black Georgio Armani suit. His hair was freshly cut and his mustache was neatly groomed. The shoes were shined and his pearly white teeth twinkled when he smiled. His cologne was pungently pervasive and seductive...

Carmen stood before him donning a full length Donna Karan fitted black dress with spaghetti straps and splits on each leg that allowed the visibility of her shapely calves. Her hair was pinned up and back off her face showing off her cheekbones and the new makeover she had received earlier at the salon. She had accessorized with long draping rhinestone earrings and a matching bracelet. She didn't wear a necklace because her bare neck was more sex appealing with the dress.

Carmen and Kyle sipped champagne and danced to the tunes on Lark's and Alex Bugnon's CD's to get in the mood for the concert. The atmosphere was particularly festive because of the holiday season. The glitz and glamour of the holidays would certainly compliment what was sure to be a romantic evening.

After the SAAB was handed off to the valet parking attendant, Carmen and Kyle proceeded to enter the concert hall. All eyes were staring at them because they made a handsome couple. Even if people weren't staring at them as a couple, Kyle was getting the stares from the ladies and Carmen was receiving stares from the men. Although, Carmen was certain she was getting stares from women as well because women love to check out what other women are wearing. She thought...no, *knew* she was looking ravishing.

The curtains went up and there was the band playing softly before the spotlight found Lark standing atop a staircase. Instantly, she resounded her first note which captivated the audience. She sang so beautifully. Carmen had known Lark since college. Her real name was Linda Durham. Everyone used to tell her what a beautiful voice she had. One of her music teachers once told her she sang like a lark. From that point she adopted it as her stage name. Devereau was her mother's maiden name. Carmen, Nikki and Lark were in the same sorority. Whenever they had fund-raisers, Lark would perform and Carmen would design and paint the posters to advertise for the event. They used to always tell each other how their gifts from God would someday make them famous. Nikki used to say that she would be each of their accountants and that they would have to pay her top dollar for her services in order for her to sustain her lavish lifestyle.

Lark sang her signature rendition of Roberta Flack's 'Killing Me Softly'. Alex Bugnon played another one of Carmen's favorites, a Brenda Russell tune, 'Piano in the Dark'.

Kyle seemed to enjoy the concert as much as Carmen. Amidst the beautiful music and romantic ambiance, all of Kyle's unfavorable behavior was forgiven. Carmen had never felt closer to him. The season was magical. She couldn't wait to enjoy the entire holiday season with him. Having him in her life was the best Christmas gift she could have.

After the concert climaxed, Carmen found her way backstage to see Lark and to show off Kyle. Lark was very surprised and happy to see Carmen. Carmen, too, was happy to see Lark. Seconds after they saw each other, they embraced and cried tears of joy. "Lark, you still look like a million bucks," said Carmen. "And you still can blow, Girl! I didn't even know you were going to be in town until I got the tickets from Nikki for my birthday. Oh, let me not be rude. I'd like for you to meet my new boyfriend, Kyle. Lark this is Kyle. Kyle, my dear friend, Lark."

Kyle greeted Lark with his gleaming smile. "It's very nice to meet you. I loved your performance. I'm glad Carmen decided to bring me," he joked.

"It's my pleasure to make your acquaintance. You and Carmen make such a handsome couple," replied Lark.

"We do, huh?" said Carmen as she grabbed hold of Kyle's arm smiling and blushing. "Hey, I really like the cover on your new CD. I see you're letting your hair grow long. You look so exotic. I love it," said Carmen.

"Thank you, Carmen," Lark replied. "It's my new manager's idea. You look like a million bucks yourself. Is that dress you're wearing a Donna Karan?

"You know that's my girl," said Carmen. "And yes, it is a size 6 and no, you cannot have it. You know I love you, but you can't have Donna."

"That's OK, I'll just settle for a wedding invitation," joked Lark as she gave Carmen a wink of approval regarding Kyle. They stood around and chatted for another ten minutes and then bid each other fair well making a pact to keep in touch with each other. "Let me know the wedding date. I'll sing for you," said Lark as she watched Carmen and Kyle disappear down the corridor.

Carmen and Kyle didn't spend much time together over the

67

holidays because Kyle had left town early to spend Christmas with his family in Charlotte, North Carolina. Carmen spent part of the holidays with her family in Nashville, Tennessee. They exchanged gifts before they left Philadelphia. Kyle gave Carmen pearl earrings. She gave him a cashmere sweater. They spent most of the Christmas holiday over the phone. They had originally planned to celebrate New Years together in Atlanta, but Kyle had a difficult time getting away because he said many of his relatives from Florida were visiting and he thought it would be rude to leave them. Carmen, however, wasn't able to reach him on the attempts she made to contact him on New Years Eve. She assumed he was busy entertaining his cousins and aunts who seemed to worship him. Kyle did, however, find time to call her and wish her a happy New Year on New Years day, citing his hectic schedule with running around doing things for his father and mother and other family members.

The holiday season turned out to be, yet another, unfulfilling special event for Carmen with Kyle. Valentines Day would be next. Carmen didn't know what to expect. Her stint in Philadelphia was near completion. Feeling torn between her career and her coveted relationship with Kyle, Carmen knew she had to make decisions based on facts. She knew she had to clear the areas of concern she had about Kyle. She would constantly see him in the company of Robbi, yet, he insisted they were just friends and that she was barking up the wrong tree because Robbi was not a factor to be considered. If Kyle was being truthful, then she didn't want to blow any opportunities they may have to be together by creating the obstacle of distance between them. Thus, Carmen decided to be on her best behavior leading up to Valentine's Day because in her mind, this would be the tell-all day. If Kyle blew this, she swore to herself that she would move on with her own agenda. After all, her promotion was eminent and she would get the opportunity to move to Atlanta, which was closer to her hometown and family.

"Would Kyle prefer romantic or sexy?" Carmen asked herself as she contemplated what type of gift she would give Kyle for Valentine's day. She knew he wouldn't appreciate flowers; he wouldn't consider that romantic or sexy. He didn't really like cookies, so that blossoming cookie arrangement thing was out of the question. Silk boxers were trite. Dinner for two at a nice restaurant was his job to do, she thought. The more she thought about it, the more she decided that it was Kyle who should be romancing her. She decided she couldn't go wrong with sexy. "That's it," she thought. "I'll do something sexy."

During one of her trips to New York City, Carmen visited the district where sexy things were in abundance. Everything seemed so raunchy. She wanted to be sexy, but classy. Luckily she ran into one of the salespeople in the Sensory Oils & Gifts shop who understood exactly what she was looking for. "I can tell you're a classy lady," said the salesperson. "So am I. Everything I carry in my shop is classy. People come in here all the time looking for an alternative to the dildos and whips. Good sex doesn't have to be raunchy. People shouldn't have to feel embarrassed when it comes to purchasing adult products. Wouldn't it be nice to pick up a little something naughty, but nice, while you're purchasing a nice piece of sexy lingerie?" Carmen agreed.

"Come over here, I got something for ya'," the salesperson said as she walked over to one of her display cases. "Please take a look at this new line of sexual enhancement oils and candles called *Ambrodisiac*. Ambrodisiac is derived from the words ambrosia and aphrodisiac. Now the term ambrosia means the food of the gods. It's something with an especially delicious flavor or fragrance. An aphrodisiac is something that stimulates sexual desire. " The salesperson went on to explain how the candles were used for ambiance and how the oils were used for the enhancement of oral sex. She explained that oils were gender specific. "The oils are in pink and blue for differentiation. For example," she explained, "for men we have Rock Candy...get it? The names are connotative and represented in good taste…no pun intended. You put the oil on the penis and now it's something good to taste. The man's penis is now rock hard and you get to eat "Rock Candy." Carmen begged for more examples. The salesperson was happy to oblige. "Well, also for the man, we have CoCo-nut, Lick-or-Wish (licorice), HoneySUCKle, Candy Cane, Nuts-n-Honey, Sugar Cane, Banana, Banana Nut, and Raise 'n' Nut. Now for the woman we have, Cherry, Black Cherry, Hot Chocolate, "P-Whip" Cream, Sweet Cream, I-Scream (vanilla, strawberry and chocolate), Juicy Fruit, Cotton Candy, and Banana Split. Now, for either gender, when you really want to be kinky, we have Sticky Buns." Each of the oils is not only full of flavor, but is aromatic, as well. Would you like samples of each?"

Carmen accepted. She knew instantly what she would do.

———————

When Carmen returned to Philadelphia, she rushed into one of the drug stores near her apartment to purchase a heart-shaped box of Valentine's Day chocolate candy. She didn't bother to see what assortment of chocolates the box contained. She just needed the box.

She could barely wait until she got into her place before she started tearing away at the plastic on the box of candy. She felt giddy as she emptied all of the chocolates out of the box onto her kitchen counter top. She then replaced each piece of candy with one of the labeled samples of *Ambrodisiac* oils. The oils smelled sweeter than the candy she had replaced. She knew this gift would be as unique as the gift she had given Kyle on his birthday. He loved sexy and erotic things. Thus, this concept was sure to please.

———————

Valentine's Day had finally arrived. Carmen had received a lovely bouquet of roses at her office from Kyle. But never mind all of that, she was looking forward to the evening. Carmen had successfully convinced Kyle that they should spend a nice quiet evening at her place because all of the nicer restaurants were sure to be crowded with all of the lovers celebrating Valentine's Day. Kyle didn't protest at all. To set the tone for the evening, Carmen left Kyle a sexy voicemail at work, "Hi, Sweetheart. Thank you for the beautiful roses. I love them and I love you. Oh, by the way, I saw you downstairs in the cafeteria. You look good enough to *eat*." Carmen then proceeded to make a playful slurping noise before she hung up with a seductive giggle.

A nice hot bubble bath awaited Kyle when he arrived at Carmen's apartment. He was still wearing his suit and tie because he came over straight from work. The bathroom was filled with lit candles. Carmen was wearing a short red robe that was wrapped loosely to allow the visibility of her cleavage. So what if one of her breast popped out accidentally…this was all part of the seduction. Since she only wore a 36B, she might have to do a little leaning to help with the "popping out". "Baby, you have on too many clothes. Why don't you slip on something a little more comfortable," Carmen flirted. Kyle beamed with approval of Carmen's sex appeal. He took another glimpse at the bubbles and candles. Kyle began to disrobe.

Now fully undressed, Kyle begin to kiss Carmen passionately as he started to undo the sash of her short silky robe. "Wait, I have something I want to give you," said Carmen. She knew that once they were in the tub it wouldn't be long before they would be making hot passionate love to each other. She wanted to make sure **Ambrodisiac** was part of the act. "I bought you a box of sweet things," she said reaching for the box of Valentine's Day "candy". Kyle accepted the box as he continued to tug at her robe. "Can I open that later?" he panted. "No, now," insisted Carmen. Kyle was obedient to his commanding partner. He began to open the box. His eyes lit up when he figured out what was going on. Carmen reached in the box. "I want to eat this flavor, " she said. "Rock Candy!" said Kyle with a devilish smile. "Hey, these are neat. This smells like Rock Candy, too." Kyle began to laugh with amusement. "Come here Baby, you never cease to amaze me," he said as he reached for Carmen to kiss her. "I think I'm in the mood for some...lets see," said Kyle as he sorted through the pink labels, "...some Black Cherry." He was clearly amused. Carmen was happy. "Bon Appetite," she said.

Carmen felt like Valentine's Day had given her the security she needed to consider requesting to remain in Philadelphia to head up another assignment. She even considered the possibility of resigning from the company if they declined her request. Kyle seemed to be more attentive to her. Although he was spending more time in Bentford overseeing the upgrade project at the apartments, he was spending more time with her during the week. She decided she wouldn't move too swiftly with a decision about her career until she was certain there was a need to. Kyle just might be thinking about making their relationship more permanent. Something like marriage.

———————

It was one cold night during the week when Carmen had requested to spend the night with Kyle or even that he spend the night with her. He declined both options, indicating that he just felt like being alone. It would be those nights when Carmen slept alone in her apartment that submitted her to loneliness and depression. Carmen watched the snow continue to fall outside her bedroom window as she imagined what it would be like to be in the arms of the man she so loved. It seemed the more she saw Kyle the more she wanted to see him. She found it very difficult to sleep. She had thought of painting, but her mood was gloomy, so she sat up watching television and flipping through magazines. She eventually drifted off to sleep on her couch. When she awakened, it was around 5:30am. Unable to return to sleep, she decided to get up and get ready to go into work. She tried to call Kyle, but got the usual answering machine on the first ring. She didn't bother to leave a message.

Carmen was dressed for work by 6:30. She had to brush the snow off her car before she could get going. This was one of the things she disliked most about living in northern states. In route to work, she decided to drive by Kyle's apartment to write *I love you* on the windshield of his car. But to her surprise, there was no snow on his windshield. "What's wrong with this picture?" Carmen thought to herself. Her heart began palpitating. "Had Kyle been out all night? No wait," she thought as she rejected that thought. "Let me think, what other explanations are there? Maybe he came out earlier this morning to brush the snow off his car and went back inside to get dressed for work. Maybe he didn't want to brush the snow after he was dressed in his work attire." Searching frantically in her head for answers, she had to follow her hunch. She parked her car behind Kyle's. Then she walked around to the front of his car to touch the hood. It was warm. Noticing only one set of footprints leading from Kyle's car to the apartment, Carmen quickly discounted her theory that he walked from the apartment to the car to brush it off and then walked back in to get dressed. Because then, there would be two sets of prints: one to the car and one to the apartment. Even though Carmen knew now that Kyle was probably seeing someone else, she felt like she needed concrete proof. As much as she wanted to confront Kyle, she knew he would lie. He would tell her that he was out all night with the fellas or worked all night at the office. He would absolutely deny being out with another woman.

The time was nearing for Carmen to receive notice if she would be receiving her promotion and whether or not her next assignment would take her to Atlanta. Kyle's behavior had been typical: hot, cold, abundant, sparse, inviting, rejecting, simple, complex. Carmen was obsessed with finding the truth. The ambivalence of the situation was too unsettling. She had considered following him to track his whereabouts, but she generally couldn't get enough information out of him far enough in advance to set things up.

Carmen was visiting Kyle at his place one Saturday afternoon. They were both growing hungry. They had discussions of the other going out to grab something for them to eat. Kyle didn't want to go and leave Carmen unattended in his apartment. She agreed to the task. She successfully convinced him to let her use *his* car to go get them Chinese food for lunch. She also convinced him that it would be a good idea to rent a movie. Assuring Kyle that she would be right back, she grabbed his keys and made a mad dash for the door. She proceeded straight to the hardware store where she requested a reproduction of every key on Kyle's key ring. While she waited, she used the pay phone at the store to call ahead on the order of Chinese food. She was extremely nervous about what she was doing, however, she felt that she had no other choice.

Finally, Carmen departed the hardware store with seven freshly made keys. All she needed was one - the one that would open the door to Kyle's apartment - the key that would provide her with the answers she needed. She had to hurry to make up for the time she had lost. She rented the movie, *Jungle Fever* before she rushed to the Chinese restaurant to pick up her order of Sweet and Sour Chicken, Hunan Shrimp and Egg Rolls. They spent the remainder of the afternoon together before Kyle had to go to his fraternity meeting. She felt overwhelming compunction about what she had done. She could hardly finish her food. All she could do to ease her guilt was convince herself she would never allow herself to feel compelled enough to go through with her plan to enter Kyle's apartment without his permission.

Rumors continued to run rampant about Kyle and Robbi's involvement. All of which Kyle denied. All of which Carmen could neither confirm nor discount. Per Kyle, Robbi seemed to create more and more reasons for him to remain late at the office to work on "critical" projects. He insisted that she was being intentionally evil because she was angry that he refused her suggestions that they should get back together as a couple. Since Robbi was merely a co-worker, Carmen couldn't understand why he would allow her to have such control over him in the workplace. However, the morning Carmen saw Robbi leaving Kyle's apartment after they had supposedly "worked" all night was the last straw. Carmen needed answers and she needed them fast!

Carmen's flight had returned early one afternoon from a trip to her New York headquarters office. She called Kyle from the airport to check out how busy he was and what his schedule for the remainder of the day looked like. "Are you real busy this afternoon? Do you think you could leave work early?" Carmen asked. "I'm really tied up this afternoon, Baby. I probably won't get home until around seven or so." Kyle replied. This was exactly the response Carmen wanted to hear. "Oh, that's too bad," Carmen said pretending to be disappointed. "It's only a little past 2:00. I'm just going to run a few errands and then go home afterwards. If you're able to get off earlier, just call me. If I'm not home, just leave a message," she continued.

Carmen hurriedly paid the parking attendant at the airport as she set out on her mission to find peace of mind. As she approached Kyle's apartment, she could feel her palms becoming sweaty. She fumbled through her purse to find the seven keys she had reproduced. She stood at the front door trembling and breathless. What would be behind these doors? Did she even want to know? Could she deal with whatever she found? Why was she even at this point? Why couldn't her overwhelming doubt be enough? What if she found nothing ... could she even confess to Kyle to what she had done. If she found something, how could she confront Kyle? How could she explain how she obtained the evidence? What if she got caught trespassing? What if? What if? What if? Carmen felt like a criminal as she looked down at her gloved hands trying to select which key to try first. She had already eliminated two keys, the car key and the trunk key. The first of the five remaining keys did not fit. She felt a sense of relief almost. It was if she needed something to hinder her from this unspeakable act. Key number two didn't work either. "These must be the keys to his parents' home in Charlotte or keys to the apartments he owns," Carmen thought to herself. The third key turned and clicked the lock. Heat flushed through her body. Carmen had to make a decision. The only thing now that stood between her and the other side was her conscience. The need to know was overwhelming. She turned the lock and proceeded to enter Kyle's domain. She felt the quiet and stillness of the room. All she could hear was the noise of the bubbles and the pump from the aquarium. Afraid to exhale, she stood still and panned the room with her eyes. Kyle was very neat and meticulous. Nothing was out of place. She began to walk slowly to the back of the apartment towards the bedroom. Her legs felt like spaghetti, her head was buzzing. As she entered the bedroom, her eyes immediately focused on a picture of a woman on his dresser! Her heart stopped, because it was obvious that it was not a picture of her. Stunned and momentarily immobilized, Carmen took a deep breath as she moved closer to get a better look. "Who is *this* woman?" she thought to herself with confusion. "This is not Robbi!" The woman on the picture appeared to be college-aged. She had big hazel-colored eyes, long brown cascading hair and very pretty straight teeth. The picture looked like it had been taken with a 35mm camera and blown up to fit the 5x7 frame it was in. "Who is this bitch?" Carmen said to herself as she transitioned from shock to anger. Her first instinct was to began trashing the apartment, but she knew she had to gain composure and remain calm. She began to look through the closet for women's clothing. There were none. Everything was so neat. She had to be extremely careful not to disturb anything to even hint she had been there. She then went into his bathroom where she saw a shower cap and two wash clothes. She looked down on the floor in front of the sink where she saw hair that was too long to be Kyle's. Having seen enough, Carmen made sure everything was placed back to its original state and then retreated to her home where she drowned in her tears and sorrow.

Almost in a trance, Carmen ignored her ringing phone as her wrinkled body soaked in a tub of what was now room-temperature water. She tried to sort through everything that went through her mind. Who was this woman? How could she be special enough to have her picture displayed in his bedroom? How did Robbi fit in? "How do I fit in?" Carmen lamented.

Even though Carmen had vowed to get on with her life if she

discovered Kyle to be unfaithful, she found it unsettling to not know who the woman in the picture was and what she meant to Kyle. Carmen refused to accept that her relationship with Kyle was meaningless. She made it up in her mind to get back to Kyle's apartment on another occasion to gather more information. She had also decided to continue to see Kyle. She wanted to believe that she was only seeing him so that he would not become suspicious that she was on to him, even though she knew she was really seeing him because she loved him and wanted to win him over.

A week later, Carmen returned to Kyle's apartment while he was at work. She stopped by on her way back from visiting a client. To her surprise, the picture of the woman was not up. Instead, there was a picture of Robbi! "What the hell was going on here?" Carmen thought. Bewildered and broken hearted, she began to sob uncontrollably. Somehow the pain of seeing Robbi's picture was much deeper than the pain of seeing the unidentified woman. Perhaps because Kyle had denied any involvement with her other than friendship. She stared at Robbi's smiling face, as it seemed to come to life offering a gloating expression. She felt encouraged to knock Robbi's picture off the dresser, creating the false sense of triumph for herself over the existing situation. As she watched the picture hit the floor, she realized that Robbi felt no pain, for the picture was merely an image of a real life person who was present in Kyle's life. The image continued to smile as Carmen continued to wail. She was in pain.

Carmen began to pull herself together. She began thinking about how she would proceed with her life, as she returned objects, including Robbi's picture, to their original location. Suddenly Robbi's image wore a smile of stupidity. Carmen got a kick out of knowing that Robbi was being cheated on by the other woman and vice versa. Even though she, too, was being cheated on, she felt vindicated because she knew what the others didn't. A step ahead is what she felt. She knew Kyle's dirty little secret.

Soon Carmen's self-proclaimed triumph had progressed to a

dangerous obsession.   She was visiting Kyle's apartment unauthorized more frequently.   She felt misinformed if she didn't know which woman Kyle was seeing during which time period.   She had learned the previously unidentified woman's profile.   It was the personalized plates on her light blue rusty Chevrolet Impala leaving Kyle's apartment early one morning that provided the necessary leads to verify her identity. "Now I know she's country...personalized plates on that raggedy piece of shit," said Carmen.   The woman's name was Lauren and she worked in the gift-wrapping department at Arpel's department store.

When Carmen first learned of Lauren's identity, she visited Arpel's and bought twenty-five sets of fine crystal candles holders and spitefully requested each of them to be specialty wrapped because of their fragility.   She also expressed a sense of urgency to have the gifts wrapped while she waited.   She waited and watched as Lauren rolled her eyes and huffed as she carried out the tedious task.   As soon as Lauren completed the wrapping, Carmen graciously accepted the bagged merchandise and then proceeded to the Customer Service counter where she politely returned the items and had her charge card credited. Although senseless and childish, she felt a small victory.   The perception that Lauren was irritated made her victory all the more rewarding.   So whenever Lauren's picture was displayed in Kyle's bedroom, Carmen would remember her encounter at Arpel's and get a chuckle.

Carmen had begun to find the games and pretense less and less amusing.   She wanted very much to confront Kyle, however, the last thing she wanted was for him to become angry at her and retreat to the arms of Robbi and/or Lauren.   She could explain it to herself, but she still wanted Kyle and felt like she was the best choice.   She felt as though Robbi was a spoiled, pushy broad and Lauren, a wannabe, was a young, inexperienced liability.   She couldn't understand why Kyle would be involved with either of these women.   Thinking that if she could somehow clear the deck, Kyle would be forced to run to her awaiting arms.   As time passed, it seemed as though Carmen spent as much time being a private investigator as she did as an artistic designer. "Obsessed" is the term Nikki used to describe her. Nikki also tried to convince Carmen that Kyle was not as classy as she wanted to believe. A lowlife, low budget, womanizer is the description she assigned to him. Nevertheless, Carmen felt convinced Kyle was the only man for her.

Carmen had pretty much figured out Kyle's pattern for cheating. She would use this knowledge as a weapon to help her emerge victorious in her battle with Robbi and Lauren. One day, she told Kyle that she had to go to New York for a couple of days on business. She was certain that Tuesday night would be Robbi's sleep-over night. She told Kyle that she was leaving out Tuesday morning and be returning the following Thursday afternoon. When in actuality, she worked from her home. She had told her boss she was experiencing a virus and didn't want to contaminate the office.

On Tuesday night, Carmen sat in her car just down from Kyle's apartment. Just as suspected, Robbi arrived at Kyle's place at around 9:00p.m. She carried in an overnight case, which clearly suggested she wasn't just over for dinner. Even though everything that was happening was according to plan, Carmen's heart was no less injured. The hurt and anger fueled the malice. She soon went home assured that Robbi would settle at Kyle's until morning. She set her alarm for 5:00a.m.

It was approximately 5:30am. Carmen had gotten up and driven back over towards Kyle's place. She stopped at a gas station close by the apartment complex to use the phone. She called Lauren's number. "If you want to catch your boyfriend cheating, I suggest you get over to his apartment right away," Carmen said before she quickly hung up the phone. She hurried back to Kyle's apartment to establish her hidden ringside seat. Within thirty-five minutes, Carmen heard first, then saw a big blue car swerving around the corner in haste. She saw Lauren emerge from the car with no make-up, dressed in red sweats and white sneakers and her hair pulled back in a ponytail that swung at the pace of her swift walk to Kyle's front door. Carmen could see Lauren knocking forcefully on the door with a serious look of anger and rage. She imagined that Lauren had probably attempted to contact Kyle by phone but reached his answering machine. Lauren ran down the stairs and began to pick up pebbles from the landscaping beds. She then started tossing them with precision at Kyle's living room window. His bedroom was on the back. She knew he was home because his car was parked right outside. Robbi's navy blue 318i BMW was right next to it, probably just like her body was next to his behind the doors of his apartment. After several attempts to get Kyle to acknowledge her presence at his apartment, Lauren returned to her car where she appeared to wait for Kyle and his woman to leave for work. Carmen was thoroughly amused. She could see Lauren's perturbation. She also felt certain Robbi was kicking Kyle's ass right about now. To be a fly on the wall and hear Kyle explain his way out of this one would be like winning the lottery.

About fifteen minutes later, Robbi exited the apartment. She looked angry as she panned the parking lot. Without much hesitation, Lauren got out of her car. She bypassed Robbi so as to minimize her significance and headed straight for Kyle's apartment. Robbi, quickly realizing that Lauren was the woman in distress, turned to reenter Kyle's apartment. A cat fight was eminent, Carmen thought to herself amusingly. Neither woman acknowledged the other as they stood at the door waiting for Kyle to answer. Kyle obviously did not anticipate both women to be standing at his door. When he finally answered, Robbi barged in, taking advantage of his surprise. Lauren followed suit. Carmen thought of joining the party, but decided she was in the safest place should bullets begin to fly. Besides, she couldn't join in anyway because she wasn't even supposed to be in town. Finally, Lauren emerged from the apartment in tears. One down, Carmen thought to herself. Shortly thereafter, Robbi emerged looking pissed off, yet somewhat triumphant. Unsure of how to assess Robbi's demeanor, Carmen became concerned. Perhaps Kyle's demeanor would help her decide what to feel. Before she could become comfortable with that idea, Kyle emerged from the war zone looking as cool as a cucumber.

Carmen felt her only recourse now was to investigate the damages inside Kyle's apartment once he left.

Once inside, she discovered Robbi's things neatly lying in a chair in his bedroom. Her picture lay face-down on the dresser. Carmen concluded that Robbi elected not to take her things with her to avoid looking defeated in case Lauren was outside watching. The look of triumph she wore on her face was probably for this same reason. As the dust of the morning settled, Carmen began feeling less than victorious. Mostly ashamed. Kyle's love, she thought, would make her feel all better.

Carmen's plan seemed to have worked. Kyle began taking her out more, buying her things and even letting her sleep over late. By the same token, her plan created a situation that would cause her to have to choose between her career or her love for Kyle. She had been informed of the new office being opened in Atlanta and the open position for an advertising consultant. This position would also groom her for the coveted advertising executive opportunities. This was the opportunity she had worked so hard for. She felt certain she would be officially offered the job during her performance appraisal, which was due in a couple of weeks. She would make significantly more money, the cost of living would be less expensive, she could buy some property and gain the experience she needed to help her pursue her goal of owning her own advertising company for artistic expressions such as painting, poetry, music, and dance. Going back to work at the headquarters office in New York would give her opportunities to work on high visibility accounts, however, she would be faced with the barrier of competing with more senior employees. Success would be eminent, however, it would take much longer. To remain in Philadelphia would mean quitting the company altogether and working with another company with offices in that city. While all the pros of accepting the job in Atlanta rang in her head, she could not ignore the fact that she was extremely nubile. She knew in Atlanta that she would have to start over again searching for a mate. She also acknowledged the rumors she had heard about the competition between women being fierce. This was primarily due to the 6 to 1 ratio of women to men. Evaluating the odds, it appeared more likely for her to be able to find a suitable job in Philadelphia versus finding a suitable man in Atlanta. Her number one goal now was to get a firm commitment from Kyle. Perhaps Robbi and Lauren would then get the hint that they were never serious contenders for the honor of being Mrs. Kyle Sealy. Carmen had pretty much resigned in her own mind that Robbi, Lauren and whomever else were nothing more than flings. She hadn't decided how or if she would ever confront Kyle about his clandestine relationships. She couldn't decide if she would get more satisfaction out of revealing to Kyle her knowledge of Robbi and Lauren or just gloating to Robbi and Lauren, especially Robbi, that she had become the woman of choice.

Feeling a tremendous amount of anxiety about what to do with her life, Carmen turned to her close friends and relatives for advice. Her parents were absolutely advocates of her getting out of the north with all those "city-slickers". She was not surprised when her mother said, "They have jobs down here. I want my baby to be closer to home." Even though Carmen's parents never intruded in her personal life, she had called home crying about Kyle one time too many for them to be proponents of her staying with him, especially since no proposal for marriage had taken place. "Times aren't like they used to be. Women are making their own way now. They don't have to run behind a man to take care of them," Carmen's mother would tell her. "A person can fix their mouth to say anything. What they *do* is the true test of what they are really about," Carmen's father would always tell her, especially when she would defend Kyle by interjecting that he tells her that he loves her… She never mentioned that he usually told her that when they were in a horizontal position. Nikki would always suggest that what he was really saying was that he loved the nooky. Nikki told Carmen to take Kyle to the nearest jeweler and select a very nice *expensive* engagement ring and then gauge Kyle's seriousness about a commitment by his reaction. She told her that if he didn't react positively that she should "kick his ass to the curb."

While all the advice Carmen received provoked thought, none of it helped her make up her mind. She was confused. She felt in love, yet she yearned for professional success. Kyle didn't seem to share her sense of urgency about any of her issues. All she wanted was for him to help her decide. That way, she could hold him accountable for a wrong decision. She prayed for a sign from God.

--- Chapter 8

Carmen sat at the airport waiting to board the plane to Atlanta. While she stared at her one-way ticket, she grew sorrowful. Her eyes began to well up as she remembered the sequence of events that led to her departure from Philadelphia. She recalled the morning she drove by Kyle's apartment while on her way to work. She arrived just in time to see Robbi leaving with a colossal bouquet of roses. Kyle walked along side of her with what appeared to be a large gift-wrapped box. They kissed each other as he helped her into her car. Kyle proceeded back inside. As Robbi drove out of the complex, she noticed her gaping in shock. Realizing her surprise, Robbi smiled with ridicule and drove off with confidence. It was Carmen's first instinct to go knocking at Kyle's door to demand an explanation. She didn't need one, the evidence was clear. Kyle was a liar. She felt like a fool for putting herself through the trauma. In her search for answers, she learned from Phyllis, who was able to get the information from the receptionist on Kyle's floor, that Kyle had convinced Robbi that Carmen was nothing more than a person who filled the void while he dealt with the devastation of losing her over the incident and "misunderstanding" with Lauren. He had also told Robbi that Carmen was very jealous of her and was trying to do any and everything to fill her shoes. Regarding Lauren, he told Robbi that Lauren was just some young girl trying to find herself a sugar daddy. He "admitted" to lending Lauren some money once because she was going through some hard times and that he couldn't seem to shake her from that point onward. Robbi was extremely flattered by Kyle's explanation and agreed to dating him again. The fact of the matter was that Robbi and Kyle had never really broken up for any extended period since they began dating two years prior. Just when Carmen's heart began to bleed at the thought of Robbi being special, Phyllis also shared with her that Kyle had provided a similar story to Lauren about Robbi. "Kyle covered all the bases," said Phyllis. "He told Lauren that Robbi was jealous of her because she was young and pretty and that Robbi was just a spoiled rich girl who was looking for someone to take care of her. He "admitted" to spoiling her one time too many and couldn't seem to shake her from that point onward. Lauren swallowed the story hook, line and sinker. She and Kyle resumed dating." Carmen remembered how Kyle had offered her the same lines about Robbi. He had no idea she knew about Lauren. He also had no idea she had keys to unlock the truth. Phyllis had reluctantly revealed to Carmen how Kyle had represented her to Robbi. "He told Robbi that you were a crazy woman who couldn't take the hint that he didn't want to be with you. Please don't take that personally, Carmen. That's the "great escape" line that men use when their asses get caught," said Phyllis. Carmen had also learned that Kyle didn't own any apartments in Bentford. It was just a part of his charade...an excuse for disappearing while he philandered. She remembered Kyle insisting that he was not clear that she thought they were in a committed relationship.

Phyllis encouraged Carmen to learn from her mistakes and to get on with her life. She assured her life would be sweeter to her if she were sweeter to herself.

"This is the final boarding call for all passengers for Delta's non-stop service to Atlanta, Georgia," announced the agent as Carmen began boarding the plane vowing to look ahead for greater things to come.

———————

The plane touched down in Atlanta on schedule. Carmen was greeted at the airport by her friend, Ava. Ava was waiting at the gate. Carmen spotted her immediately. She was still tall and skinny. She wore a big T-shirt and leggins with no socks and a pair of sneakers. She could have easily been a model...she stood 5'11" in her stocking feet. Her hair was swept up in a bun and she wore very little makeup...she was naturally pretty. Ava was now around thirty-one years old. She didn't look a day over twenty-five. She and Carmen had known each other for many years. They originally met in New York. Ava worked for the agency as a financial analyst before resigning to move to Atlanta to marry her college sweetheart, Jerome "J.B." Briggs, who was now a successful obstetrician. Everyone thought Ava was foolish for quitting. Jerome was fresh out of medical school and was making very little money. A fair amount of the money he was making was being used for paying back school loans. Six months later, it became apparent why Ava and Jerome married so hastily...she gave birth to twin girls, Toria and Tamia. The twins were now four. Ava taught aerobics, was the wife of a physician, the mother of two beautiful daughters, and lived in a palatial home in the Cascades, a beautiful suburban community.

After their jubilant reunion, Carmen and Ava proceeded to baggage claim to gather Carmen's luggage. Carmen had five large suitcases. Ava's Range Rover had plenty of room to transport all the bags. Carmen could hardly wait to get to Ava's house to see the home she had only previously had the luxury of viewing in pictures. They had a lot of catching up to do. Since Carmen would be staying with Ava and J.B. for the next few weeks until she found a condominium to purchase, they would have plenty of time to do just that. She was also dying to see the twins. Carmen would be a virtual leech for a couple of days because she was going to have to depend on Ava for transportation until her SAAB arrived. She was having it shipped to avoid putting all the miles on it by driving from Philadelphia to Atlanta. After only a few minutes in Atlanta, she realized everything was so spread out, high mileage on the SAAB was inevitable.

Carmen's visit with Ava and J.B. was therapeutic. She was amongst friends who loved her and wanted to see her do well in life. Watching Ava and J.B. interact gave her hope that relationships actually do work. She asked Ava if she ever felt threatened that J.B. was an Ob-gyn and looked at naked women all day. Ava replied, "Whatever he looks at all day doesn't seem to be enough to keep him from coming home to me." J.B.

referred to Ava as the queen of his world. The Royal Highness wore a two-carat rock suitable for a queen. Ava and J.B. had a lot of material things, however, they were extremely down-to-earth people. Toria and Tamia had chores even though Ava had a housekeeper to come in once a week. J.B. was a tall well-groomed man. He wore a shadow beard and had very nice low-cut wavy hair. He stood about 6'3" and could have easily been a model, as well. He coached little league baseball with inner city teams and gave large donations to many inner city development projects. He also participated heavily in the Big Brother programs.

The fairy tale couple seemed too good to be true, but they were truly in love with each other and planned to be that way forever. Ava was quick to say that marriage was not an easy institution, that it required work. When asked if she felt she and J.B. married too quickly, she replied, "While we can always blame the bad times on the fact that we married young, we can also take responsibility for any situation and deal with the present rather than dwelling on the past. J.B. and I could have chosen to split many times when the road got rough, but splitting doesn't guarantee you paradise. Problems are a part of life; you either deal with them or you just create that many more problems for yourself. Besides we love, respect, and most of all, trust each other. If we didn't have trust, we would have nothing."

"I see. So when is J.B. going to introduce me to some of his nice doctor friends?" Carmen joked with a hint of seriousness.

"Do you just want a doctor or do you want a man who will treat you right?" answered Ava.

"For starters, I'll take both," Carmen replied as if she were placing an order.

"Most of our doctor friends are married. The one's that are single aren't necessarily your type.

"Why do you say that?" asked Carmen as if she couldn't figure out what Ava was eluding to.

"You know you have always had a thing for tall, very good looking men. And you know, they can't walk funny, talk funny, act funny, dress funny, and so on," Ava replied. "And the one's that you would find interesting, so would every other woman. But you know what's even funnier?

"What?" asked Carmen as she listened intensely.

"The second that one of the least attractive ones finds a woman who isn't so caught up in physical and material things, then all of a sudden he's *desirable* to other women. It seems as if women always want the man they can't have or only want a man once he has been *pre-qualified* by another woman; be it a girlfriend or a wife! Women are trips!"

"Wonder why that is," said Carmen. "All I know is I'm not going to settle for no ugly, broke man. Ugly men will dog you out just like the good-looking ones will. You know why?... *'Cause ugly people don't think they're ugly!"*

"I suppose you have a point. All I know is I am holding on to my man," joked Ava.

For the next couple of months, Carmen engrossed herself in her work. She often thought of Kyle. Many times she wanted to contact him, but somehow found the strength not to. Her main focus had become her job and finally settling on a condominium to purchase in the Buckhead area. She had found a condo she liked on Lenox Road. It was on the top level of the ten-story building. It had a beautiful white marble foyer. The living room was spacious and had a large window that provided a panoramic view of the nature that surrounded the property as well as a partial view of downtown Atlanta. It also had a fireplace with a rich white marble landing. Three skylights provided the natural light. The carpet throughout the condo was white and plush. Imported ceramic tile covered the floors in bathrooms and kitchen. The master bedroom had vaulted ceilings with beautiful recessed lights. In the wall was a small fireplace that provided for many romantic possibilities. The master bathroom had a black toilet, sink and Jacuzzi tub with gold fixtures. It also had mirrors on three walls making the room appear very large. The guest bedroom was small enough to deter a roommate. She decided she would use it for her painting room...she could always put things away if she had guest. The kitchen and dining were also pretty small. Carmen didn't mind since not much space was required to prepare cereal, which was generally her main course. The condo was quite pricey, however, she would have the opportunity to buy it relatively cheap if the current owners, who were friends of Ava and J.B., were able to close on their new property within the next couple of weeks. They were expecting a baby and were trying to buy a ranch way outside of Atlanta. Carmen knew she could qualify for the property because she basically had no debt other than her SAAB, which was almost paid for. If this deal did not come through, she had her sights on another condo on Peachtree Road.

Dating in Atlanta was something Carmen had planned to embark on very soon since she had begun to feel incredible loneliness. Her travel schedule and lack of privacy because she lived with Ava and J.B. were the excuses she had created for not dating thus far. She couldn't decide whether her reason for really not dating was because she needed time to get over Kyle or whether it was to make sure she was free should Kyle decide to beg forgiveness and another chance to be a part of her life. In either case, she was lonely and felt she needed to do something about it.

———————

Carmen received the good news that she had qualified for the loan to purchase the condominium on Lenox Road. Nikki suggested that she give a house-warming party and to put her in charge. She told Carmen all she would have to do was round up all the fine, rich men in Atlanta....and, for balance only, women who posed no competition. Little did Nikki know, the only man she really wanted to share in her celebration was Kyle. Carmen was too embarrassed to admit this to anyone. She felt stupid for feeling this way herself after the way he had treated her. She hadn't spoken to him since she left Philadelphia, but felt now would be a good time to call him up to brag about how well she was doing with full intentions of letting him know what he had given up by letting her go. She wanted to call him up to let him know that she was doing quite well in life without him. "If only I had a man," she thought, "then I could *really* drive the stake through his heart." As Carmen contemplated her revenge, it became apparent to her that any man who was good enough to make Kyle jealous was good enough to replace him. Kyle was sure to suspect her motives for calling him if she really had another man and was so happy. "Oh, but what the hell," she thought. "Kyle won't have to know I don't really have a man. I can just do a good job of making one up. Since I don't have one, I really have nothing to lose."

Carmen moved into her new place successfully. Although the condo was not nearly as spacious as Ava and J.B.'s, it was considerably larger than her apartment in Philadelphia. The efficiency apartment she once had in New York could almost fit into the guest bedroom. Having more space made her realize just how much furniture she didn't have. She figured a few large plants and a few nice pieces of art on the walls would provide the fillers she needed until she decided on a color scheme and a style of furniture she could afford. Looking at her finances after closing on the property made wooden crates appear to be all that she could afford at the moment.

Ava and J.B. had given her a beautiful framed art piece as a house-warming gift. It was so huge, there was only a couple of walls it could fit on. It was a limited edition serigraph of a woman who appeared to be deep in thought. They had purchased the piece from the William Tolliver gallery in Buckhead, which was not very far from where she lived. This picture would no doubt be her main showpiece in her soon-to-be home gallery. She had the jazz piece she had purchased in Philadelphia. It looked like a mini-print compared to the Tolliver piece. She also had a few of her own pieces she felt were good enough to display. A couple of them needed reframing. It was always amazing how the framing could make or break the artwork. Despite her lack of furniture and decoration, Carmen knew she had accomplished something great, she had purchased her first piece of property. Driving a convertible and continuing to live in an apartment had gotten old and, quite frankly, showed no stability in her life. The wait for a man to come along and take care of her seemed to get longer and longer. She felt she had to make some investments into her own future. She had money in an IRA account and now some property. She was feeling pretty good about herself.

It would be only a matter of time before she would contact Kyle to let him know just how good she felt. She decided she would contact him during work hours. She felt that if she tried to contact him during the evenings or the weekends he would either not be reachable or, if he was, wonder why she has so much time on her hands... particularly if she had a man.

"Kyle Sealy," he answered on the second ring. Carmen's heart skipped a beat.

"Guess who," she managed to utter. Immediately recognizing her voice, Kyle responded, "To what do I owe this surprise? ...Well, Hello, Ms. Layfield. It is still *Miss*, I'm assuming."

Slightly amused by his sarcasm, she decided to toy and probe. "It might be. So, if men changed their last names when they got married, what would yours be, Gant or Lauren Whatchamacallit?"

"Ha Ha, very funny. I wish my name could be Kyle Layfield. But you left me. You really hurt me, Carmen."

"I hurt *you*?...You're obviously a very confused man," she quipped.

"Carmen, I know you're not going to believe this, but I was very confused...really, I'm serious. I knew I loved you and still do, but I was afraid to make a commitment to you because I knew you were only in Philly for a short period.

"What about Robbi?" asked Carmen seeking to understand.

"What about her...Robbi and I are just friends. I will admit that when you told me that you were up for your promotion and it would take you out of Philadelphia, I started to back off our relationship because I didn't want to stand in the way of your aspirations. Robbi must have sensed that because she started hanging around more. However, she *was* also having a lot of problems with her family and she was having problems at work. She turned to me for support because, lets face it, we have known each other for a long time. But I don't want her, Carmen...she's just a friend. True, she wants more than that, but I don't. I really miss you, Baby. Why did you have to leave me?"

Carmen felt completely diffused. She was armed with an attitude when she placed the call. Now she felt like putty in Kyle's hands. She hadn't planned for this type of reception. How could she resist his charm? How could she stay focused? How could she brag that she had gone on without him? Instead, she felt like begging for forgiveness for ever leaving him. Her loneliness seemed to cloud her better judgment. "Kyle, you didn't give me many reasons to stay," Carmen said. Kyle went on to explain to her how he went through such a depression period after she left. He said that by not knowing how to contact her added to his pain. He suggested that he wanted and needed to see her and that he would be willing to pick up the tab for any of her travel expenses if she came to visit him in Philadelphia. She told him about her new place and had agreed to him coming to Atlanta before she realized that she had completely deviated from her plan.

Carmen waited anxiously at the gate for Kyle's arrival. Thank goodness he was flying in on Delta airlines because she didn't have to travel too deep into the airport in order to be on time for his arrival. Delta occupied Concourse A, which was the first stop on the airport underground rails. The last thing she wanted was to have to back track and search feverishly for him in the baggage claim area. This would only add to her anxiety and overwhelming desire to see him right away. While she waited, she removed her compact from her purse to check her makeup. The beads of perspiration over her top lip warranted a little touching up. The bright yellow linen dress she wore was now full of wrinkles, but she didn't mind because wrinkles in linen somehow added to the look of comfort. Her hair swept up off her shoulders into a bun and her ankle strapped sandals completed her look of summer.

Passengers began to emerge from the plane. Carmen could hardly breath. She chewed up the entire pack of Tic Tacs while she waited for Kyle. Suddenly, there he was…tall, groomed, handsome and *edible*. He was wearing a blue denim, tab-collar shirt and black jeans with black Kenneth Cole shoes. He cracked that sexy and seductive smile when he laid eyes on her. Kyle was in Atlanta…as he had promised. Carmen glided towards him as quickly as she could, for if she did not hurry, her feet and legs would melt beneath her. She reached up at him as he reached down at her. Suddenly, she was lifted off her feet and kissed passionately by whom seemed to be the only person in the world other than herself. All seemed to be forgiven. The SAAB was outside waiting to take them to the place Carmen had prepared as a love nest, her new condo.

Upon entering through the front door of her condo, Carmen took Kyle by the hand and led him to her bedroom where they could really kiss and makeup. And so it was, they made passionate love for what seemed like an eternity. Carmen was back in love again.

Within three months of Carmen and Kyle's "reunion", the relationship began to fade to black. Kyle seemed to still be full of promises he either could not or would not keep. He was still just as private, or rather, secretive as he ever was. Carmen had visited him twice during their brief second-time-around courtship. Each time, she felt as if she was being smuggled in and smuggled out. While she would visit, it disturbed her when Kyle turned off the ringer on his telephone. He also turned down the volume to the answering machine. He said he did this because he had with him the only person he wanted to talk to; everyone else would have to wait. While Carmen felt flattered, yet suspicious, she wanted to be able to answer the phone to proclaim her territory to any woman who was trying to be a part of his life. She wanted so much to be seen in public with him. She wanted it to get back to Robbi and Lauren and whomever else that she and Kyle were seemingly working things out despite the distance between them. None of her wishes materialized. She soon realized that trying to work things out with Kyle was probably a big mistake. The pain was still too fresh. After all, it was her loneliness that got her into this situation. She knew it was not the brightest thing she had ever done. Being "just friends" was probably best for right now.

Carmen would periodically call Phyllis, the receptionist at her old job, to say hello and to get an update on Kyle. Phyllis was often vague and evasive. Carmen knew she was putting her on the spot each time she inquired about Kyle and Robbi, however, her desire to know overruled her sensitivity to involving Phyllis in petty gossip. Phyllis casually mentioned to Carmen that she had run into Robbi at the mall recently and learned that Robbi was looking for an outfit to wear to a wedding she had been invited to attend in Atlanta. Carmen's antennas went up because she knew that Kyle was planning to attend a wedding in Atlanta in a couple of weeks. He was going to be a groomsman in his buddy, Langston's wedding. Kyle had originally invited Carmen to the wedding, but they got into an argument when she pressed him about why he couldn't act right so they could be in love and get married like normal people. So he uninvited her saying that he didn't feel like dealing with her drama. She and he had since then made up, but he said that the bride's mother had taken a final count and was not adding anymore people to the list. He vowed to Carmen, however, that he would be sure to spend time with her as soon as the wedding was over. He said he wouldn't be able to spend time with her before the wedding because he would be busy with rehearsals. Carmen didn't want to believe that Robbi was attending the same wedding...let alone as Kyle's guest! But she had to know. Thus, she transitioned into private investigator mode once again.

It was Friday afternoon, the day before Langston's wedding. Kyle called Carmen from the Atlanta airport to let her know he would come to her place as soon as he picked up his rental car. Although Carmen was happy to know that she would be seeing him soon, she felt extremely uncomfortable. She felt like she should be going to the wedding with him. Something seemed wrong. Maybe it was her imagination. Maybe Kyle was going to surprise her and take her to the wedding anyway.

Kyle arrived at Carmen's place at around 5:30p.m. As always, the passion between them ignited at first sight. As always, they headed straight for the bedroom or the first horizontal platform available once enough of their clothing was removed.

After they made love, they lay on the bed talking about whatever was going on in each of their lives as it related to work. Let Kyle tell it, he had no personal life because he worked *all* the time. After about twenty minutes of small talk, Carmen asked about the wedding. Kyle insisted that he had done all he could do to get her an invitation, but to no avail. He took this opportunity to remind her that he could not stay long because he had to go to the rehearsal which was scheduled for 8:30p.m. When Carmen asked if she could join him for rehearsal, he quickly told her no, once again reminding her that he would be completely busy with the wedding party and also the bachelor party which was scheduled for later that evening. He said he didn't want her to feel left out. She had considered going to the church anyway, but could never get a clear answer from Kyle as to the name of the church. All she could determine was that the wedding was going to be held in a church in the metropolitan Atlanta area, which wasn't much help at all since there were at least a zillion churches in the area.

Carmen got one last hug and kiss from Kyle before he walked out her front door on his way to rehearsal. He told her that he would probably not get a chance to see her until Sunday since he would be tied up with the wedding all day Saturday.

As she sat alone in her condo, Carmen could not rest. She had a very uneasy feeling about Robbi. She called the airlines to check if Robbi was confirmed on any flights out of Philadelphia for Friday evening...she knew which airline to check because Kyle had mentioned before which one she preferred. The airline representative would not provide her with this information. Not to be outdone, Carmen called the airline back pretending to be Robbi requesting a confirmation of her reservation out of the connecting city of Pittsburgh into Atlanta. Bingo. Carmen was able to get the confirmation that Robbi was scheduled to arrive in Atlanta at 10:45p.m. Carmen called the airline once again to make sure the flight was on schedule. She learned that due to some type of problem, passengers destined for Atlanta were rebooked on the first flight out of Pittsburgh the following morning. The new arrival time would be 9:48a.m. on Saturday. Now she had the rest of the evening to plan how she would deal with the situation before her. She thought of going to the airport to watch Robbi get off the plane and then follow her to her destination. This idea seemed stupid and psychotic. The whole thing seemed psychotic, really. Besides, she wasn't certain that Robbi was attending the same wedding as Kyle, although it seemed strangely coincidental that Robbi would be coming into Atlanta during this time period. Desperate to know the truth, she decided she would just go to the airport to see who would be there to pick Robbi up. "Dealing with Kyle reduces me to my personal *worst*," Carmen said to herself when she acknowledged her previous and planned behavior.

Carmen arrived at the Atlanta airport at around 9:00a.m. She parked her car and hurried inside to check the monitors for gate arrival information. Robbi's flight appeared to be arriving on time. She then took the airport train to Concourse B where the flight would be arriving from Pittsburgh. Before she went to the gate, she stopped by the ladies room to make sure her hair and makeup was in order. For if Robbi were to spot her, she would have to look her personal best. She had to look successful and, of course, happy. As she proceeded down the Concourse toward the gate, she checked her watch to make sure she would have time to position herself to have a clear view of Robbi without being noticed. She was feeling a little hungry so she decided to stop off at the bakery to pick up a quick snack. As she paid the cashier she looked up and out into the Concourse. Her eyes must have deceived her ... she saw Kyle pass by! He was wearing the same clothes she had seen him in last night when he left her house. She quickly grabbed her food and ran to the door to make sure she was not hallucinating. It was him indeed. Carmen could hardly catch her breath... this could not be happening. She watched Kyle as he took a seat across the isle from the gate where Robbi would be arriving. He grabbed the newspaper in the chair beside him and began to read it. He checked his watch while he anticipated Robbi's arrival. Carmen could hardly hear herself think. How could she deal with this? Why did she seem surprised?...She knew there was a possibility Kyle would be there. Maybe deep down she was hoping he wouldn't be. In any case, there he was. If she revealed herself to him, how could she explain why she was in the airport? One option was not to reveal herself at all, but to follow them both. But her mind told her there was nothing to conclude by following them. It was pretty obvious that Kyle was at the airport to pick up Robbi. It was pretty obvious that he had planned to pick her up the night before, but was not able to do so because the original flight out of Pittsburgh was canceled. He must have spent the night in the airport.

After weighing her options, Carmen felt she had nothing to lose. It was ten minutes before the flight was scheduled to arrive. She decided to approach Kyle. However, she had to stage her alibi first. She sneaked over to the nearest pay phone to call Nikki. When Nikki answered, Carmen explained that she didn't have much time to talk. She told Nikki that she would explain later. "Nikki, I need for you to do me a favor. In about fifteen minutes, I want you to call the airport here in Atlanta and have me paged. Oh, do it a couple of times to make sure it's heard," Carmen instructed nervously.

"Are you OK?" asked Nikki sensing the urgency and stress in her friend's voice.

"I'm not really OK, but I will have to tell you later. It's a trip. Please just do this for me and I'll call you later. Are you going to be home later this afternoon?"

"This sounds juicy, I'll stay right here. You better not forget to call me," ordered Nikki.

"I won't. Hey, I gotta go. Don't forget to call in fifteen minutes. Well make that ten minutes now. I'm gonna run. Talk to you later. Thanks for helping me." Click.

Carmen did the best she could to collect herself as she initiated movement toward Kyle.

She had decided to present the surprised-to-see-you-here look rather than the what-the-hell-are-you-doing-at-this-airport-to-meet-Robbi-Gant look. Carmen started to walk hastily through the Concourse as if she were hurrying to meet someone. As if she were cued to do so, she looked over at Kyle and created the shocked look along with the theatrical squinting of the eyes...pretending to be making sure her eyes were not deceiving her. She tried to ignore the shock on Kyle's face when he looked up and saw her...she didn't want to lose her concentration.

"Hi, Baby. I *thought* that was you...," Carmen said as she inched toward Kyle pretending to be surprised. "What are you doing here?"

"Oh, hey," Kyle said clearing his throat. "Nothing, I just came down to the airport to just chill out," he continued, obviously struggling to respond on his feet without the luxury of preparation.

Trying not to sound completely insulted and pissed off at his asinine response, Carmen gave a fake chuckle while pretending to give credibility to what he said, yet sound confused. "You came down here to read the paper? What? Why here?"

Kyle immediately jumped up as he realized the plane from Pittsburgh had arrived at the gate and passengers were about to deplane.

"I'm kind of hungry. Let's go get some breakfast," Kyle

said as he guided Carmen by the shoulders toward the exit escalators down the Concourse. Kyle was so nervous, he didn't bother to ask Carmen why she was in the airport or even if going to get breakfast would impact whatever she was there to do.

"Why are we going to get breakfast?" said Carmen as she kept pace with Kyle leaving the scene.

Trying to appear cool, Kyle said, "I just thought it would be nice to go some place and sit down and have a nice breakfast. I'm tired of being at this airport anyway."

"Baby, you are so sweet. I was just telling my mother last night what a terrific man you were and how I felt bad for ever doubting you since we got back together. I really love you, Kyle. I will never doubt you again because I know that you are sincere about making our relationship work," Carmen rambled knowing full well that Kyle was lying and so was she. She got pleasure out of watching him squirm as she went on and on about love and trust. As they went down the escalators to catch the underground train to the baggage claim area, she thought to herself that Robbi was probably off the plane by now and probably not too far behind them. She wanted to slow up to give her time to catch up, but Kyle was stepping fast! As they approached the exit doors in the baggage claim area, Carmen heard a page for her over the PA system. "Thank you, Nikki," she thought.

"Kyle, Baby, hold up. I got so caught up in the moment with you I forgot why I was here," Carmen lied. "I'm here to pick up my friend, Nikki. That's probably her paging me wondering where I am. Let me get that and she can go to breakfast with us, OK?" Kyle never stopped moving. With a nervous twitch in his face he said, "I don't want to wait, I'm hungry now." He proceeded out the doors without Carmen. She would have followed him, but she wanted to see Robbi instead.

Carmen stood in the baggage claim area stunned that Kyle just disappeared. She knew why ... he was busted! She was sure he didn't know that she knew about Robbi. Within a couple of minutes, Robbi emerged from the crowd. She still has zero style, Carmen thought as she checked out Robbi from head to toe. Robbi was wearing a tight, pale blue T-shirt with very tight, black pleated pants. Her hair was still styled with the tight curls Carmen remembered. Carmen quickly moved near the baggage carousel where Robbi would pick up her bags. She pretended to be waiting for someone.

Robbi soon recognized Carmen as she approached the carousel. "Hi Carmen, did you hear a page for you?" Robbi said to Carmen as if they were old friends. She seemed completely unfazed that Carmen was in the airport.

"No I didn't, actually," she lied. How long ago was that?" Carmen acted unfazed to see Robbi, as well.

"Just a few moments ago... right after I got off the plane," said Robbi.

"Oh, I'd better go check," Carmen said as she began to walk over to a phone to pretend to check the page. Within a couple of minutes, she returned to the carousel pretending to not have a message and also pretending to continue to wait on her friend.

"So what are you in town for?" Carmen asked pretending to make conversation.

"A wedding," answered Robbi.

"Oh, that's nice."

Carmen noticed Robbi checking her watch as she waited for her bags. "So, is someone picking you up? Do you need a ride somewhere?" asked Carmen realizing the answers to both questions.

"As a matter of fact, Kyle is picking me up," Robbi boasted.

"Oh really? So that's why he was here. I guess you should know ... Kyle left when he ran into me. I guess he didn't want me to see him with you," Carmen ridiculed. "Now he might come back...who knows. Perhaps after I leave. He's probably embarrassed," Carmen continued while loving the sting she was injecting into Robbi. "Where is that Nikki?" said Carmen to introduce a distraction to her venomous stings. "Let me go check my answering service at home just in case she called." Carmen walked over to a pay phone and again continued her theatrics. "Oh well, she missed the flight," Carmen said as she returned to the side of a fuming and abandoned Robbi. Carmen would not relent for long. "Oh, Robbi, should Kyle show up, could you give him his shades?" she said as she reached into her purse. "He left them at my home last night." Robbi appeared shocked, but as usual tried to appear unfazed and composed. Carmen could tell that she was really agitated. "Well, I better get on with my day, since my friend didn't make it. Are you sure you don't need a ride?" Carmen said sarcastically. "Kyle said he was going to get breakfast, but he is probably somewhere watching us waiting for me to leave. I'll do that so you won't have to be stranded here. But, if he doesn't show up, we do have taxis here in Atlanta. Good luck."

Carmen exited the airport. The pleasure of zapping Robbi was turning into the painful reality of what was really going on. Kyle was still the same liar he ever was. She knew she had to get on with her life. Boy, where had she heard this before? She decided whatever explanation Kyle would give for this episode would be a lie.

--- Chapter 9

During a conversation Carmen had with her mother, she learned that Lewis was living in Atlanta. Her mother told her that Lewis had called for her number and revealed that she could reach him in Atlanta. Carmen was elated to have her good friend to hang out with, however, she didn't get too excited about being introduced to any of his friends, for they all were sure to be gay. Although, she thought, meeting his friends might not be such a bad idea. At least she would know for *sure* who was gay and still in the closet. After all, Lewis was a prime example of a man who you would never suspect being gay.

Carmen finally decided to get in touch with him. He had always been a good friend to her. Now was the time she could use a good friend the most. Besides, Lewis was a great companion. When she contacted him, she learned that he lived in a high-rise apartment in Midtown. Carmen had heard that Midtown Atlanta was a section of town that was heavily populated with gay men. So his place of residence came as no surprise.

Carmen had agreed to go by Lewis' apartment to pick him up for their night on the town. The two of them had not seen each other for years. Neither of them knew what to expect the other to look like. So when they talked over the phone, Carmen was careful not to make any fat jokes. In the past, she and Lewis could joke about anything. She was hoping they would just pick up where they left off. All indications during their phone conversations suggested there would be no problems. Lewis was as humorous as he ever was. He was excited about seeing her. She was almost ready to leave her place to go pick up Lewis when the phone rang. She answered it. "Hello."

"Carmen Layfield, this is Lewis."

"Hi Lewis. I'll be there in about twenty minutes."

"Twenty minutes! What are you trying to do... squeeze your big ass into a girdle?"

Lewis joked as he burst into laughter. Carmen burst into laughter, as well.

"You are sick," she commented. "And besides, I don't have a big ass. I'm assuming that because you are so willing to make jokes about mine, your ass doesn't look like it's pregnant with twins," Carmen retorted. "Seriously, I'm almost ready. When I get there, I'll just park and then come up to your place. Did you need me to stop and get something along the way?"

"Yeah right! ... and make your always-late ass even later? No, I'll just wait until you get here. Now hurry your late ass up."

Carmen felt like she was going out on a date, even though she knew Lewis was not a prospect. When she arrived at Lewis' apartment building, she buzzed him to let him know she was on her way up. She could hardly wait to see him.

When Lewis answered the door, he stood there still drop-dead gorgeous. "Damn, why does he have to be gay?" she thought. He was good looking, very well-groomed, intelligent, witty, insightful and any women's best friend and any man's best friend. The two hugged each other with joy and elation. They both joked how relieved they were that the other was not fat. Lewis told Carmen she looked like a celebrity. Although she knew he was exaggerating, she accepted the compliment because she knew he was saying that she looked like she had been taking care of herself. She had been...externally.

They started their evening off with dinner at Houston's restaurant in Buckhead. The wait was an hour and a half, as usual. It was a very popular place to eat. So they put their names on the list for the non-smoking section and decided to order drinks and wait outside on the patio. Since they had so much catching up to do, the hour and thirty minutes would go by in no time. She told him all about Kyle, Robbi and Lauren. Even though she felt emotional pain, Carmen always knew how to tell a less-than-happy story with such amusement. Lewis seemed to love the drama of Carmen's life. He never discussed his gay relationships, however, he shared stories of dates with women. This provided Carmen with a great lead-in to her topic of concern, unknowingly dating a gay or bi-sexual man.

"So, tell me, Lewis, do you think you will ever get married?"

"Probably not. I would love to have kids, though."

"So, would you adopt?" Carmen asked trying not to initiate the topic of him being gay. She wanted him to begin and she would surely chime right in.

"Perhaps, but I would really like to have kids of my own. By the way, I can tell you're trying to avoid the subject of my sexual preference. So let me make it a little easier on you. No. I do not plan to marry a woman just so that I can have my own biological children. Could I do this with a woman with her knowing that I am involved with men? ... Absolutely. Some women don't care. Carmen, you would be surprised what some women are willing to accept just to have a man."

"You gotta be kidding me?" challenged Carmen. "You mean to tell me that there are women out there who would continue to be involved with you and know that you could possibly mess around on them with another man?" said Carmen in disbelief.

"What do you mean "*could* possibly mess around"? Not only that, some women know that you actually *are* seeing a man and they *still* want to be with you. Like I said, some women will put up with anything to have a man. Remember I told you once how some women try to convince themselves that I'm too fine to be gay, and deny the possibility. Or some women think that I must be gay because I haven't met the *right* woman yet. Then they go on an all-out mission to try to change me. Women are a trip."

"So now, Lewis ... how can I tell if a man is bi-sexual?"

"Easy, just look to see if he has titties *and* a dick," joked Lewis. "I'm just kidding. There's no easy way to tell if he's in the closet unless you patrol his every move. You could ask him, but that doesn't mean you will get the truth...kinda like how married men lie about being married. You should never make any assumptions…Every man that's feminine is not gay and every man who's masculine is not straight. One way to find out is to get to know a man before you go jumping into bed with him. Control giving up the cooty so fast. Look at our situation. I didn't tell you I was gay. I'm sure during the process of getting to know me you suspected it. You just kind of hung around long enough to confirm it. Now, aren't you glad you didn't give up the cooty? "

"I'll say," said Carmen with a sense of relief.

"Do you see now that you can apply the same thing to getting to know a heterosexual man. Now, I don't mean to be hard on you Carmen, but you can't convince me you didn't know early on in your relationship with Kyle that something just didn't add up…you probably still gave up the cooty knowing something was suspicious. The only difference is that he was sleeping with another woman, or shall I say with *a couple* of them. Giving up sex early does not secure you a place in a man's heart. What it most likely secures you is a place in his little black book. Wear your raggedy panties for a while."

"What do you mean?" inquired Carmen.

"Well, since you asked, I think a lot of women use sex as a tool to get men and cry victim when men hit it and quit it. Maybe if you wear your raggedy panties, instead of being so ready to show off your recent purchase from Victoria's Secret, you will force yourself not to allow your precious bodies to be used and abused. You'll then allow the man to get to know you and respect who you are. Also, you will give yourself time to learn something about the man. Hopefully, you will determine if he is even worth having you. You'll see if he is even remotely interested in getting to know you better or even respecting you. I think women should take more control over giving up the cooty. All too often, if the cooty goes first, the mind is next. You all go crazy because of what you expect from the man once you have laid down with him. Now if sex is all you want and expect, that's one thing. But, if you're looking for a story with a happy ending, sex should not be in the first chapter of your relationship. Do you understand what I'm saying?"

"I do," acknowledged Carmen. "Everything you've said makes sense."

"Then act like you have some sense," said Lewis.

"I know, I know. I just wanted to give the relationship a chance. Kyle seemed to be everything I ever wanted. I just think I came into his life at a bad time. Who knows, maybe some day our paths will cross again."

"Carmen, don't let me have to start talking about your ass for being crazy over a man. You have too much going for yourself. If Kyle Sealy doesn't know what he had when he had you, then that's his loss. You should remind yourself of that every day," Lewis insisted. "Stop running around here trying to change people."

"Are you through preaching?" joked Carmen. "I told you I am trying to move on from Kyle. My friends Ava and J.B. are trying to hook me up, except most of their friends are married or in committed relationships. The ones that are available seem to be too nerdy."

"Who's your benchmark for a man, Kyle?" asked Lewis in an effort to determine if Carmen was really trying to move on.

She, of course, denied any suggestion that she was looking for a clone of Kyle. "Look, I will admit that I think Kyle has a package, but I would like to have someone who's local and who has at least *some* attractive qualities. Lewis, I'll gladly take a man like you, except I want him to be straight."

"If you were a man, I'd want you too," joked Lewis.

"Stop kidding," said Carmen. "I'm serious. I want a healthy relationship with a person of the opposite sex. I'm telling you right now, that if I find a man I like, I want you to tell me if he's straddling the fence. I don't need any surprises." Lewis looked at Carmen and said, "Like I said, if you women would keep your drawers on long enough, chances are you will discover a lot about a man *before* you give up the ass. Otherwise, don't be surprised about anything."

--- *Chapter 10*

Although Carmen loved the holiday season, she found this time of the year to be particularly lonely. This would be her first Christmas in her new home. She never imagined she would be alone. However, not getting into the spirit was not an option. She had selected and decorated her tree all by herself. Her home was filled with brilliant red poinsettias. She burned wood in the fireplace even though it wasn't that cold. The weather in Atlanta made it feel more like springtime. She had done most of her Christmas shopping for her family and sent out Christmas cards to several friends. To secure the position she believed she had with Kyle's family, even though she had never met them, she managed to get off a few kiss-up Christmas cards to the key influencers, Kyle's mother and his aunt.

Spending time with her loved ones was always something she looked forward to. The only bad thing about being around all of her family members was being constantly quizzed about when she was going to get married and have kids. In addition to that, they would ask about Kyle and comment on what pretty children he would have made. If they only knew the truth about Kyle, they would never consider the idea of him being a part of the family. Carmen never shared any details because she knew that family members never forgive and some never forget. She knew that keeping silent about Kyle was her own way of holding on and hoping that someday they could get back together. Maybe she could get through the holidays with her family since she would only be there for a couple of days. Besides, her parents had plans to come to Atlanta for New Years. One of her father's fraternity brothers had invited them to a New Year's Eve ball at one of the downtown hotels.

Carmen had been invited to a New Year's Eve party at Ava and J.B.'s house. Most of the people who would be there were sure to be coupled off. Carmen, of course, didn't have a date.

She had thought of inviting Lewis, but he told her he was going to a gay New Year's Eve party. He said he was going with his "friend". Carmen remembered thinking, "Just look at this shit…what's wrong with this picture…Lewis has a man and *I don't*!" Ava and J.B. swore they would have a good mixture of people in attendance. Only time would tell. Anyway, she had an excuse to go shopping for a new outfit. Since she was going to a house party, she wouldn't need a real formal ensemble.

————————

Carmen was a social butterfly at Ava and J.B.'s New Year's Eve party. The scent of cedar and the sounds of holiday music all over the house made her spirit festive. The ten-foot Christmas tree was beautiful and still looking fresh. The poinsettias and holly that lined the curved staircase and fireplace were still vibrant and decorative. The fireplace was all ablaze creating a romantic ambiance.

Carmen felt very confident in her holiday outfit. She wore a black velvet, two-piece midriff pantsuit with black sequins pumps. Her hair hung long and just below her shoulders. Her diamond stud earrings and rhinestone watch were her only jewelry accessories.

Ava and J.B. didn't lie about having a variety of people. Everyone was well educated and were pretty well established career-wise. However, no sparks seemed to fly with any of the cute men who said they were still single. Carmen decided not to assume that being *single* was synonymous with being *available*. She wanted to believe she had learned her lesson with her experience with Kyle.

As the clock approached midnight, Carmen couldn't help but wonder what Kyle was doing and with whom. What she did know was that she was in a house full of people, yet she still felt somewhat very much alone. J.B. began to make sure everyone had a full glass of champagne in preparation for the New Year's toast. "Hey Carmen, you have an admirer," said J.B. as he filled her glass.

"Who?" asked Carmen, feeling mildly flattered.

"His name is Justin... Justin Gray. He was asking me a lot of questions about you. I told him I would check to see if you were interested in meeting him. If so, then I'll introduce the two of you."

"J.B., I haven't seen anybody mildly fine who has expressed any interest in me. Point him out to me and circle back over here after we toast the New Year and I'll let you know."

"He's the tall gentleman with the black turtleneck sweater and black slacks. He's a friend of a buddy of mine. I don't know very much about him except that he's single and he seems like a nice guy. I'll check back with you in a few. OK?"

"OK, I'm gonna go find Ava and get the scoop on this so-called admirer," said Carmen. I need the *woman's* perspective.

Ava didn't know much about Justin except that he was interested in meeting Carmen. She decided to let J.B. handle the screening and introductions. She figured a man would be able to tell whether another man was legitimate or not. Besides, she didn't want to be responsible for setting Carmen up with a loser if he turned out to be one.

Shortly after the New Year rang in, people began to mingle. Carmen could see that Justin was keeping a close eye on her no matter where she turned. She was still trying to size him up to see if she really wanted to meet him. He was about 6'1". He had a brown look...light brown hair, light brown eyes, and light brown skin. He wore a goatee, which was kind of sexy. The black outfit looked nice against his earth toned body canvas. His shoes looked nice, too. "He might be all right," she thought. She decided that J.B. and Ava were too busy playing host and hostess to be overly concerned with playing cupid. So she decided to make herself available for Justin to approach her. She decided that this would be his first test... Would he be the kind of man who went after what he wanted or was he shy or even a wimp?

Justin made his move. He walked over to Carmen and introduced himself. He also shared with her that he had been admiring her all night and was waiting to see who she would pair up with as they toasted the New Year. He said he concluded that she was available as he watched her hug Ava and J.B. when the countdown was completed. Carmen thought his attitude was pretty presumptuous, but nevertheless a reason to justify an inquiry.

They exchanged the typical questions shared between strangers when each is screening the other as a prospect. There were questions like, are you from around here, do you live here, what do you do, where's your man, where's your woman? They both decided that the other was available enough to now explore common interest. Carmen shared with Justin that she was an advertising consultant, that she loved to paint, that she loved jazz music, liked to travel, enjoyed church, and loved to skate and snow ski. Justin shared with Carmen that he was a publishing agent and that he too, loved jazz, that he enjoyed traveling for pleasure, dancing and race-car driving. He said he was trying to get more into church.

Carmen assessed the things they had in common. She determined they both liked jazz and could attend concerts together. Since they both loved to travel, she thought they could go on a few trips together, provided they liked the same places...and they could have separate hotel rooms. She knew she wouldn't be joining him in a fast car. It seemed too dangerous. Although, snow skiing was not exactly a leisurely sport either. So, they both liked racy things. So, he liked to dance. "I wonder if he dances as well as Kyle," Carmen thought to herself.

For the next month, Carmen and Justin dated. While she liked him, she didn't give him much of a fair chance because she compared everything about him to Kyle. Justin was a nice guy, so she decided to try to stick with the relationship. She thought Justin would grow on her eventually.

It was February in Atlanta. Winter didn't seem to get into full swing until then. Although January was cold, forecasts of snow didn't seem to come around until the month of cupid.

Justin had friends who were planning to attend a ski summit

in Vail, Colorado during the week of Valentine's Day. He knew that Carmen liked to ski, so he offered to take her there as a Valentine's Day present in lieu of roses and a box of chocolates. Carmen was extremely flattered. She thought that was very thoughtful and romantic. There could be something to this man after all. Lewis didn't have any knowledge of Justin being gay or bi-sexual, thus that hurdle was crossed. Justin really seemed to like her…That was another plus. On the surface, he seemed to be an OK guy. They had never been intimate, so she didn't know his credentials in the throw-down lovemaking department. She had kissed him, though. He was decent. Carmen decided to accept his invitation to go to Vail.

One evening Carmen had come home from work and was too tired to cook, so she decided that a bowl of Raisin Nut Bran cereal would suffice. Exhaustion and laziness were not her only excuses for eating cereal for dinner…She was trying to lose a few pounds so that she could fit into her ski wear. After all, you never knew just who would show up at the Summit. The men would be well represented. There would be lawyers, doctors, pilots, businessmen and, of course, wannabes. Many women would come looking for husbands. The men knew that, so they would come to behave like the eligible bachelor who's looking for a wife and the mother of their unborn children. Amongst the vultures would be good, Christian men. Except they would usually come with their wives or girlfriends. Nevertheless, Carmen wanted to look good for vanity's sake. She knew that the women would look like they had been poured into their outfits. She didn't want to look like she was in overflow. Besides, if she was going to be there with a man, she wanted his attention to be on her and not other women. She had to admit to herself that she was anxious to see what type of women Justin would find attractive. She hated to admit to herself that she was also interested in what type of women would find him attractive. She decided if women didn't check him out or flirt with him, then maybe he's not that interesting to have. Carmen remembered what Ava had said about women not wanting men until he's taken or desirable to other women. Oh well, at least she was not the first woman, nor would she be the last, who felt this way.

As Carmen fished out the last raisin in her cereal, her phone rang. It was Nikki who was calling to tell her that she would be attending the Summit as well. Carmen was thrilled to know she had someone to ski with in case Justin turned out to be boring.

"So tell me, Carmen, is this Mr. Right?" asked Nikki. "This must be pretty serious. I mean, this man is taking you to a ski resort for Valentine's Day. Do you plan to give up the nooky?"

"Is that all you think about?" joked Carmen.

"Is that a yes or a no?" quizzed Nikki.

"How about a "nunya" as in none of ya' business," replied Carmen. "By the way, who are you going with?"

"I'm going with the Chicago ski club. I'm not taking a man. That would be like taking sand to the beach."

"So do you plan on meeting a husband?"

"Absolutely. That's why I have to control the kitty cat. I don't want the prospects to think I'm loose. So to control any urge I may have to give up the nooky, I'm taking the advice you got from Lewis…I'm taking all of my raggedy panties."

"Are you really?"

"You heard me, I'm taking my raggedy panties, nothing sexy. I figure if I get myself into a situation where one thing leads to another after soaking in one of the hot tubs or the hot springs, I will be able to resist just by knowing that I can't allow myself to get undressed, revealing my embarrassing raggedy lingerie."

"Hold up. You can always say they are crotchless and were purchased that way," joked Carmen.

"Uh-huh. So how will I explain all that broken elastic?" Nikki said laughing.

"I just have one more question. Why would you wear panties underneath a swimsuit? I mean, you *do* plan on wearing a swimsuit in the hot tub, right. The only other alternative is to get in *nude*. Then what would you do?"

"Wear a tampon," Nikki answered sarcastically.

"Oh, Nik, you are disgusting," laughed Carmen. Anyway, I

can't wait to go. I'm just letting you know right now that I'm going to come looking for you if Justin turns out to be a bore.

Carmen had enjoyed her trip to Colorado. She was able to enjoy Justin's company without being sexual, although Justin tried several times. She wanted to prove to herself that she could resist moving too fast. Although, she had to admit she was scoping out other prospects and didn't want to get too involved with Justin in case something better came along. She could tell that Justin was really getting into her.

For the next couple of months, Carmen pretty much took Justin for granted. He was dependable and for the most part thoughtful and respectful. The only thing she identified as a fault was that he wasn't a challenge. He was boring to her. She seemed to look for reasons not to like him because she was too embarrassed to admit publicly that she was bored with a man who treated her nice. She often pointed out to Justin things in her home and in her car that needed repairing. She had always found it to be a turn-on to watch a man fix something. Each time Justin looked perplexed while observing a broken or malfunctioning item and then resorted to the yellow pages for a repair service, she became turned-off. She argued to her friends that a man should know how to fix things even if he had the money to hire someone else to do it. Her friends would argue back that her comments were sexist and then remind her that she was a woman who couldn't cook.

Carmen's feelings for Justin were completely changed on the night they retreated to his place for a night cap after attending a play at the Fox Theater. While making herself right at home in his kitchen after agreeing to prepare the drinks, she gazed over at Justin sitting on the couch in the living room. He had already loosened his tie and removed his shoes. She remembered how Justin looked especially nice that evening when they were at the Fox. He was generating stares and double takes. She had gotten her usual amount of attention, as well. The slinky red Donna Karan dress certainly created the visual effect of a stunning, elegant woman. As always, she welcomed the compliments. She also liked the feeling of power she had felt knowing that Justin had eyes only for her, especially when other women tried to make eye contact with him during the intermissions. Even when they tried to sashay in front of him, he would turn and kiss her on the cheek to reassure her that she was his lady.

After pouring two glasses of wine, she carefully carried them into the living room, trying not to spill any of the wine onto her dress or onto the carpet. She kicked off her shoes as she approached Justin who was now slouched back on the couch. She smiled at him as she handed him his glass. "For you," she said softly. She then took a place beside him on the couch and proceeded to raise her glass. "I'd like to propose a toast to a wonderful evening," she said with a smile. "I'll drink to that," he replied.

Shortly after they had taken their first sip of wine, Justin received a phone call. He started not to answer it, but decided to anyway. Carmen detected by Justin's tone that the caller was a female. Justin told her that he was busy and would have to get back to her later. Then there was a long period of silence, as Justin appeared to be listening to the caller talk. Carmen listened for his next comment. "Well, you should have thought about that before you over reacted. Look, you said you wanted to see other people, right. I'm not interfering with your life. I have gone on with my life. I wish you well," Justin said to the caller. Then there was silence again. "Yes, I do have company and would like to get back to them. I have the rest of your things, I'll put them in the mail tomorrow, OK. I gotta go, now. Bye."

"What was that all about?" asked Carmen. Justin went on to explain that the caller was his ex-girlfriend, Elaine, who had broken off their two-year relationship because she wanted to see other people. "Now that she realizes the grass is not greener on the other side, she wants to try and work things out between us," he said. Carmen immediately wanted to know how long the relationship had been over. He told her they had broken up in early December. "And no, I didn't create the environment for the breakup to avoid having to buy her a Christmas gift," Justin interjected jokingly as if he anticipated Carmen's next question.

Justin wasn't exactly a mind reader, Carmen thought to herself. What she was actually thinking was that she was just as much a rebound to him as he was to her. Now Carmen was interested in pictures. She wanted to know what the "competition" looked like. Without further delay, she asked for the visuals.

"Why do you want to see pictures of her?" Justin inquired.

"No particular reason. I just want to know what she looks like."

"There are some pictures of her in that box over there," Justin said as he pointed to a box at the end of his coffee table.

While viewing pictures of a happy Justin and a beautiful girl, who also looked happy, Carmen became jealous. She somehow felt threatened that this woman still had access to Justin. The fact that she was beautiful didn't help. Then the "twenty questions" began. What's her name, again? What does she do? Where is she from? Where is she now? How old is she? Did she ever want to marry you? Did you ever want to marry her? Does she still love you? Do you still love her? Are you still friends? Is she seeing anyone else? Are you jealous? What Carmen really wanted to hear was what a bitch the woman was and how he could never go back to her.

In a nutshell, Justin told Carmen that he was very hurt by the breakup, but he could never go back to her because he could never trust her love for him or commitment to their relationship.

"Justin, you need to make a point to her about how you have moved on. The fact that you still have her belongings only encourages her to think you are still hanging on and that she has a chance of weaseling her way back into your life. You need to Fed-Ex this box to her tomorrow!...Regular mail won't do. Also, you need to certify it so she won't be claiming she never received it, which would only provide her with another excuse to keep calling you," Carmen instructed. "I know how women are," Carmen continued.

Carmen's motives were completely selfish. Suddenly, Justin had become more attractive to her since another woman wanted him. Sadly, the events of the evening surrounding the other woman would be the impetus behind Carmen giving in to Justin sexually.

Chapter 11

"You are the star that brightens up my world, without you, I have no light." These were the words of Nikki to Carmen as she read a hand-written card she had just received from her "dream man", Drew Collins. Nikki had met Drew during her ski trip to Vail. She had purposely not discussed Drew with Carmen because of his circumstances. Specifically, Drew had told Nikki that he was going through a bitter divorce during the time of the summit. He told her that the divorce from his wife was almost final. He mentioned that the holdup was due to the custody of their daughter. Nikki was impressed with the fact that he was a father who was not trying to abandon his child despite the fact that he no longer wanted to be married to the mother. The greeting card to Nikki was Drew's way of letting her know that she would become the lady in his life as soon as the divorce proceedings were finally over. Now that Nikki felt like she could avoid being labeled as a home wrecker by Carmen, she decided that it was now safe to reveal her new man. Carmen was happy that Nikki seemed happy, but felt a bit skeptical about the situation. She knew that far too often married men claim to be divorced or going through a divorce to prey off desperate women. Because of her concern for her best friend, Carmen felt that the ritual of twenty-questions was very much in order.

"So, Nik, tell me about this Drew guy. I know you can anticipate all of my questions, so I will spare you having to listen to me ask them. Just give me the answers. Go."

Eager to defend Drew, Nikki began providing answers and explanations. "Well, like I said, he's getting a divorce. He has moved out of the house and I *am* able to call him at home. I know she lives twenty miles away from him in Denver. He has a daughter named Jessica. She's almost three. He was married for almost four years. His soon-to-be ex-wife is named Tracy.

From what I hear, she's a crazy bitch. She got pregnant on purpose while they were dating because she really wanted to marry Drew. Because he's such a wonderful guy, he married her when she was six weeks pregnant, trying to do the right thing for the baby. They had a small ceremony in her parents' back yard ... nothing elaborate. Well, she lost the baby shortly after they got married. So, instead of divorcing her because he really didn't want to be married to her, he stayed with her because he thought he would stay and make the best of a not-so-great situation. Then, she got pregnant with Jessica a few months later." Nikki paused to take a sip of her diet coke. "Don't stop, " said Carmen. "Hold on, I'm going to continue - my throat is getting dry," replied Nikki as she sensed the anticipation in Carmen's voice. "Now where was I..."

"Baby Jessica is in the belly oven," Carmen said jokingly to remind Nikki.

"Yeah, yeah. So ... Now ... she's pregnant with Jessica. He and Tracy aren't really getting along that great. Tracy insisted to Drew that once the baby came, things would be better between them. Well, sure enough, when Jessica was born, Drew was the happiest man alive."

"So then why is Mr. Happy trying to get a divorce?" asked Carmen with interrogation.

"Well, he fell in love with his little girl and then Tracy started to complain that Drew was spending more time with Jessica than with her or even with them as a family. Drew started to realize that he was only married to Tracy because he felt that she would try to take Jessica away from him if he tried to divorce her."

"Uh-huh. So then, if he has this fear, why is he divorcing her now? I mean, how would Tracy be able to prevent him from seeing Jessica anyway. I would think they would have joint custody at a minimum," said Carmen.

" I don't have all the details, but from what I understand, Tracy accused Drew of every woman walking. She made it up in her mind that because he didn't want her that he must have been screwing around. Because she could never peg him with any one woman, meaning she never found any evidence, she accused him of everybody."

"Oh, come on, Nik. You can't tell me that this man wasn't cheating on his wife if he claims to have been so unhappy."

"Well, from what I understand, Drew said that Tracy is unfit to be a mother," said Nikki trying to change the course of the dialog and to defend Drew.

"Unfit?" Carmen blurted out.

"Yeah. He said she's a crazy bitch."

"There go those words again... "crazy bitch". OK, so now tell me what makes her a crazy bitch?" probed Carmen.

"Well he did tell me that he cheated on her once. He said that even though he was unhappy with Tracy, he still felt bad about it. He said that he felt so bad that, one night, he confessed voluntarily. He said that Tracy was hurt but was glad he told her. She pretended to let by-gones be by-gones, but he said that since that day she never let him forget it. He says that she made his life a living hell ever since. She spied on him, trashed his clothes, threw temper tantrums, trashed the house, cussed him out in public and in front of Jessica. She would throw things at him almost hitting the baby and on and on. Oh! He said she would call up women she suspected was sleeping with him and cuss them out. He hung in there longer than I would have."

"Maybe he hung in there because his ass was guilty," said a skeptical Carmen. "Nikki, I don't know about this Drew person."

Nikki became even more defensive. "See, I knew you would judge. Drew is really a nice guy. I wish you could meet him. I'm sure you would agree. He's just caught up in a bad situation. This really feels special, Carmen. I want to give it a chance. Besides, I supported you when you were dating Kyle."

"That's a low blow," said Carmen. "Besides, Kyle wasn't married and didn't have any children. If I had told you these things about Kyle, you would have expressed the same concern for me and my well being," Carmen retaliated. "Before you say anything, I would like to comment on something. Please don't take this the wrong way. Usually, Nik, you are turned on by what a man has as far as material possessions. You launched right into Drew's marital status and went on and on without a peep about what he does for a living or what kind of car he drives. You haven't even commented on the way he looks! What's up?"

"Carmen, I know you. You weren't interested in hearing about his material possessions. You were more interested in the information I gave you. And if you will notice, you didn't actually *interrupt* me to ask me what type of car he drives or even what he looks like."

"OK, OK. Then let me hear the reasons why you *really* like him," joked Carmen.

"Ha, Ha, very funny," Nikki said sarcastically. "Well, since you asked ... he is a regional sales manager. He makes six figures. He says he's driving a "Merc" right now. He's going to get a brand new car once he's divorced. Probably a Porsche or something like that. He might get another Benz. He knows if he gets it now, Tracy will hit him up for excessive child support. Of course, she wouldn't play fair. He's living in an apartment right now, but he says he's going to be buying this really nice house on a ranch outside of Denver. I have no idea what his taste in furniture is since I haven't seen his place yet. He wants me to help him pick out some things when I go visit. And he's gorgeous! He's 6'2" and fine. He's really intelligent. I'm sure he will do very well in life. I figure if Tracy gets a great amount of money in child support, he'll still have a lot left over for us. Besides I bring something to the table myself. So together, we should do pretty well financially. And Carmen, I can tell he's really into me. We have so much fun together. When he visited me last weekend, Girl, I fell in love."

"Did you give up the nooky?"

"Carmen, it was beautiful. He is such a gentleman.

"You're in love because he makes love beautifully?"

"No silly, because of the whole package. I know he comes with a little baggage but he's worth it," drooled Nikki.

"Are you having protected sex?" asked Carmen. Nikki paused.

122

"Well are you?" Carmen asked again.

"I'm on the pill."

"The pill! A pill isn't going to protect you from herpes and AIDS!"

"Look who's talking. Did you have protected sex with Kyle? Are you having protected sex with Justin?" attacked Nikki.

"I admit it. I did not have protected sex with Kyle. Knowing what I know now, I should have. And yes I am having protected sex with Justin ... whenever he's in town. Anyway, I'm just looking out for you Nikki. You really don't know Drew and he is long distance!"

"I can see why you would regret having unprotected sex with Kyle and why you are having protected sex with Justin, but my situation is different," said Nikki.

"How!" shouted a shocked Carmen.

"Carmen, he was married, so he was in a monogamous relationship." Carmen held the phone in disbelief. "Nik, are you crazy? Get a grip. Even if he was monogamous doesn't mean that his wife was. You don't know what diseases she may have passed on to him as a result of her being unfaithful...assuming she was. And you just said he cheated!"

Nikki was silent. Carmen realized Nikki was too far gone to listen to reason. It was as if she would have to crash and burn before she knew what she had gotten herself into. Carmen couldn't understand why things seemed so clear to her. Yet, they were so foggy to Nikki.

"Nikki, I love you. Hang in there, Girl. Please keep your eyes open. Use your head. I'm gonna run now. Talk to you later - call me if you need me. I'll always have an ear for you."

Chapter 12

Carmen had managed to stay on top of her work at the advertising firm. The bonuses just seemed to keep coming. She was able to rebuild her savings after purchasing her home and she was also able to buy the really nice bedroom and living room furniture she had seen while visiting the Merchandise Mart with Ava. Although she had an eye for decorating herself, Carmen allowed Ava to help her with the overall interior decorating project of her condo. Rich scarlet accents were chosen to enhance the virgin white foundation. One of her other outstanding projects was to reframe some of her pictures. She and Ava had picked out beautiful moldings to have the pieces custom framed. Everything was selected to go picture perfect with the decor. Also with her bonus money, Carmen had thought of taking an exotic vacation, but she didn't want to travel alone. Justin couldn't get the time off.

With summer in full blaze, Carmen finally decided that she would display some of her art during the up and coming Atlanta Arts Festival at Piedmont Park. With Justin always traveling, she had extra time on her hands to create several pieces. Painting always gave her a sense of peace. Today was a good day to stay inside and play on her canvas. It was too hot to be outside. To prepare her mood, she showered and then put on one of her colorful workout leotards and a pair of white boxer shorts. She pulled her hair back into a ponytail and then tied it into a knot on top of her head. Then she made a pitcher of lemonade mixed with cranberry juice. She laid out a tray of *Oreo* cookies to munch on. Then she put on her head phones to listen to a smooth jazz CD to allow herself to be completely absorbed in the rhythm. The rhythm of the music gave her art rhythm and expression, a meaning, a reason. Her art allowed her to escape many of her worries in life.

Having too much time on her hands made Carmen concerned that Justin wasn't paying as much attention to her as he once did. Even though Justin lacked many of the qualities she admired in Kyle, she wanted to believe their relationship could work. She thought she could grow to love him the way she loved Kyle. She didn't understand why he seemed to be drifting. All she knew was that she wasn't getting any younger, she would be thirty on her next birthday, and there weren't any other prospects for a husband in her life. She had made up in her mind that if Justin didn't start paying more attention to her, she would have to resort to 'Plan B'… Kyle! Besides Kyle had been calling lately. He had mentioned that he was thinking about moving to Atlanta. She had not taken him seriously and didn't want to set herself up for disappointment.

Justin had grown tired of Carmen complaining about them not spending time together. So he returned home early one Friday to surprise her with dinner for two at the Buckhead Diner. After dinner, they returned to Carmen's place where they made passionate love throughout the night.

To keep the magic going, the next morning, Justin surprised her with breakfast in bed. She watched him walk into the room with the bed tray. He wore Calvin Klein pajama bottoms with no shirt. His sexy brown chest hairs lay flat on his body. His slightly bowed legs made him look even more amorous. He had made her his secret recipe French toast along with bacon and fruit. This was a welcome change from her usual *Eggo* waffles. He fed her berries with his mouth, following up the contact with a fresh wet kiss. She could feel heat surge between her legs as his tongue danced with hers. He took another berry into his mouth and began to suck her nipples while occasionally rolling the berry over the entire surface of her breast. Then he grasped the berry between his teeth and slowly returned the chastened fruit to her lips and mouth for consumption. Not able to resist him any longer, Carmen moved back the tray. "So you like to play with fruit, I see," said Carmen. "I have a treat for you." Carmen reached inside her night stand and pulled out a sample of *Ambrodisiac* oil. "How would you like to taste some *Black Cherry*?" said Carmen as she rubbed the oil between her legs.

"What's this *Ambrodisiac* stuff?" asked an intrigued Justin.

"Ambrosia means food and scents of the Gods. Need I say more..." Justin placed his face between Carmen's thighs and took her to ecstasy.

The remainder of the Saturday was filled with them roller blading in the park and playing softball with teams made up of any interested kids who happen to be in the park. Carmen and Justin volunteered to play the umpires.

Being in the park reminded Carmen of the Art Festival that she would not be a participant in. Her worrying about her relationship and her job had taken up a lot of her time. She had only completed half the paintings she had planned to exhibit. She decided that she would display her art in another arts festival at a later date. She concluded that an arts festival was something that would always be... she would always have other opportunities to display her talents.

Later, Carmen and Justin returned to his place where they would get dressed to go to the Kenny G concert at the Chastain Park Amphitheater. Lark had contacted Carmen to let her know she would be in town and that she was one of the opening acts. She said she had arranged for Carmen to pick up table tickets at the box office if she were able to attend. Carmen invited Ava and J.B to be their guest for the evening. They were both fans of Kenny G and Lark. Carmen was beginning to feel real magic with Justin. She was glad she had decided to hang in there even though she never really felt he measured up. Although he was not her first choice, having him was better than being alone.

Later that evening, Carmen and Justin met Ava and J.B. at the concert. The table was set beautifully with food and candles. The lily-white tablecloth draped the table adding to the elegance of the star-lit evening. As Carmen sat and listened to Lark sing her rendition of Brenda Russell's *Piano in the Dark*, she began to daydream about Kyle. She remembered the time they had attended Lark's concert in Philadelphia. She reached over and grabbed Justin's hand trying to regain her attention to him. They had had a wonderful weekend thus far and here she was thinking about another man. Justin commented on how beautiful Lark sang. Carmen agreed. "I'm really glad things are looking up for her. Think of all the exposure she is getting here tonight. I'll be glad when she can be the headliner instead of the opening act. I really want her to make it big. Do you hear how effortlessly she hits all of those notes?" said Carmen.

"Yeah. She's truly under rated," replied Justin. "Some things about life just don't seem fair. I mean, listen to her. She sounds way better than some of these wannabe singers who have chart-topping recordings. Ya' girl Lark might need a new manager. How long has she been with the manager she has?"

"I'm not really sure. I know she's been dating him for a while. I wonder if he ever gets pissed off at her and then threatens to stifle her career just to be evil."

Ava and J.B. tuned in. "Surly you don't believe that," said J.B. That would be like him cutting off his nose to spite his face."

"I mean really, every gig he doesn't land for her affects his pocket book," added Ava.

"Not necessarily," said Carmen. "Lark is not the only act he manages."

"Damn, Carmen. You are so jaded when it comes to men," said J.B.

"No I'm not. I just worry that Lark puts too much faith in this man to manage her career mainly because he's her boyfriend. I mean look at this, she is *one* of the opening acts. She is not *the* opening act. Lark has been at this for years. She has a CD out but she is not the household name she should be. This is, of course, one woman's opinion," said Carmen with a smile in an effort to lighten the conversation.

Later, Kenny G took center stage. Cheers resonated. Couples began to lean into each other preparing to be serenaded by the sounds of love. Kenny G was classic. He was mellow and rhythmic. The stars seemed to twinkle brighter with every note. This was music for falling in love. Carmen looked up at Justin to gaze into his eyes. He appeared to be in another world. He was completely mesmerized. She thought she would tap into his mind by catching him in mid-thought. "What are you thinking?" whispered Carmen as she postured herself for a romantic response.

"My ex-girlfriend and I used to love to listen to Kenny G. I bet she realizes what a good man she lost every time she hears one of his songs," said Justin as he gazed up to the stage.

Carmen just sat there, stunned! She couldn't even respond. "How the hell can he be sitting here with me at a concert that I invited him to thinking about another woman!" Carmen fumed to herself. The fact that she was thinking about another man earlier had little significance to her because she never let on to Justin that she was doing so.   So then, for the remainder of the concert, she sat there fantasizing about making love to Kyle to Kenny G tunes, of course.

"Nikki, can you believe this crap? This jackass had the nerve to let me know he was sitting there thinking about another woman," said an appalled Carmen.

"Maybe he still has a thing for her. You did say *she* dumped *him*. You know men don't like rejection," replied Nikki.

Carmen agreed. "Girl, men are all the same. They never want the woman who loves them. They always want to chase after the one they can't have."

"What makes you think he's chasing?" asked Nikki.

"Nik, I haven't said much about this because I just wanted to see what was going to happen."

"What do you mean?" asked Nikki.

"Well, I know for a fact that they have been calling each other."

"How do you know that?"

"Now Nikki, you know I'm very resourceful. You can never tell anyone how I know this because the person who helped me would get into trouble."

"What? What? Tell me! Stop stalling!" demanded a curious Nikki.

"Well, my friend Lewis has a friend who works for a long distance phone company. He can look at Justin's and Elaine's phone bill. They have been having conversations that last as much as two hours! 'Hi, how ya' doin' doesn't take two hours. Justin has been going out of town a lot on business. I know he's been going to Huntsville, Alabama a lot. I'm not sure if he's been going by way of Birmingham, if you know what I mean. That's where she lives."

"What are you gonna do?" asked Nikki.

"I don't know yet. I will tell you this though. My baby has been calling me pretty often lately."

"You mean Kyle?"

"Who else?" replied Carmen. "He said he's planning on moving to Atlanta by the end of this year to start a law firm with his friend, Langston. He says the distance between us has really made him realize how much he loves me. He thinks the timing and distance added to the stress of our relationship."

"Hold up. Didn't he have this same revelation of love the first time there was distance between you," Nikki said sarcastically. "Is lover boy coming to his senses *again*?"

"I said the same thing to him. He said he understood why I wouldn't believe him, but he was going to work hard to prove himself to me."

"Are you sure, Carmen?" said Nikki with skepticism. "You have gone on with your life. I know how much you were hurt the first time...and the second. Why would you go back to that? Are you a glutton for punishment?"

"Absolutely not, I just want to be with the man I love like any other woman would."

"So what are you going to do about Justin," inquired Nikki.

"I'm not sure, Nik. A part of me wants him and the other part doesn't know what I want."

———————

Carmen couldn't figure whether to hate Justin or thank him

when he came to her about a month later and broke the news that he and his ex-girlfriend, Elaine, had decided that they had never reached closure in their relationship. As a result, they each said they found it impossible to go on with their lives with other people.

"Why did you involve me in your life and tell me you loved me if you knew all along you had feelings for your ex-girlfriend?" Carmen asked Justin as she felt rejected. Her feelings were so familiar to her. She didn't understand why men seemed to love her on the rebound. She couldn't understand why her love wasn't strong enough for a man to want to be with her instead of another woman.

Justin apologized to Carmen for the situation, but insisted that he really did love her, just not the same way he loved his ex. "Oh, this is supposed to make me feel better?" she cried. Carmen felt hurt by the rejection, but at the same time relieved that Justin had provided her with an out to be with the man she really loved. Justin seemed a little irritated that Carmen wasn't more devastated by his announcement. She found that somewhat flattering, but she didn't care very much about displaying the role of the distraught woman. She decided to save the drama for another time and place when it was genuine. She also felt like she had a "one up" on Justin because she would not be alone…she could always swing right back over to Kyle.

Chapter 13

Carmen could hardly keep her mind on anything else except Kyle. He was calling her very often and sending her romantic greeting cards and flowers on a weekly basis. Kyle seemed to be keeping his word about making a believer out of her. He told her that he could really see them being engaged by the end of the year, and definitely married in the following year. The end of the year was only a couple of months away. All of this sounded wonderful and enticing, but she couldn't help thinking about Robbi and where she did or didn't fit into the picture. She didn't want to end up in the same position she was in with Justin, and more importantly, she didn't want to end up in the same position she was in on the first go round with Kyle. On the other hand, she didn't want to miss out on the opportunity to rekindle their love. She began to feel that all she had to do was open up her heart and give it a chance. After all, he said he had learned from his mistakes of the past. And now, he was the one who was doing the chasing. All she had to do was let him catch her. She knew she would be subjected to criticism by her friends, family, and colleagues regarding her decision to re-enter a relationship with Kyle. However, she decided that they all would "eat crow" once she and Kyle got married.

The end of the year had arrived. The holiday season was in full blossom. Carmen and Kyle had spent lots of money on phone bills and plane tickets to cultivate their newly seeded relationship. Life couldn't be better for Carmen: She had gotten another raise at work, although she hadn't put a lot of energy into her work since she had gotten back together with Kyle. She was getting major attention from the man of her dreams. Kyle had made her thirtieth birthday very special. Also, per Kyle, the details with him starting the law firm in Atlanta were being finalized. Everyone in her family was in good health. Again, life was good.

For the holidays, Carmen and Kyle decided to spend Christmas with their own families. They also decided to spend the day after Christmas through New Year's in Atlanta... This was a nice arrangement to her since she was sure that she would be getting a proposal for marriage before the New Year.

It was New Year's Eve. Carmen and Kyle spent most of the day doing last minute shopping for the New Year's Eve party to be held later at the Swissotel. Carmen combed Phipps Plaza looking for accessories for the dress she would don. Kyle searched for the perfect cuff links to accent his tuxedo. Carmen took every opportunity to stop at a jewelry store to skillfully remind Kyle that she was expecting a ring. The two of them visited jewelry stores before, so she was fairly certain he knew what she wanted ... something big and sparkly and not Robbi's diamond in a different setting.

Later at the ball, they sat back and enjoyed the entertainment as they enjoyed a five-course dinner. As Carmen sat mesmerized by the band, she couldn't help but think about Kyle's words, "I can see us getting engaged this year and definitely getting married next year." She thought to herself, "This year is about to be over." Kyle couldn't disappoint her because she had told all her friends, family and co-workers that she expected to return to work as an engaged woman. How would she ever be able to save face if she had to return to work empty handed? If Kyle didn't propose tonight, she had three more days before she would have to return to work. She thought that Kyle would opt for the excitement of a New Year's party to engage her versus trying to cram the event into the next three days before he would have to return to Philadelphia. Well, he had about thirty minutes before she would know.

"They're opening up the dance floor. Would you like to

dance, my princess," said Kyle as he reached for Carmen's hand to guide her to the dance floor. She beamed a smile as she replayed his words, "my princess", over in her head. She checked her fresh manicure to make sure her hands looked perfect, especially her left one.

The band played love song after love song. Carmen and Kyle mouthed, I love you, and kissed after each melody.

"Ten, nine, eight, seven, six, five, four, three, two, one, Happy New Year!" Confetti sprinkled through the air, balloons poured onto the floor, couples embraced and kissed, the crowd cheered and toasted as auld lang syne resounded in the background. Kyle looked Carmen directly in her eyes after kissing her. "This year is going to be our year, Baby. Just hang in there with me. I'm going to make you the happiest woman alive."

"I love you, Baby," Carmen replied with mixed emotions. She thought to herself, "Where's the ring to make me believe what you just said?" She managed to shield her disappointment. She didn't want to spoil the evening or any chance she might have of getting the ring at a later date... hopefully before she went back to work.

For the next three days, Carmen interpreted everything as an opportunity to be surprised with an engagement ring. When she and Kyle went to McDonald's, she would go from searching the bottom of the bag to looking inside of her Chicken McNuggets box for a ring. When she would get up in the morning she would rush into the bathroom hoping to read 'Will you marry me?' written on the mirror of her vanity. Sleeping would not commence until she had searched underneath her pillow. In desperation, she searched his luggage from the inside out looking to see if he had it stashed away. She turned up nothing. It was beginning to set in that a proposal was not eminent before Kyle left to return to Philadelphia. She thought to herself, "Maybe he's waiting until Valentine's Day."

--- *Chapter 14*

Nikki and Drew had been dating for almost a year. His divorce from Tracy was still not final. He told Nikki that the divorce proceedings were still being complicated by issues associated with the custody of Jessica. Nikki speculated that Tracy was making Jessica an issue because she knew that Drew wouldn't just walk away from his daughter. She felt all of the issues Drew was having with Tracy and Jessica were putting stress in her relationship with him. She felt this was, no doubt, part of Tracy's plan. Nikki concluded that Tracy felt that if she couldn't have Drew, then no one else could.

"Nik, I'm a little confused," said Carmen. "You say that the custody over Jessica is the only thing that's holding up his divorce, right? You also said that he describes her as a crazy bitch with questionable motherhood skills, right? Then what's the holdup? To me, it seems as though *he* should get full custody and *she* should get some visitation rights and some counseling coupons. This looks like a no-brainer."

"That's easy for you and me to assess," replied Nikki. "However, it's my understanding that it's not that easy. You know what people say, "marriages are easy to get into but hard to get out of.""

"Really now? If marriage is so easy to get into, then how come I can't seem to get into one?" said Carmen referring to her relationship with Kyle. "But then again, I guess we could all be married if that's all we wanted. Think about all the men who we *don't* want... They all would be *honored* to have us as their wives. It's the ones we want that we can't seem to have. I wonder why that is?"

"Who knows?" answered Nikki. "All I know is that I refuse to settle for less than what I want. My preference would be to have a man who has never been married and who has no kids, but if the rest of his package is tight, then I'll make the sacrifice."

Carmen changed the subject slightly. "Hey, so tell me all about Drew's place. Did you help him decorate it when you went to visit? Did he let you drive the Merc?"

"Well his place was pretty empty when I got there. He had a couch and a bed. I bought him some plants and some pictures for his walls. He likes Jazz almost as much as you do. I'd like to get him a nice jazz painting for his birthday. Can I commission you to do a piece for me?"

"Sure," replied Carmen. "Since I know your man is loaded, maybe I'll up the price," Carmen joked.

"I beg your pardon. *He* won't be paying for it. Your living-from-paycheck-to-paycheck friend will. So I expect you to lower the price ... significantly," said Nikki with a chuckle.

"So tell me about the Merc, "said Carmen.

"Well, he didn't have it while I was there. Tracy had it because she said she needed it more than he did because it was more reliable. And since she had Jessica most of the time, she thought it should be hers."

"Yeah, right. So what unreliable car is he forced to drive when he has Jessica?" said Carmen sarcastically. "Does he drive the Merc-*ury* instead of the Merc-edes?"

"Ha, Ha, very funny. He drives the Toyota Celica," said Nikki defensively. I think it's a smart move actually."

"How so?" asked Carmen.

"Well think about it. If he had the Mercedes now and she complained to the courts that she was left with the more unreliable of the two vehicles, he might be forced to buy *her* a new Mercedes instead of one for himself."

"So when did you say that his divorce was supposed to be final?" asked Carmen.

"It's hard to say right now. I'm sure when things are worked out with his daughter. Most likely things will work out as soon as Tracy realizes it is silly to use her daughter to hang on to a man. I mean women always claim they want to hold on to a marriage for the sake of the children, when they know full well it's more about holding on to the man. I wish this Tracy would get a life."

"What, get a life so *you* can get her man?" joked Carmen.

"He doesn't love her," said Nikki feeling defensive and offering a reason why it was OK for her to be involved with Drew.

"How long do you plan on waiting for this man, Nik?" asked Carmen. "And who's to say that he is going to want to marry you once he is divorced. And are you prepared to deal with the possibility of a scorned ex-wife, who is the mother of his first born... I might add, being in your lives forever? I mean, you know that little Jessica is always going to need yet one more pair of shoes and a lifetime of piano and ballet lessons, and for sure, a college education at Harvard.

"No one said it would be easy. I don't have all the answers. Anything worth having is worth waiting for," said Nikki. "Besides you can ask yourself the same questions you're asking me.

"What do you mean?" asked Carmen.

Nikki retorted, "How long do you plan on waiting for Kyle? How do you know that he's going to marry you once he gets to Atlanta? Do you even know if he's ever going to get to Atlanta? How do you know that Robbi is still not on his trail? How do you feel about the possibility of Robbi always thinking that it should be *her* that's Kyle's wife and not you?"

"Point well taken, Nik. I'll attend to my own business and stay out of yours. Deal?"

--- *Chapter 15*

Carmen sat in the chair at the beauty salon growing more and more disgusted with her beautician, Bridgette. Once again, Bridgette was trying out yet another technique for taming Carmen's moody mane. This time, Bridgette thought she would set her hair in jumbo rollers to give it the conditioned look of a set and the body and straightness of a blow-dried hairdo. Carmen knew it would turn out too curly or too bouffy. She couldn't understand why Bridgette wouldn't just find the right conditioner and learn how to blow dry her hair without it looking dry and frizzy. Then again, she did understand, Bridgette was too lazy to take the time to blow each strand to make sure all of her hair was dry, including the roots. This jumbo roller hairdo was just a way for her to hurry up and stick Carmen underneath the dryer so that she could put another patron in her chair.

As Carmen sat only half way underneath the dryer because the rollers were too big, she could hear the conversations of several women in the salon. Almost every conversation was about a man or a man problem! Even if a woman was talking about shopping, she was talking about shopping for the right outfit to catch a man or to look good for the man she was trying to keep. She found the dialog very interesting and most entertaining. The women seemed to talk so freely about their personal business. The beauty salon was a breeding ground for gossip. One woman spoke very freely about how good her man was in bed and how no matter what, she was going to hold on to "that good dick." Carmen wondered to herself if the woman listening to this was a loyal friend or possibly someone who was thinking how interesting it would be to find out if what the woman was saying was really true. Hmm.

Bridgette became engaged in a conversation with one of her other clients about how they were going to leave their "no-good" men. They went on to gossip about some woman named Vesta being a damn fool for staying with some man named Skip. Bridgette openly discussed the details of Vesta's woes. Carmen couldn't help but think that Bridgette probably gossiped about her to other clients when she wasn't around. She was certain Bridgette wouldn't be discussing Vesta's private affairs if Vesta were present. The other question was how did Bridgette get all the details of Vesta's relationship? Did Vesta come into the salon and seek therapy from a bunch of nosy women? Do beauticians purposely make you spend an entire day waiting to get your hair done so that you will grow weary and resort to having girlfriend conversations with complete strangers? Is it that every woman is going through similar trials and tribulations with life and relationships that she is inclined to chime right into a conversation that she can relate to? Do men sit around discussing their private business, or are they discussing how many points Michael Jordan will score at the next Bulls game? As all of these thoughts went through Carmen's head, her cerebral moment was interrupted when she heard Oprah's name. She couldn't believe her ears when she heard these women speaking authoritatively about how Stedman was *never* going to marry Oprah.

"How the hell would they know?...It might be Oprah who was never going to marry Stedman... And just maybe Oprah and Stedman were happy not being married at all," Carmen thought to herself. All she could think of now was how glad she was she had not parted her lips to share with those gossip-hungry women that Kyle had finalized the details of starting his new law firm in Atlanta and would be relocating in a couple of weeks.

Carmen felt nervous as the flight attendant announced that her flight was making its final descent into the Philadelphia airport. She wanted to make one final visit to the lavatory to make sure her hair and makeup were in place, but everyone else seemed to have the same idea and the line was too long. She fumbled around in her purse to locate her compact mirror to make sure her facial shine was under control. The gentleman next to her began to make conversation. "Are you meeting that special someone?"

"Yeah, I can't believe how nervous I am," answered Carmen. "You would think I was meeting him for the first time with the way I'm acting," she continued.

"When was the last time you saw each other?" asked the gentleman.

"A couple of weeks ago."

"How long will you be in the Philadelphia area?" the man asked attempting to keep the conversation going until they landed.

"Actually only a couple of days. I'm coming up here to help my friend drive back to Atlanta," Carmen said happily. "I'm not really looking forward to the drive, but I'm really looking forward to us being together in Atlanta," she said.

"Will wedding bells be ringing soon?" asked the man.

"I hope so," said Carmen as she felt the plane touch down sending her heart into a flutter.

Overcome with excitement about seeing Kyle, Carmen managed to subdue her feelings of insecurity about where her relationship with him was heading. Although she was thrilled about him moving to Atlanta, she was not comforted by the fact that there had been no proposal for marriage. Kyle was still doing the usual dangling of the carrot. Moving forward was always contingent on something that she had no control over. Kyle had suggested that they should live together before they got married to make sure they could get along. He offered that he just didn't want to go through another broken engagement as he had with Robbi.

Carmen was not entirely comfortable with Kyle living with her or "shacking up" as her mother would say. She agreed to allowing him to do so because she didn't want him to come to Atlanta and be totally available to all the man-hungry women who always welcomed additions to the selection pool. After all, she concluded that living together was somewhat of a commitment. She decided that if he didn't propose marriage within a certain period, which she had not yet defined, she would terminate their living arrangements and possibly their relationship.

Kyle was standing at the gate when Carmen emerged from the plane. He welcomed her with a bear hug embrace and a tongueful kiss. As she kissed him, she knew that it wouldn't be long before they would end up in his now empty apartment, and they would be making passionate love on the bare floors and countertops. This would be symbolic to her. No matter what had taken place in that apartment before, it would be their togetherness there imprinted in his mind as the final episode of the past and the beginning of the future. Although she was happy to be there, she and Kyle couldn't leave fast enough for her. She was happy to be the one to help him say goodbye to Philadelphia. She could hardly wait to claim her man by taking him back to Atlanta.

Kyle seemed saddened as they loaded the last piece of luggage into his car. When asked if he was okay, he replied, "Yeah. It feels kind of funny. I have many memories here. I'm leaving behind a lot of friends. That's all."

"Are you having second thoughts about coming to Atlanta?" asked Carmen in an attempt to gain reassurance.

"No, Carmen. I'm not having second thoughts. Atlanta is going to be great. Langston and I are going to have the serious law firm, I'll be closer to my family and of course, we'll be together." Kyle answered. "All I'm saying is that it feels weird because I'm leaving something I'm familiar with and leaping into the unknown." Carmen tried not to be concerned with where she fell in the order of why he thought moving to Atlanta would be great. "You've always wanted to be a partner in your own law firm and you're making that dream a reality. I think that's admirable," said Carmen. "Most people don't have the guts to go after what they want out of life. I think that you and

Langston are going to make a great team. As entertainment attorneys, you guys are going to have lots of clients in Atlanta. My friend Lark is very connected in the industry. I'll have to conncct the two of you. I know she can send you major business."

"Thank you, Baby, for looking out for me," said Kyle. "How is your art project coming?"

"What art project?" asked Carmen.

"Your project. The one where you said you would showcase your talents at the Atlanta Arts Festival. You *do* still plan on doing that, right?" inquired Kyle.

"Yeah, of course. I just need to get focused. The agency is keeping me really busy, but it is a goal I have, so I'll just have to make time," Carmen offered as an excuse.

Kyle placed Carmen into the car on the passenger side and then got in on the driver's side. "Well Baby, this is it. Thank you for coming up here to be with me. Let's get this show on the road!" exclaimed Kyle.

Chapter 16

A kiss on the cheek and a whisper of "I love you" was the daily ritual for Kyle as he prepared to leave for the office. He would also double check to make sure his tie was on straight and that the cuffs of his dress shirt extended the proper distance below the sleeves of his suit jacket. "I'll call you later to let you know around what time I'll be home" was what he would say as he walked out the door. However, he would never call in enough time to allow Carmen to make plans to do other things if he was going to be late. She always felt like she was on hold and many times like she was a hostage to his lack of communication. She felt like if she did go ahead and do something else, she would miss out on the opportunity to spend time with him if his plans changed and he was available to spend time with her. What was even worse was when he would call and say that he would meet her at home for dinner, he would show up at 9:00 or 10:00 o' clock at night with no phone call in the interim letting her know he would be late. She knew that he was at the office because most of the time when she called to check on him, he would answer or Langston would answer informing her that Kyle had run out for a moment and would be back shortly. Langston and Kyle always seemed to be busy working on making the law firm successful. As much as Carmen felt like she was in the back seat in Kyle's life, she didn't want to let him go. The primary reason was because she loved him and also if the law firm turned out to be very successful, she felt like Kyle would be making enough money to support the two of them so she wouldn't have to work.

Even though Carmen looked forward to the affection of Kyle's good-bye kisses in the morning as he set off to make a fortune, and even though she looked forward to sharing in his success, all of this was no consolation to the enormous hole she felt in her heart when she had no encouragement they were going to be married. She had hoped she wouldn't have to resort to issuing an ultimatum, but as the old saying would go, "He's going to have to piss or get off the pot." Speaking of "pissing or getting off the pot," she wondered how Nikki was coming along with Drew. Nikki usually called at least once every two weeks. A phone call was definitely due, be it initiated or received.

"How are things coming with Drew?" asked Carmen.

"To be honest with you, I'm getting a little sick and tired of waiting on the damn divorce to become final. If it's not one thing, it's another," cried a disgusted Nikki.

"What is it now?"

"Drew says Tracy is trying to get even more of a child support settlement and alimony!"

"Ooh, she must have read or seen *Waiting to Exhale*," joked Carmen. "How long will this drag out?"

"Longer than I'm willing to wait... That's for damn sure," exclaimed Nikki.

"Now that's a change of heart. I thought you were willing to stick by Drew."

" I *was* when I thought the bitch would only get *half*. Now she wants blood. She told Drew that she owed it to herself to make his life miserable," said Nikki.

"She *owes* it to herself?" said Carmen. "So she's just going to dedicate the rest of her life to being scorned instead of getting on with it?" Carmen continued.

"Girl, all I know is I'm not going to put up with this much longer. There's something to be said for standing by your man, but he needs to *be* your man first. Drew says that I should understand that marriage is much more difficult to get out of than it is to get into. I told him not from my perspective, because I would have just as hard of a time getting into a marriage with him as he is having getting out of his with Tracy. He told me he understood and for me to hang in there with him just a little while longer."

"Are you going to?"

"I don't know, Carmen. I'll think about it later. He's taking me to Cancun with him in two weeks," said a gleeful Nikki. "What's the deal with you and Kyle?"

"I'll find out tonight. I'm planning to open up a discussion with him about marriage and how it pertains to us," said Carmen. "I've decided that if he doesn't engage me in the next two months, I'm going to start dating other people.

"How do you plan to do that with him living with you?" asked Nikki.

"He's just going to have to move out. I'm beginning to feel like the only reason he wants to live with me is so that he can keep and eye on me or rather keep me in check. Meanwhile, he can just run around Atlanta and do whatever the hell he wants," said Carmen. "Kyle is having his cake and eating it, too... and I'm letting him. This crap must end."

Carmen prepared the final touches on the gourmet dinner she was making for an intimate evening with Kyle. To create the ambiance, she artistically placed several candles throughout her condo. The drapes were drawn open to expose the evening skyline of Atlanta. A table for two had been set directly in front of the large picture window in her dining nook. On the table set the wine bucket with a bottle of Alize'. Towering on the table were two candles with flames that flickered rhythmically to the soft jazz music sounds that filled the room.

Carmen continued the presentation of elegance by wearing a sleek lingerie gown that very closely resemble the gown donned by John F. Kennedy, Jr.'s bride, Caroline, during their wedding ceremony. She strategically placed on the coffee table a copy of _People_ magazine with the newly married couple gracing the cover. She was hoping this would provide a good lead in to her discussion of nuptials. She was also hoping that the evening she had prepared for Kyle would give him a taste of what he would be missing if he decided to move out.

The telephone rang. It was Kyle calling to say that he was in his car and would be home in less than five minutes. Carmen rushed to make sure everything was in place. A spry Carmen freshened up her perfume by spraying one last time on her neck, between her breast and near the nooky zone.

Kyle was very impressed with what he saw when he arrived on schedule. When he asked what was the occasion, Carmen simply replied, "Love."

Kyle spent most of the evening talking about the business. Just as that topic began to reach the level of adnauseam, he somewhat changed the subject by expressing to Carmen how grateful he was for all her patience and support. He went on to say how all he was doing was for the two of them and their future.

Carmen, stunned, couldn't believe he was talking about a future between the two of them. She dared not interrupt before he had an opportunity to finish.

"Carmen, you have really put up with a lot from me since the first day we met. I know that I'm very lucky to be sitting here with you right now. I know I gave you a lot of reasons to never want to have anything to do with me. I'm glad you were willing to work with me.

Carmen sat quietly as she picked up her glass of wine to take a sip to shield her anxious face. She took another sip to calm her nerves. Kyle was notorious for saying all of the right things. She wanted to hear substance.

"Carmen, I'm no fool. I know you've been trying not to bring up the subject of marriage. I *know* you want to get married and so do I. I also know you want to have children and so do I. I might add that I want all of this with *you*."

Carmen could hardly breathe. She felt like she was going to pass out. She was afraid to anticipate what would come out of Kyle's mouth next.

"I know you probably want a big wedding and a big ring. I want you to have those things. I know how you like romance and sentiment. I've been really nervous about bringing up what I'm about to say because I am afraid of your reaction. But here goes... How would you feel about us trading in the ring that I gave Robbi to get you a ring? I don't have a lot of money on hand right now because I have been pumping it into the business."

Carmen hated the thought of Robbi's name being mentioned while they discussed their relationship, but she didn't dare rock the boat. "Well, as long as you're not planning to give me *that* ring and you plan to give me something nicer, I don't see a problem," said Carmen trying to appear as a team player.

"So that you don't think I'm trying to pull a fast one, I would like for you and I to go looking at rings this weekend," Kyle said.

"Are you proposing to me, Honey?" asked Carmen. She didn't want the evening to end with a misinterpretation. "I guess I am, Mrs. Sealy," said Kyle playfully. "I will make sure I do it formally with the ring. So before you go announcing our plans to the world, *please* let me engage you officially.

Carmen was ecstatic that she was finally going to be marrying Kyle. Although she didn't have her ring yet, she thought she would take advantage of every free moment to plan her wedding. Every time she went to the supermarket, she would pick up yet another bridal magazine. She spent countless hours looking at fabric samples to find the right color and fabric for her bridesmaid dresses. She had decided Nikki would be her Maid or Matron of Honor, depending on her marital status at the time of the wedding. With the way things were going with Drew, Maid of Honor would be more likely. Ava, Lark, and Kyle's two sisters would complete the bridesmaid court. Langston was sure to be Kyle's best man or at least second in line to Kyle's brother, Chris. Two of his fraternity brothers and her brother would complete the groomsmen court.

Carmen decided that it would be cute to have Ava and J.B.'s twin daughters, Tamia and Toria as flower girls. Kyle's little nephew, Brandon, would be the ring bearer.

Although Lark would be a bridesmaid, Carmen couldn't pass up the opportunity to have her sing at the wedding. She was sure that Lark's beautiful voice would fill the air with love and romance. There was sure not to be a dry eye in the house.

Carmen had narrowed her wedding dress down to two choices. One was extremely vogue, contemporary and fashionable. The other was more like a Cinderella gown, more traditional. She couldn't decide whether to use white horses and carriages or several white stretch limousines. She thought if she chose the Cinderella gown, then the horses and carriage would be complementary to that look. The limousines were more appropriate for her vogue, chic ensemble. No matter which choice she made, her wedding would be the fulfillment of a fantasy, a dream come true. She would get her prince charming and all the world would know it.

--- Chapter 17
YES!

Happy to be finally engaged to Kyle, Carmen couldn't bring herself to speak publicly about her slight disappointment with the size of her ring. The thought of size never entered her mind on the evening she received the ring. But now, since that evening, she had feelings of insecurity and somehow thought that if only her ring were larger, it would make more of a statement. Somehow the ring could speak the love or security she was missing. Did he really go all out for Robbi when he engaged her? Why didn't they really get married? Did Kyle take her on a high and then let her down? Enough about Robbi -- Why was Kyle hedging on setting a date with her? How could he have professed his love for her the way he did on the evening of the engagement and hedge on setting a date to make their dreams a reality? His excuse for not setting a date was that he needed to get a handle on the business of the law firm so that he could be sure he could have enough security and make enough money to support his family. He said that he wanted to bring his new bride home to a house he provided rather than to a condo she owned. "Carmen, let me be the man," he insisted.

Carmen reminisced about how Kyle executed the proposal. He had called her from work on a Friday to tell her he would be home in thirty minutes and that she should have her bags packed and ready to go. He would not reveal where they would be going. Without this information, she didn't know what to pack. Since they were only going away for the weekend, that made it a little easier. So she packed an outfit for all possible activities. He arrived on time and they were off to a location yet still undisclosed. The destination couldn't be too far away since they were taking the car.

About three and a half hours later, Kyle pretended to be lost as he drove through the woods on a winding road. "I must have taken a wrong turn somewhere," he insisted. "I'll turn around as soon as I find a spot that won't scratch up the car."

As they approached the top of the hill, a small house emerged. Kyle proceeded to the driveway of the house. Above the door was a sign that read, Welcome to Lover's Paradise. Kyle shut off the engine. Still not knowing what was going on, Carmen waited patiently for him to explain what was happening. Instead, he got out of the car, walked around to Carmen's side and opened her door. "Miss, would you please step out of the vehicle," Kyle said as he extended his hand.

Realizing that this was part of Kyle's surprise, Carmen was overcome with joy. She began to cry tears of happiness. Lover's Paradise was a chalet in the Smokey Mountains of Tennessee that Kyle had rented for the weekend. He helped her out of the car and asked her to stand right there for two seconds as he ran inside.

Upon entry into the chalet, Carmen noticed *Cristal* champagne chilling in an ice bucket that sat on a candle-lit table. Red, black, and green grapes draped from a basket filled with assorted breads and cheeses. She was speechless. Across the room was a heart-shaped tub lined with scented bath oils and candles. She could also recognize a couple of **Ambrodisiac** oils. The evening was sure to be erotic as well as romantic. It was.

The next morning, Kyle insisted that she hurry up to get dressed. He suggested she wear something casual and comfortable. "You don't have to spend a lot of time on your hair. Just pull it back or something," he suggested.

The day was filled with a romantic helicopter ride over the Smokey Mountains, a horseback ride through the woods along the streams, romantic strolls in the woods watching animals, shopping, and spontaneous acts of affection. She didn't know why Kyle was doing this and she didn't want to risk spoiling it by asking. Was he guilty of something and trying to soften the blow? She didn't know. She decided to just go with the flow.

As dusk fell upon the day, Kyle escorted her back to the cabin where they changed for dinner. She had enjoyed the day, but knew that their weekend getaway would be ending soon.

"How soon do you think you can be ready for dinner?" asked Kyle.

"Well, it depends on how dressed up I need to get. I can't say that I have a whole lot of choices as far as things to wear. I have my black dress and my black dress," Carmen said jokingly. "I can't imagine that I will have to get too dressed up for the "Smokey Mountains," continued Carmen, making fun of Southern accents.

Carmen and Kyle took a quick bubble bath. Kyle kissed and caressed her like she was the most precious thing on earth to him. Carmen reciprocated. The evening grew magical by the minute.

Kyle watched Carmen put on the final touches of her makeup. He had already put on trousers and a white dress shirt. His hair was neatly groomed. His bronze skin was as smooth as silk. He waited until Carmen walked over to the closet to slip into her black dress when he walked up behind her and begin to kiss her on the back of her neck as he sniffed her perfume.

"You smell so sweet, I can taste you. Your skin is so smooth and soft. I love you so much, Baby," he said as he held her tightly from behind.

"I love you too, Kyle. You are the love of my life."

Kyle put his fingers over her mouth. "Shhh, I want to tell you and show you how much I love you. You have always told me. I know you love me, Carmen. I *know* you love me. I want you to know how much I love and appreciate you. I bought you something. Close your eyes." She did. "Now turn around," he whispered.

Carmen turned around on cue. Kyle was holding a full length, fully beaded evening gown designed by her favorite designer, Donna Karan. It was red and most definitely hot. She was speechless and breathless. "My God, Kyle, it's beautiful! Oh my God, it's simply gorgeous. Why?"

"It's just a little something I picked up. Please put it on," Kyle requested.

"Where are we going?" asked an excited Carmen.

"The sooner you get dressed, the sooner you will see."

No sooner than Carmen slipped her foot into her second shoe, there was a knock at the door of the chalet. She was startled. "Oh my goodness. Who knows we're here?" She said with a twinge of fear.

"Wait right here," Kyle said as he approached the door to investigate. "Okay," he murmured with a smile. He closed the door and walked back to the closet to grab the jacket to his suit. There he was looking like the prince to Carmen's eyes.

"Who was that?" asked Carmen with concern.

"It was just a couple who was lost. They thought this was their chalet."

"Oh," said Carmen expressing relief.

When Carmen stepped outside, she was not prepared for what she saw. Before her very eyes was a beautiful, shiny, black stretch limousine! The knock at the door was the chauffeur letting Kyle know that he had arrived. Once again, she was speechless. Kyle was loving every minute of it. He could tell he was blowing her mind. The chauffeur proceeded to open the door of the limo and gestured for her to enter. Almost in a daze, she climbed in. "Kyle, what are you doing to me?" "Just trying to make you happy" Kyle said with a gleaming smile as they drove off.

The full moon lit the skies. The stars were bright and shimmery. The air was fresh and clean and so was Carmen's mind. All she knew was that she felt right. Everything about life felt perfect. Kyle popped a bottle of champagne and poured a glass for Carmen and himself.

"Here's a toast to us," said Kyle. Suddenly, the limousine pulled up to a hillside where there seemed to be a staff of waiters and a chef. Kyle had arranged for a private catering staff to provide a fine dining experience for him and Carmen on top of a hill which provided a spectacular view of the mountains beneath the decorated skies. The table had already been set with candles and appetizers. Carmen tried to hold back the tears in an effort to preserve her makeup, but lost the battle. Tears were gushing everywhere. "Baby, you're making me feel like a queen," she said with a trembling voice. "My God, I've never felt this way before. My heart is beating so fast. I can hardly breathe."

Kyle took her hand and pulled her out of the limo. Suddenly, she could hear one of her favorite songs began to play. It was an old song by Al B. Sure, _Night and Day_. Kyle began to mouth the words, *"I can tell you how I feel about you Night and Day... how I feel about you."* The two of them danced and played for the duration of the song. Carmen began to speak. "Shhh," said Kyle as he placed his finger over her mouth and then kissed her softly. "I don't want you to speak. I can hear what's inside of your head just by looking in your eyes. This evening is yours. Here are the rules. You will only get to speak *one word* in the next forty-five minutes. Until that time you can only speak with your eyes." The glow on Carmen's face spoke a novel.

As the evening progressed, her eyes spoke a sequel. The French chef served Saumon fume' (smoked salmon) and Me'daillon de Saumon farci (stuffed salmon medallion) as the appetizer. A presentation of Filet de vivaneau Dugle're' (fillet of red snapper with Dugle're' sauce) and Riz aux amandes (rice with almonds) graced the table as the entree. Carmen could hardly contain herself. She wanted to know why Kyle was being so nice. What could she have done to deserve this magical evening?... Or even what could Kyle have done? Was this evening a kiss-up apology for something he had done that he knew she would have trouble forgiving him for? Whatever the reason, he seemed to be enjoying every minute. She decided to enjoy every minute as well. The reason was sure to manifest eventually.

She checked her watch. Forty-five minutes was almost up. She began to think about the one word she would be allowed to speak. The words that came to mind were *Thanks*, *Gee*, *Whew*, *Wow*. She could be greedy and say, *Next*. Maybe she could be inquisitive and say *Why*.

"I'd like to dedicate this next song to you," said Kyle as another one of Carmen's favorite songs began to play. It was a composition by the jazz artist, Stanley Jordan, _The Lady in My_

<u>Life</u>.

"Carmen, I never knew real love before I met you. We've really been through a lot together. I haven't always known what I wanted, but right now, I've never been surer about anything. You are the lady in my life. I want you in my life forever," Kyle took hold of Carmen's trembling hand. "Carmen Layfield, will you marry me?"

Carmen gasped. Her eyes began to well up with tears. She sat there with her mouth gaping. She wasn't speechless because she was originally instructed not to speak…She was astounded! Taking a deep breath was her attempt at harvesting enough energy to respond. A confident Kyle looked on and waited patiently.

"Yes!" said Carmen as she exhaled. Her lip continued to tremble. Tears began to stream down her face. She was so astonished. She hadn't even realized that she had not yet been presented with a ring.

"Look there's a falling star," said Kyle as he pointed over the mountain at the sky. "Quick, close your eyes and make a wish."

Although she didn't see the falling star, Carmen closed her eyes anyway. She could hear the waiter removing the dome from the desert platter in front of her. Before opening her eyes, she completed her wish for eternal happiness. She then opened her eyes slowly. Sparkling like one of the stars in the sky, her engagement ring lay in a bed of orchids. "The star has landed," said the waiter.

"Oh my God, Kyle, this is so incredible. I can't believe this is happening," said Carmen as she struggled to speak through the excitement in her voice.

Kyle slid the ring onto her finger. "Mrs. Sealy, whatever you wished for, the answer is *yes!*"

Chapter 18

Dawn introduced the new day as Carmen peeled herself out of bed after being on the phone all night with Nikki. She remembered their conversation. She thought Nikki was in dire need of some relationship counseling. She and Drew were on the verge of breaking up. It was appearing that the closer he got to his divorce being final, the further he seemed to be pulling away from Nikki. The frequency of his visits to Chicago had diminished. Whenever she called him, he was always either "just about to walk out the door" or "just getting in and too tired to talk". Nikki had slipped and mentioned that she had found ladies underwear in his dryer during her last visit. Drew offered her some excuse about how the panties must have been mistakenly packed in little Jessica's overnight bag by Tracy. When asked if she believed him, she said that it was possible. She said she didn't put anything past Tracy. *"Denial"* was the best description for Nikki's mental state, Carmen thought.

Nikki described Drew's new furniture. She spoke of leather couches and animal skin rugs. Dimmer switches had been installed in all the rooms. The place was laden with incense and candles. Carmen thought to herself, "If I hear that he has a lava lamp, I'm going to scream." The clincher for Carmen was the bottle of bubble bath. "Since when did Drew find it necessary to indulge himself in a bathtub full of bubbles... alone?" she thought. Nikki mentioned that the bottle was not full and that she and Drew had only taken showers... (hmmm).

Nikki dismissed Drew's behavior as that of a man longing for the woman he *really* loved. Carmen thought, "Oh, now when Nikki, Lark and I were in college, we always said to each other when we saw a woman being a fool for a man... "If you ever see me being a fool, *please* knock me up side my head. Tell me. Don't let me walk around looking *that* stupid.""" Carmen thought this was a good time to remind Nikki of their promise to each other. Somehow she thought saying anything negative about Drew would incite Nikki to prove her wrong. Then Nikki would involve herself even deeper into the relationship. It wouldn't stop there, Nikki would probably get angry with her and cease communication. Carmen would be viewed as the adversary rather than the ally. She remembered how Nikki dismissed any suggestion that she might be co-dependent. Drew was obviously not the man for her, but Nikki wasn't hearing it. Carmen had concluded that Nikki's outreach for counseling from her was nothing more than a request for an audience to listen to her diagnose her own situation. Carmen knew that Nikki's "heartbreak and pain" should be classified on the same level as *cardiac arrest*, but Nikki dismissed her pain to be as minor as a little gas and indigestion. Nikki didn't want advice, she wanted an amen corner. If today was the let's-hate-Drew-and-consider-him-to-be-the-scum-of-the-earth   day,   then everyone should agree. On the other hand, if today was the Drew-is-the-best-thing-since-ice-water-in-the-Sahara day, then let the church say, "Amen." What Nikki was in need of was divine intervention.

"Enough of Nikki and Drew," Carmen said to herself as she proceeded to the bathroom to wash her face. She remembered that Kyle had left his pager number for her in case she needed to contact him over the weekend. He and Langston had left Atlanta to attend an attorney's convention in Seattle. Since the time zones were different, it was difficult for her to catch him. She tried not to let her mind wonder and think negative thoughts. She remembered how she felt about pagers. She once told Nikki that she should be careful not to develop some false sense of security just because Drew had provided her with his pager number. She explained that a page sent is not always a page returned. For some people who carry pagers, the pager is merely a tool for helping them understand during what time period a lie needs to be concocted. And of course, if before the page is returned and one is unable to devise a story that's somewhat believable, then the ol' "I left the pager in the car," if you're supposed to be inside, or the ol' "I left the pager in my room" if you're d to be out, or the ol' "I had turned the pager off," or the ultimate, "You paged me?... I never got it" is used as the bail out.

Carmen didn't want to be too pushy or smothering with Kyle. She decided to take him at his word that he was always handling business. She had to believe he was indeed handling business in Seattle. After all, the sooner Kyle got situated in his career, the sooner she could set a wedding date. She wanted to show Kyle that she could be the supportive mate. If he was going to be a successful entertainment attorney, then he would have to travel on many occasions. She didn't want to complain now and give him an unfavorable snapshot of what life would be like with her after the *I do's*. One of the things her mother would always say came to mind, "You can draw a man to you or you can drive him away from you."

Beginning to feel depressed, she went through her mental list of things she could do to take her mind off her woes. Her idle mind was turning into the devil's den. Her heart and head were in battle. She needed a distraction. She thought of going to get her nails done, but the salon was sure to be filled with a bunch of women in denial about a bad relationship or a bunch of women plotting how to win a man over. If she went to the mall, she wanted to avoid any salesperson who would try to convince here to buy something because it would look good to or attract "that man." Carmen wanted to scream. "I don't want to think about a relationship. I don't want to talk about a relationship. I just want to have a positive and uplifting day," she thought to herself. "I can do this. I can get through this day without thinking about what Kyle is doing or who he's with. I can do this. I *will* do this. I will have a happy day. I will not engage in a pity party."

The phone rang. It was Kyle calling to tell Carmen that he loved her and missed her. He told her he had made a lot of contacts and that he saw enormous opportunity for a successful law firm. After a few minutes of small talk, Kyle solicited a kiss, told her he couldn't wait to see her and that he would be home soon. Carmen felt better already.

No sooner than she began to nod off into a much-desired afternoon nap, Carmen was awakened by a phone call from Ava inviting her to join her in an afternoon of shopping. Not able to resist the temptation of being able to seek out a bargain for an awesome outfit, she accepted. Since Ava agreed to pick her up, that gave here a chance to compose herself and remedy her lethargy. Ava was sure to be dressed to the nine and looking stunning in an outfit that showed off her physically fit body. Carmen decided that she could not allow herself to look worse than a woman who was older *and* had two kids. Thus, she combed here closet for an outfit that looked classy, yet subtle. She didn't want to appear to be *trying* to look fabulous. She wanted a look that said, "Sure, I look this great all the time... I just threw this on and I look great effortlessly." None would be wiser. No one had to know this look and attitude was manufactured. It's just something that women do... try to look attractive to the opposite sex while making sure you don't allow your girlfriends to run rings around you. Thus, try to look good to be admired by other women as well. "I wonder if men do this," Carmen thought to herself.

While Carmen was putting on the final touches of her makeup, she received a call from Ava indicating that she was going to be bringing along one of her girlfriends who was also an aerobics instructor. She said her name was Amber.

"Amber. That sounds like a name of someone who's pretty," Carmen said to herself as she hung up the phone after suggesting she was excited about meeting her. She wasn't really. As she sat and waited for Ava to arrive, she picked up the phone to call Nikki.

"Hi Nik, whatcha doin'?" asked Carmen.

"Nothing. What's up?"

"Nothing really. I'm just calling to kill a little time before Ava gets here. We're all going shopping. She's bringing some woman named Amber. Doesn't that sound like someone who's cute?" Carmen said with envy.

"Now Carmen, you know that mothers look at their ugly newborn babies and give them *cute* names every day. You know that a person's name is no indication of what they look like. Remember how you refused to meet that guy named Buford Dozier because you thought he would be fat, ugly and country? You found out that he was tall, gorgeous, and sophisticated *after* he started dating someone else. Why do you care if she's cute anyway?"

"Oh, come on, Nikki. You know that competition is fierce here in Atlanta.

"Why are you worried about competition. You already have a man. Or did you forget to tell me something?" asked Nikki.

"Girl, you know how men can be. Kyle is no exception. Just in case he decides he wants to act up, I need my 'Plan B' ready. I just need to scope out the potentials," answered Carmen with determination. "The only thing about having this Amber woman in my company is that if she tries to become friends with me, then any man she spots first or any man who finds her attractive will be off limits to me," continued Carmen.

"Then don't befriend her," said Nikki. "But then again, maybe you should because that way you can make sure she keeps her hands off any man you spot first or any man who may find you attractive."

"You have a point," said Carmen as she massaged this thought in her head. "I just thought of something. This woman might already be heavily involved with someone."

"What's your point? *You* are already heavily involved with someone and you're still looking. She might be, too. How do you know she's not married since she's friends with Ava? You know married people only like to be around other married people. You know how some married women are. They swear that all of their single friends are interested in their husbands or their husbands may be interested in their single friends," said Nikki with an attitude.

"First of all, Ava and J.B.'s marriage is as solid as a rock. Second, I know she's single because Ava mentioned that she was and that we had a lot in common. That's why she thought I wouldn't mind her coming along. Ava thought we might like each other. We'll just have to see. "Call me later on to let me know how everything went," requested Nikki.

"Okay," said Carmen. "I'm going to run now so I can make sure I'm ready when they get here. They should be here any minute. I'll call you when I get back. Bye."

Later that evening, Carmen called Nikki as promised to provide her with all the details of the outing. She told Nikki that she found Amber to be somewhat nice and kind of attractive. Amber had dark hair and dark features. Her haircut was very similar to Nikki's. She was slim and stood about 5'9". Carmen explained that she thought Amber would have had a nicer body than she had since she taught aerobics. Maybe because she only did it part time was an explanation for her less-than-perfect physique. She was a Project Manager by day and taught aerobics three nights per week and on some weekends.

When Nikki asked Carmen about Amber's relationship status, Carmen explained to her that Amber was in the market for a new man. She and her boyfriend of almost two years had severed their ties about a month ago. She had recently joined the church to help her deal with her loss. She said she was looking for peace with God. Not a lot of details of why they broke up were provided. "She said she wants to hang out with me," said Carmen. "I don't know about women sometimes. We'll just have to see."

Feeling the pressure from her co-workers and family members, Carmen thought it was timely for her to start putting the pressure on Kyle to set a date for their wedding. Since Kyle had returned from the convention in Seattle, all he talked about was the goals of his law firm with Langston. The excuse for not setting a wedding date in the past had been his discomfort with the promise of a successful business venture and financial stability.

The sense of urgency for Carmen to get married came the day when Kyle came home with a brand new 740I BMW... black on black! She had no forewarning of this significant purchase. He had traded in the Probe. He claimed that the new car was necessary for the image of the law firm. He said that in order to *be* successful, you had to *look* successful. She recalled thinking, "In order to *look* married, you need to *be* married." To her, the car was sure to be a magnet for all types of competition. Now, time was of the essence. She had to get Kyle off the market. He was about to become a successful entertainment attorney. He was also going to look the part. Kyle's dreams were about to become a reality. Carmen felt like she had stood by him along the way and provided him with contacts through Lark to allow him to accomplish his goals more expeditiously. She couldn't allow him to escape her grasp. She couldn't allow some other women to just step in and enjoy the fruits of her labor.

Chapter 19

If we could look over the wall into the future, would we? If we knew what lay ahead of us, would we be brave enough to meet the challenges? If we knew of ultimate happiness, would we be willing to walk through the fires to experience it? All of these thoughts came to Carmen's mind after receiving the devastating news that Lark might have throat cancer. Lark's voice was her livelihood. It had always been the basis of her dreams and wishes. Carmen wasn't able to reach Lark to express her love and support. Lark's mother, Mother Durham, had assured Carmen that she would be sure to let Lark know that she had friends like her and Nikki who were anxious to speak with her as soon as she was able to receive guests. Carmen accepted this. However, in the meantime, she stopped everything she was doing to write Lark a letter to say all of the things she could not communicate verbally.

Dealing with the sadness of the news about Lark presented Carmen with several challenges as she tried to prepare a kick-off gala for Kyle's and Langston's law firm. She had wanted Lark to attend the gala since other entertainers would be present. However, as they say in show business, "The show must go on."

Ava and J.B. had agreed to host the party at their home. With Ava's assistance, the function was sure to be a classy affair. Trying to keep the guest list to less than two hundred people was a challenge. Carmen wanted to invite several of the powerful and influential people she knew as a result of working through the advertising agency. Kyle and Langston wanted to invite all of their friends, supporters and potential clients. Ava and J.B., of course, wanted to make sure they were able to invite their powerful and influential friends. Nikki had managed to only invite herself since she thought bringing Drew would be like bringing sand to the beach... All of these "powerful and influential" people were sure to have money, which was a magnet for her. She told Carmen, "There is nothing wrong with having options."

Carmen made sure that everyone else who was invited was extended the option of bringing a guest. She particularly wanted the women to bring a man so that they wouldn't be preying off Kyle, Langston, and J.B.. Mainly, she was concerned about them preying off Kyle; Langston and J.B. were married. But then again, some women wouldn't care, according to Lewis, they might even find that more attractive.

Glitz and glamour described the evening as the guest arrived at the residence of J.B. and Ava. Onlookers would have guessed a mini Academy Awards was taking place in the Cascades of Atlanta. The street was lined with Mercedes Benz's and limousines. The women donned slinky sequined dresses, both floor-length and above the knee. The men wore tuxedos with fashionable and trendy cummerbund and bow tie ensembles. Kyle and Langston looked especially alluring. They each wore black designer tuxedos with white wing-tip collar shirts. After all, they were the men of the evening. Carmen was absolutely stunning in her signature red. Her dress was long-sleeved with a cleavage opening all the way down to her navel. The dress hugged her hips before opening to a beautiful flow with the split from just above her knee all the way down to the floor. She wore matching red ankle-strap, high heel sandals that had just one thin strap across the top of her foot near the toes. Her only accessories were here diamond stud earrings and her engagement ring. She had made sure she got her ring cleaned earlier that day to ensure that its brilliance would be seen and that she would be clearly recognized as Kyle's fiancée.

Although Carmen wore Kyle's ring, she didn't really feel totally secure because they had not officially set a date. She didn't concern herself with this excessively because after tonight, she would be able to approach the subject and not have to receive the excuse Kyle had been using about wanting to feel secure about the business. If Kyle didn't feel secure about the business now, then he wouldn't be announcing to the city and citizens of Atlanta the launching of his new law firm.

"Carmen, come here for a minute," said Ava as she pulled her into a room where they had a brief moment of privacy. "I was just thinking, what would you think of introducing Kyle's brother, Chris, to Amber?"

"Amber?" said Carmen. "I haven't seen her here."

"She isn't yet," explained Ava. "She just called and said she was on her way. She originally thought she wouldn't be able to make it because she had a date to go to the concert at the Fox Theater. Her date didn't make it into town. He missed his flight. She thinks he may already have a girlfriend and just couldn't get away for the weekend."

"Is she upset?" asked Carmen.

"Yeah, she's kind of in a blue funk about men right now. Chris seems like a nice guy. I thought he might be a nice guy for her to meet. He did say he was looking to meet a nice, attractive woman."

Carmen, not really thinking Amber was all that attractive, played along. "Yeah, he did say that. Although, he doesn't seem to be having too much trouble. I've seen a few women flirting with him tonight. I think my friend, Nikki, has made herself the woman in charge of finding Chris a mate. I'll tell her to introduce Chris to Amber when she gets here.

"That was another reason why I asked you what you thought. I wasn't sure if Nikki was interested in Chris," said Ava.

"Girl, Nikki only has eyes for Drew. I guarantee you she will find something wrong with every available man in there... unless he happens to be rich," Carmen quipped.

Amber arrived on the scene about twenty minutes after Carmen had learned she was on her way. Carmen greeted her at the door. They exchanged compliments. Carmen's adulation for

Amber was exaggerated and, quite frankly, fabricated. "Amber, Hi. Come on in. You look like a million bucks," said Carmen as she really thought, "You really look like an advertisement for Sears or sewing pattern number 0000 from Simplicity or Butterick." Frumpy was a description that came to mind. Amber was wearing a white, loose-fitting sequins pant outfit. The sleeves on the top were short. The pants appeared to be a little too short. Her flat-heeled shoes seemed to indicate that she might have been aware of that fact. Her tapered haircut looked fresh and pretty nice. "Amber has potential," Carmen thought. Figuring out what Amber had potential for was the mystery.

Nikki had already revealed to Chris that she had someone she wanted him to meet.

Not long after Amber's arrival, Nikki was deep into the introductions. Carmen was certain Chris wouldn't like Amber. To her surprise, Amber snubbed Chris! She told Ava he acted young. She wanted someone much more mature and had more going for himself. Carmen was appalled, "Talk about beggars being *choosy*!"

The party ended at around 2:00a.m. Everyone seemed to have had a great time. Kyle and Langston were experiencing shear bliss. The objective for the evening appeared to have been accomplished. Carmen felt very proud to say Kyle was her man. She admired his perseverance to achieve a goal. There had been many things that could have discouraged him, but he was persistent. He would no doubt be as successful as he desired.

Although a cleaning crew had been hired for the evening, a few close friends hung around to help out just the same.

"So Nikki, did you meet anyone interesting?" asked Ava as she, Carmen and Amber tidied up the kitchen.

"Not really. All the good men were taken," said Nikki.

"What about you Amber... did you meet anyone interesting?"

"I'm with Nikki, all the good men seemed to be taken. They were all married or seriously involved. When is your

170

wedding, Carmen?" Amber interjected.

Carmen felt embarrassed that she couldn't answer that question with confidence. "We've had a lot of things to work out. Kyle's business was one of them. Now that we've instituted it, we can concentrate on us," she said.

"You are so lucky. You have stuck by your man and look at your reward. You better hurry up and marry him before someone comes along and snatches him up," said Amber. "I would ask you if he had any brothers, but I've already met Chris. He has a long way to go before he is a Kyle. I hope I can meet someone like Kyle one day. Once again, you are so lucky."

Carmen smiled, "Thank you, Amber. I do feel lucky. I'll tell Kyle to keep a look out for you. I'm sure he'll be meeting a lot of interesting people. I too, will keep and eye out for you."

"You can keep the other eye out for me while you're at it," Nikki said laughing.

Carmen began to reflect. "I was just thinking how Kyle has always wanted to be an attorney and then he became one. He later decided he wanted to become an entertainment attorney, and now he *is* one. I can't help thinking about Lark. I don't know what she's going to do. She has always wanted to be a singer. She has a growth on her larynx. It is very possibly malignant. Her dreams will be shattered. I'm so worried about her. She must be devastated. All we can do at this point is pray for her."

Nikki began to feel somber. "Let's hold hands and say a quick prayer for Lark." They all grabbed hold of each other's hand. Nikki led them in meditation. Then in unison, they all said, "Amen."

The relentless pressure of trying to deliver positive activity and results for the social report card created an agony Carmen could no longer withstand. People wanted to know when, where, how much, what colors, how many... everything associated with her wedding. All she was really concerned about at this point was *if* she were ever going to be married. If so, to *whom*? Kyle seemed to be slowly drifting away. He had become more and more evasive whenever the subject of setting a date came up. Love wasn't supposed to be like this. She had to work hard at even getting him into a relationship in the first place. Then she had to give ultimatums to get a ring and a proposal. Now she was having to labor just as intensely to get a date. Would she have to work this diligently after they were married to get him to behave like a husband, she thought.

Carmen had promised herself to never spy on Kyle again. She knew that trust was a key element in the survival of any relationship. But she needed answers. "What was really the hold up? Why is he stalling? If Kyle didn't want to be married to me, he should never have moved into my home. He should have never given me a ring," she thought. She had thought of hiring a private investigator to track his comings and goings, but they were too expensive. She wanted to follow him herself, but Kyle would surely recognize her car. He would think her behavior was excessive and that she had mental problems. "To hell with Kyle and what he thinks," she thought. "I wouldn't be the first woman to spy on her man. If he would just tell the truth then I wouldn't have to resort to these measures."

Carmen had decided not to go into the office today. She had a few personal errands to run since she had been out of town for the last couple of days. The real reason she stayed home was because she was feeling depressed. She couldn't face the world. She was tired of dodging questions. She was tired of trying to make people feel like they were invading her privacy when they asked when was the big day. This question was no more of an invasion into her privacy than someone asking a pregnant woman when her baby was due.

She and Kyle didn't have a chance to talk last night since her flight had gotten in pretty late and Kyle was asleep when she got home. They also didn't get a chance to talk this morning because Kyle left at around 6:30a.m. Carmen was still asleep.

While sitting at the table in her pajamas having breakfast,

Carmen read the nutritional facts on the side of her box of cereal as she stirred the spoon around lazily in the bowl. She picked up the cordless phone to check her voice mail at work. She had several messages. Some were business-related, most were personal. She scrolled through all the messages deleting those that were of little significance and saving those that required her attention. She chuckled as she listened to the last message. It was from some guy she had met in the airport. She remembered he had on brown pants, a mustard colored shirt with matching mustard shoes. He looked like a corn dog! Delete!

Like a ritual, Carmen fished out the last raisin in her cereal before drinking the remainder of the milk from the bowl. For whatever reason, she suddenly felt energized. She decided not to let her dismal mood get the best of her. A nice long, hot shower would shake off any remaining anxiety. She went into her bedroom where she took off her pajamas and tied her hair to the top of her head. In route to the shower, she searched for the remote, even though she stood right in front of the television, to get a glimpse at CNN to see what was happening outside of her world. She found it underneath the covers at the foot of the bed. As she pressed the up arrow to advance the channels, she witnessed a series of talk shows. "How could these people get on national television and expose all of their personal problems," she thought. "Don't they have jobs to go back to? How do they face their co-workers or even their bosses? Do these people even work? If so, do they use their hard-earned vacation days to become guests on these shows? Heck, if these people can face the world after bearing their souls to a million strangers, surely I can handle the people in my circle," Carmen said as she turned on the water to the shower allowing it to get hot.

She thought she'd better check voice mail one last time before entering the shower because she planned to be in it for a long time. She put the television on mute. While looking at the images on the screen, she grabbed the phone on the nightstand and hit the redial button. When her voicemail didn't immediately pick up, she realized she was using a phone other than the one she had previously used in the kitchen to call her office, thus, activating redial on *that* phone. As she was about to hang up to correctly dial the office voicemail, she heard a voice that absolutely paralyzed her! "Hello, you've reached the residence of Robbi Gant. I can't come to the phone right now. Your call is very important to me, so please leave a message at the tone and I will be sure to return your call as soon as possible... Beep."

Carmen stood immobilized. Robbi's answering machine surely recorded the dead silence. All Carmen could hear was the thunderous thumping of her own heart. All she could feel was the enormous lump in her throat. Growing weary from shock, she managed to place the receiver back into the cradle. A million scrambled thoughts created echoes in her head. Nothing made sense. She clutched her nude body as she lay atop the bed. She began to grab her temples so as to collect all the sounds, all the thoughts that consumed her.

"This bastard has been calling that *bitch* ... on my phone!" said a wrathful Carmen.

She couldn't understand why Kyle would place a call to Robbi knowing full well that the number would appear on her phone bill. Maybe there was nothing to this. But maybe there was. How could she know? All she knew was that her heart palpitated uncontrollably. She wanted to pick up the phone to call Kyle and demand an explanation. However, the likelihood of an explanation packed with lies was high. Her promise to herself to not spy on Kyle was about to be broken. The phone bill was due in about three and a half weeks. She decided to do some investigation in the meantime and confront Kyle with the bill once it arrived.

"Oh God, what will I do if I find out Kyle has been cheating on me with Robbi? Will I leave him? Can I leave him?" Carmen said searching within. "Maybe I don't want to know. Maybe it's just a fling, a phase, a last rendezvous before we get married. Why should I accept this as being OK if this is indeed what's happening? I'm so confused. God, please help. Maybe she hunted him down and called him on his pager and he just returned the page and it just happened to be her number. Maybe they're just friends. After all, he is engaged to me. He lives with me here in Atlanta. What could she possibly give him with her living all the way up in Philadelphia? God, I'm so scared."

Discovering that Kyle had been maintaining contact with Robbi and not having a wedding date had pushed Carmen to the edge. She couldn't wait two weeks for the phone bill. She had decided that if something were still going on between Kyle and Robbi, she had the edge. It was time for Kyle to piss or get off the pot. She had been patient long enough. There was no reason for him not to respond positively to an ultimatum. At least that's what she thought.

Kyle decided he could not take Carmen's "nagging" any longer. He said he was tired of the arguing and that he couldn't get excited about marrying a woman who constantly attacked him. "Baby, I want to marry you or I would not have asked you, but I need to be able to come home to peace. I'm going to marry you, Carmen, but you have got to show me we can get through at least one week without an argument or you questioning what I do."

"Oh, so you want to put me on trial?" Carmen asked sarcastically. "Let me get this straight. You asked me to marry you because you were *sure* you wanted to marry me. Now you want to put me on trial and *if* I behave like a good little girl, then you can be *really* sure you want to marry me. What the hell is this, phase two of the process? Then what ... *if* you decide to marry me, I get to advance to phase three ... doing the dog and pony show for your ass for the rest of my life to get you to *stay* married to me!"

"See what I mean ... look how you're going off for no reason," said a pompous Kyle.

"*For no reason?* Kyle, I told you from the beginning, I was not interested in a long engagement.   To me, an engagement should last no longer than it takes to plan a ceremony.   You don't get engaged to see *if* you want to get married; your mind ought to be made up when you decide you're ready to pop the question. *Do you want to marry me, Kyle?* If so, then we can go down to the Justice of the Peace tomorrow.   Hell, you can't seriously plan a wedding with no date.   What am I supposed to do… send out invitations with "TBD"(To Be Determined) or "question marks" where the date should be!"

Kyle bit his lip and let out a deep sigh through his nose as he stared at his fallen princess.

Carmen grabbed a calendar and walked closely up to Kyle. "Pick a date, Kyle. Right now, let's pick a date. Enough of this foolishness already.   Let's pick a date," she demanded in desperation.

"December 25th," said Kyle sarcastically. "It doesn't matter what date we pick, Carmen, I'm not going to marry you until you learn how to control your emotions. I don't want you running around screaming like this in front of our kids," continued Kyle with a condescending attitude.

"Don't you dare try to turn *your* inability to commit into me having behavior problems! You're the one who has problems and I'm not going to let you drive me crazy. It's obvious you think this is some sort of game. Well, I'm not going to be your puppet. I want you *out* of my house by the weekend!"

"I beg your pardon," said Kyle with a mild tone of shock.

"You heard me. I want you *out* of here. I'm not going to continue to shack up with you.   When I agreed to this arrangement, I thought it would be temporary. When I step back and look at it, there's no reason for you to marry me, I'm giving you everything anyway.   If you don't respect me Kyle, then I have to respect myself. I want you out!" Carmen stopped short of throwing the engagement ring at him. She remembered how Robbi had done that once and he kept it, never giving it back.

Kyle didn't offer much protest against Carmen's order. He agreed they needed space or rather that *he* needed space. Calm and collected, Kyle suggested that living together prior to them getting married had created undo stress in their relationship. He assured her he was not angry and that if they survived a hiatus, then they would ultimately be a much happier couple.

Kyle's calmness only made Carmen angrier and resentful. She felt like she was being manipulated. Suddenly, she began to physically attack him. She started to beat at his chest screaming, "I hate you! I hate you! I hate you!" Tears were pouring profusely from her eyes. Her hair became mangled as her head lunged forward with every blow of her fist.

Kyle grabbed her by her wrists in an effort to restrain her. He shook her so as to snap her out of her rage. "Carmen, stop it! What is wrong with you!" he shouted. She dropped to her knees sobbing. Her head hung forward in exhaustion while Kyle still held her by her wrists. "Kyle, how could you do this to me? Please don't leave me. Oh God, please don't leave me," she begged through her uncontrollable tears.

"Carmen, you demanded that I leave. I think it's best. You don't know what you want. This is just too confusing," said Kyle.

"There is nothing confusing about it, Kyle," she sobbed. "I don't want you to leave, but I don't want to continue to live in sin. Please let's just get married. I know things will be perfect then. Please, please just don't leave," begged Carmen as she remained on her knees looking up at Kyle's unsympathetic eyes.

Kyle, still holding her wrists, pulled her up off the floor. "Carmen, this is just too much drama for me," he said as he remained completely composed. "I have an idea. Tell me what you think. First, go wash your face and try to calm down so we can talk like civilized people. Carmen, feeling slightly encouraged complied.

"I'm listening," she said.

"Carmen, we have to figure out a way to make both of us happy or neither one of us will be happy. I think one thing we agree on is that we want to be married to each other. What we disagree on are the conditions. I need to feel more comfortable. I'm sure that *I* will feel more comfortable if *you* can feel comfortable. But, you can never get comfortable as long as I live here. I was thinking I could move out into my own apartment and only sign a six-month lease. Now, I know you've always wanted a big wedding, but I think that's probably adding to your stress. I was thinking that you and I could just decide at some point during the next six months to just elope. We don't have to resort to going to the Justice of the Peace. Knowing you, you can find a beautiful spot on this earth for us to exchange vows and honeymoon at the same time. Yes, our families will be upset, but we can always have a reception when we get back ... I just think this plan is a *minor* inconvenience compared to what we stand to gain. Don't you agree?"

"Kyle, I'm just so afraid of losing you. What you've said makes sense, but it feels risky," said Carmen with intense doubt in her voice. "I want to trust in our relationship ... believe me, I do."

"Then let's show each other we're worthy of the others trust. Everything will fall right into place," said Kyle. "Come over here. All of a sudden you look so sexy to me. Would you like for me to taste you?" Kyle said in his seductive voice while changing the subject. Reading Carmen's silence as an inviting 'yes', he began to caress her breast. He then pressed her chest to lean her back onto the couch. He spread her legs apart and began to kiss her between her thighs. The silence was no longer. Panting and moaning resounded.

--- Chapter 20

The flickering candles provided a soft light to her seclusion. A glass of sparkling cider sat on the edge of her bubble filled garden tub. *Sade* sang her usual woes from one selection to the next. Carmen flipped through the pages of her *Essence* magazine. How to love yourself, How to pamper yourself articles filled the pages between the covers. Susan Taylor's In The Spirit was as usual, inspiring for the moment. This scene had almost become prosaic for Carmen. It was her attempt to escape the heartaches of life. Listening to *Sade* provided the misery-loves-company element... she could count on *Sade* relating to her pain. The song *Is it a Crime* had become her anthem ... *"Is it a crime that I still want you, but I want you to want me, too,"* Carmen sang. *"My love is taller than the Empire State...My love is wider than Victoria Lake."* were the lyrics of the song she also sang because, to her, they described her love for Kyle. Each time the phone rang, Carmen hoped it would be Kyle. He had been gone for almost two weeks. "Why isn't he calling and begging to come back? Why does he always seem so happy with life whenever we speak on the phone? Why does he always seem so busy and so into the law firm that it consumes our conversation each time we get together? He is always talking about moving the firm to the next level. He is never complacent. How can he be so happy without me?" Carmen recited repeatedly. She closed her magazine in frustration. "I don't want a Milk Bath, I want Kyle! I *am* pampering myself, yet I still feel like crap. Dear God, please bring him back to me."

It was a rainy Saturday afternoon. Carmen was trying to recover from the rejection she had received from Kyle earlier when she asked him to attend a banquet with her later that evening. He said he had a lot of work to do and thought he would just spend the evening at home catching up. She was considering accepting an invitation from Ava to attend an art show being given by one of her friends in the Cascade area. Ava had always commented on what a beautiful gallery her friends had in their home and what nice people they were. She thought Carmen would love viewing some new and interesting talent as well as meeting other people who shared her interest in the arts. Ava also thought this was an excellent opportunity for Carmen to meet people who could distribute her art once she finally settled down and created a line. Carmen had learned from Ava that Amber had declined her invitation to join her, thus she felt somewhat compelled to go since Ava seemed disappointed. Apparently, Amber had been slack on keeping commitments with Ava lately. Carmen knew that one thing she and Amber had in common was loneliness and heartbreak. Thus, she understood why Amber would go into seclusion and find her own sorrow more important than mingling with others.

Ava had always been a loyal friend to Carmen. She would be extremely disappointed if Carmen didn't show up. Carmen knew that Ava was more interested in helping her deal with her void with Kyle than seeking companionship at an art show. So she decided to blow off the banquet and spend a mellow afternoon with Ava. All things considered, she had nothing to lose by going. Besides, it was sure to be a classy affair *and* it was something to do.

The afternoon turned into evening while Carmen and Ava were at the art show. The rain had subsided only somewhat, but the guest didn't seem to mind. As suspected, the art show was attended by a lot of nice, classy people. The weather conditions didn't dampen the spirits of the people who were enjoying an opportunity to comrade with people with similar interests.

Carmen was glad she came. The exhibition of art had inspired her. She knew she had been putting off doing a series from one year to the next. Here she was in a city where people had an appreciation for the arts. Finding an audience to admire her talent wouldn't be difficult at all. Her only limitations were those she placed on herself.

After the art show, Ava invited Carmen to come by her house for dinner. She said she would be making chili dogs and French fries for the twins. This was their favorite meal on Saturdays. Carmen wanted to decline so badly because she wanted to get home to be by her phone just in case Kyle called. She had already told Ava she had blown off the banquet for the evening, so she couldn't use that as an excuse. Chili dogs and French fries wouldn't take long to make, but she knew she would have to stick around and play games, play with the dolls, and possibly have to sit through _The Lion King_ yet again ... that or _The Little Mermaid_. "Boy, what a family scene," Carmen thought to herself. "I'm a single woman, it's Saturday night and this simply does not appeal to me. How can I decline gracefully without offending Ava?"

As they were about to leave the art show, Carmen took a deep breath. "Ava, I'd like to take a rain check on the chili dogs. I've had you away from your family all day. I think J.B. would appreciate a nice quiet evening at home alone with his family. I know you're just being your normal sweet self by inviting me, but I will be OK this evening. In fact, I think I will go home and work on some of my art pieces. This has been an inspirational day. Would you mind if I joined you guys for church tomorrow?"

"Are you sure you're going to be OK this evening?" asked Ava. She knew that Carmen wasn't taking this new arrangement with Kyle very well.

"I'll be fine. I promise if I need you, I will call you. Otherwise, I'll see you at the 9:00a.m. service tomorrow. I'll come by your house first so we can all go together, OK? I'm going to run now. I had a great time. Thanks for the invite."

Carmen couldn't get home fast enough. When she walked into her condo, she headed straight for her answering machine.

Her display indicated she had three messages. She nervously hit the play button. The first message was a message from her mother left at 3:30 that afternoon. The second message was from Nikki with a message to call her as soon as she got the message; it was left at 5:07p.m. Carmen began to sweat as she awaited the third message. "Oh, God, please let it be from Kyle." It was from Ava making sure she got home OK in the rain. Carmen all of sudden felt a sense of panic. She quickly pressed *69 hoping to hear Kyle's number announced thinking perhaps he called, but just didn't leave a message. She felt so disappointed to learn that the last number called was from Ava. She wanted so badly to initiate a phone call to Kyle, but she didn't want to appear disrespectful of the time he had allocated to catch up with work.

Calling Nikki back was not desirable to Carmen right now. She was slightly irritated with her because she had suggested that Kyle had handled their relationship like one of his court cases. She said Kyle treated her like the defendant and he was the prosecution who cut her some slack. She said Kyle had put her on parole ... one little screw up and she could face his sentence... LIFE...without him! Although what Nikki said made sense, Carmen felt like she was in no position to pass judgment on anyone. After all, look at her situation with Drew. He has already let her out of jail, she just won't go home!

Concluding that she and Kyle shouldn't be apart this evening, Carmen dialed his number.

Of course, she got his answering machine. She dialed again hoping he would answer. Once again, she got his machine. She left the ol', *"Hi, I just called ... didn't want anything"* message. "Give me a call if you'd like to get together later," she continued. She waited five minutes thinking he may have been screening his calls and that he would call her back. Nothing of the sort happened.

Not able to resist her curiosity, she decided that she would drive inconspicuously by his apartment to see if he was really home. This is what she and Nikki called "doing the drive-by." "What if he wasn't home," she thought. "Then what?...What if he's home, do I ring his doorbell assuring an unfavorable response? Do I go to the nearest phone and leave him a message letting him know I'm in the area?" Neither action would yield positive results, she concluded. However, she decided to drive by his apartment anyway.

As she approached the townhouse apartment, she could see Kyle's lights were on. As she got closer, her heart stopped with a thump. There was a car right out front of his place. She didn't recognize the license plates. Perhaps it was one of the people from the office. Her mind started to churn. "Who could it be? Why wouldn't he answer his phone? How can I know who it is? To hell with wondering," she thought to herself. "I'll just walk up and ring the doorbell. But then, if Kyle looks through the peephole and sees it's me, he might not answer. This is assuming he will get up to look at all."

Carmen walked nervously up to the front door. As she reached for the doorbell, she heard the laughter of a female! Then there were screams of horseplay, then laughter again. Stunned, which had become a feeling of familiarity, Carmen took a step back. One of her reactions was to start rapping on the door until Kyle answered. Another reaction was to leave. Information is knowledge, she thought. "I have to know." She walked to the side window, which allowed a view into his living room. With her back to the wall, she walked sideways until she could look inside without being noticed. Pillows and candles greeted her eyes before she saw the movement of a person. She stepped back quickly. She trembled nervously as she tried to force herself to breathe. The drizzle of the rain on her face made it slightly difficult for her to see clearly without concentration. She leaned her head to catch another glimpse. She caught the back of the head of the female. She was changing the CD in the stereo. Determined to capture the identity of the woman, she held her position until she would eventually turn around.

Carmen blinked constantly to clear her eyes of the rain. The woman apparently put on soft music because she began to sway softly from side to side as if she could feel the music. Suddenly, she did a sexy turn. Shock and disbelief would describe

Carmen's state of mind! With her mouth dropped open and her eyes locked in a stare, she squinted hoping the image would change. There standing in Kyle's apartment enjoying a romantic evening was Amber!

Carmen began to leave the scene, as her heart was about to explode. She didn't have the energy to be confrontational. Although Amber was still fully dressed ... for now, the image of the candles, the Chinese food, and Amber making herself right at home with Kyle was almost too much to bear.

Realizing she had not seen Kyle, she mustered up enough energy to walk back to the window. Kyle emerged holding his portfolio of clients. He sat on the couch beside Amber and began turning the pages, as he appeared to explain the significance of each entry. He appeared to be really into whatever he was telling her. Amber appeared amused and fascinated. As Carmen looked on, she felt somewhat relieved that neither Kyle nor Amber had displayed any real affection toward the other. But suddenly, Amber reached up and began to rub the back of Kyle's head, playing with his hair as she looked at the turning pages of the portfolio. Kyle was not responding. Kyle said something and there it was again, that loud burst of laughter. As Amber appeared to be so tickled, she leaned over to give Kyle a quick kiss on his cheek. Kyle seemed irritated that he didn't have her full attention on whatever he was talking about. "Lord, please don't let Kyle respond," Carmen prayed as she continued her peeping tom behavior. Amber began to rub on Kyle's thigh as she mouthed the lyrics of the song playing on the CD. Kyle looked up suddenly. Carmen's heart stopped. She thought for a moment that he had somehow seen her. In actuality, Kyle heard his pager going off. He reached over to get it. After he read the number, he said something to Amber. She appeared disappointed about whatever he told her. Kyle closed the portfolio and began to clean up. Carmen waited for him to go near a phone to return the page, but he kept on putting away things. Apparently, Kyle wanted Amber to leave.

Remembering that her car was parked out front, Carmen decided she'd better leave before Amber came out and recognized it. She hurried to her car trying to shake off some of the wetness of the rain. Feeling extremely confused, Carmen retreated to her home where she could collect her thoughts.

"Why does life hurt so bad," Carmen thought, as she entered her condo. Overwhelmed with emotion, she began to sob. She dropped her purse and keys on the floor as she walked over to her couch. She didn't care that her clothes were soaked when she plopped helplessly onto the sofa. She rolled from side to side with her arms clinching her mid-section. Her eyes looked to the heavens as tears found a path on her temples before streaming down the side of her face. She suddenly leaned forward and buried her face in her hands when she released a loud scream. "Kyle, I hate you!" she shouted. "OK, God, *please* make this pain stop," she said as she bellowed.

Carmen had so many questions: Why was Amber at Kyle's? When did the two of them get acquainted? What had he told her to make her disregard his relationship? Did Ava know about this? What was going on? How would Kyle explain this? She couldn't wait until church tomorrow to communicate with Ava. She had to have answers to some, if not all, of her questions ASAP!

With her hands trembling like leaves in the wind, Carmen dialed Ava's number. She could barely speak when Ava answered. Ava said hello twice before Carmen finally spoke.

"Ava, this is Carmen. Do you have a couple of minutes," she said in a faint voice.

"Oh, my God, Carmen, what's wrong? Where are you? Do you need me to come and get you?" said a frantic Ava. All Ava knew at this point was that she had said goodnight earlier that evening to a jovial Carmen and now she was speaking to someone who sounded completely despondent.

Carmen managed to compose herself enough to tell Ava what she had just witnessed.

She was somewhat confrontational until she heard the shock in Ava's voice. She could tell that Ava had no prior knowledge of Amber interacting with Kyle.

"Carmen, don't you worry. It's on! I'm going to get that

little bitch. I have to confess something to you. I did mention to her that you and Kyle were having problems and that he had moved out. I never thought in a million years she would back-door you. Oh Carmen, I feel so responsible," said Ava remorsefully.

"Ava, you are not responsible for grown people. Even if you did tell Amber about me and Kyle, she didn't have to make a move on him. And as for Kyle, he should not be making a move on her either. I mean, of all the women he could be with in Atlanta, why would he chose one of my closest friend's friends? *And* he knows that Amber and I have hung out together with you. Even though I would not consider Amber and I to be friends, he knows that she is your friend and that we could all potentially move in the same social circles. How would either of them explain this shit? I mean, would Amber really be able to face you knowing that she has made a move on the man who is your friend's fiancé?" Carmen rambled endlessly. She could not believe the gall of Kyle and Amber.

"I need to calm down before I have a stroke. Are you sure she was about to leave his place before you left?" asked Ava.

"I'm not really sure, but I think so," answered Carmen. "I was in such a daze, I'm not really sure what happened after I walked away from the window. I don't even know what Kyle did or even where he is right now."

Ava took a deep breath. "Carmen," she said. "I need to ask you not to attend church with us tomorrow. I have some business I need to attend to."

"What?" asked Carmen. "I really could use church right now. What are you talking about?"

"Well, Miss Amber is going to be at the service tomorrow. I just want the opportunity to speak with her. I'm going to act like I don't know anything. I just want to hear what this back-stabbing heffa has to say."

"What makes you think she is going to tell you anything? You said that she has been avoiding you lately. Now we know why."

Ava insisted that she knew what she was doing. Carmen

reluctantly agreed to her suggestion. She thought twice her own ability to mask her feelings if she came face to face with Amber. Lord knows she didn't want to create a scene in the church ... after the service in the parking lot maybe ... but not in the church.

"I'm going to visit another church tomorrow then. I think I'll go to New Birth to hear what the Bishop has to say. I would invite Kyle for the heck of it, but I need to be away from him right now until I can figure all this out," said Carmen. "Are you sure Amber is going to be at church tomorrow?"

"I'm sure because she has to usher. She joined the church a couple of months ago when her boyfriend dumped her. It's a little early for her to be faltering on her duties," Ava replied with confidence.

Carmen and Ava agreed to touch bases tomorrow after church. Meanwhile, despite her exhaustion, Carmen decided to return Nikki's call from earlier that day.

It was very difficult for Carmen to absorb any of Nikki's advice after she shared what had happened between Amber and Kyle. Nikki wanted to relate everything to her own situation with Drew. She insisted that Kyle had moved out with no intentions of them getting back together because that's what Drew had done with Tracy. She also insisted that Kyle must have told Amber that they had split up because Amber, otherwise, would not have gotten involved with him. Again, she related this to her own situation, stating that had Drew not told her things were over between him and Tracy, she would never have gotten involved with him.

Carmen listened as Nikki conveyed such self-righteousness. She stopped short of over criticizing Amber because that would mean she was somehow criticizing herself. She did, however, lash out at Kyle while making Drew pedestal-worthy. She said, "At least Drew was man enough to tell Tracy he wanted out of their relationship. He didn't just leave and leave it up to her to figure out." Carmen bit her lip as she almost reminded Nikki that Drew appears to have moved on from her and that she didn't recall Drew communicating that verbally. She just let Nikki have her moment of denial. She continued to listen to her confused friend. She didn't have the heart to be completely angry with her because she knew that deep down Nikki was questioning her role in Drew and Tracy not being allowed to work out their differences. She knew that Nikki had to remember the countless conversations they'd had about the roles women play in failed relationships between couples. They kidded about how a woman will justify being with a married man or a committed man by saying, "Well, he and his wife are having problems...or... he and his girlfriend are having problems"...like that was a green light to infiltrate...like couples aren't allowed to have problems! Carmen listened as Nikki said, "Girl, all men are dogs. Some are pit bulls and Dobermans while others are Chihuahuas. I would say you need to leave Kyle alone because he is definitely a pit bull! I would say Drew is more like a Chihuahua."

"You know, Nik, I find it interesting that you would consider Drew a Chihuahua because of *your* assessment of how he treated Tracy, which is based on *his* version of the story, by the way. I wonder how Tracy would describe him. I mean, if you were in Tracy's shoes, how would you describe him then? If we as women continue to deal with these "dogs" as you put it, then what are we, female dogs? ... ala Bitches!?"

--- *Chapter 21*

Carmen had returned home from church. There was a message from Kyle on her answering machine. He wanted to know if she were interested in going to brunch. Although touched by his invitation, she didn't want to respond to his call until she had an opportunity to speak with Ava. Meanwhile, she turned to a section of the Bible that she heard referenced at the service. It was *Isaiah* 40:6-8,

The voice says, "shout!"
"What shall I shout?" I asked.
"Shout that man is like the grass that dies away, and all his beauty fades like dying flowers.
The grass withers, the flowers fade beneath the breath of God, and so it is with fragile man.
The grass withers, the flowers fade, but the Word of our God shall stand forever."

Carmen realized she had put Kyle first in her life and not God. The passage in *Isaiah* resonated in her mind. She found comfort and strength in reminding herself that God would see her through her adversity if only she would believe in his word and put him first.

The long awaited call from Ava finally came. Carmen listened patiently as Ava described the events of the day surrounding Amber. Ava explained that she approached Amber after church and began to interact with general girlfriend conversation. "Girl, where have you been. I haven't seen or talked to you in almost two weeks. You must have found a new man," Ava said she said to Amber.

"Well, I haven't heard from you either. I thought *you* had put me down. I called you a couple of weeks ago to invite you to go shopping. I didn't leave a message. I know you have caller ID, so I know you know I called. Why didn't you ever call me back?" Amber offered as an explanation.

"I was out of town all last week visiting my mom. She was in the hospital for some tests," rebutted Ava. "But you still haven't told me what you've been up to," said Ava not letting her off the hook.

Amber sighed. "Well, God works in mysterious ways. I'm just following the path God has put before me."

"Oh, really," said Ava. "What's the path?"

"It's still a little early, so I really don't want to say just yet," said Amber. "So how are the girls," she continued trying to change the subject.

Ava was offended that Amber would ask about her girls as if she really cared. It was obvious she was uncomfortable with the dialog between them. She decided to cut to the chase. "Amber, I need to ask you something. I really hope it's not true. Have you been going out with Kyle Sealy, Carmen's fiancé?"

Amber's eyes got as big as saucers. "What difference does it make?" she said with defensive arrogance.

"What difference does it make! Amber, that's my friend's fiancé and you know Carmen and you know Kyle is her fiancé?" Ava said with anger and disbelief. "So you *have* been going out with him, haven't you?"

"How do you know I've been going out with him," asked Amber.

"What difference does it make," Ava replied with sarcasm. "So tell me, are you going out with Carmen's fiancé?"

Amber collected her thoughts. "First of all, it's my understanding that they are no longer together. Second, I didn't break them up, so why should I feel bad? Third, I don't really know Carmen that well, so it's not like I have any loyalty to her. Kyle says he would like to get to know me better. Things may work out and they may not, but I don't see any reason I shouldn't give it a chance."

Ava was almost speechless. She could not have predicted this response in a million years. "So let me get this right, you think this is a path God has put before you. You think God is

OK with what you're doing?"

"As I said, I don't feel I'm doing anything wrong. I'm sure God didn't like the fact that Carmen was living in sin with Kyle."

Becoming more furious by the second, Ava had to take deep breaths to keep herself composed. "Amber, I know you're not judging Carmen to justify your actions. Have you been intimate with him?"

"That's none of your business. I don't feel like I have to justify anything to you or anyone else," replied Amber.

"You say Kyle told you he and Carmen had split up. Didn't you think you should investigate his story a little further. I can assure you, that's *not* what Carmen would say."

Amber became more defensive. "Well, the way I see it is that if things were so great between them, he would not have moved out and he wouldn't be spending time with me."

"So couples aren't allowed to have problems? You see a problem in a relationship as a green light to disrespect another woman and I might add ... disrespect yourself?" said Ava in complete outrage. "How would you feel if you were Carmen?"

"I'm not Carmen and I don't feel responsible for what has happened to her," said Amber.

"So you're going to continue to see Kyle?" asked Ava with the intent of concluding the stressful conversation she was engaged in.

"I plan to follow the path God has put before me."

"Tell me Amber, do you really think you and I could be friends after this? I mean, do you think I'm supposed to hang with you knowing what you have done?"

"Ava, it's really up to you. You and I really weren't *that* close anyway."

Ava was flabbergasted. She looked at Amber with a piercing stare. "Girlfriend, I will pray for you. The Lord knows you have lost your mind." Ava walked away with total disgust for Amber.

As Ava concluded her story to Carmen, she began to apologize for even bringing Amber into Carmen's life.

"There is no need to apologize, Ava. You didn't do anything wrong. I'm shocked that Amber has graciously granted herself immunity of any wrongdoing. She actually calls herself a Christian! She will burn in hell," said Carmen.

"What are you going to do about Kyle?" asked Ava. "It should be very interesting to hear *his* attitude on this."

"I'm going to confront his ass, that's what," said Carmen, as she grew angrier.

"Carmen, my friend, I will leave Kyle to you, but I'm not through with Amber's ass. I don't know how or when, but she will get hers. What goes around comes around. I'm more concerned about *you* right now. Are you OK?"

"Ava, I don't know whether I'm going or coming right now. I'm going to call Kyle back. He wants me to join him for brunch."

Kyle was on time when he came to pick Carmen up. He had decided they would dine at *Rays on the River*, one of Carmen's favorite restaurants. He greeted her with a bouquet of fresh flowers when she got into his car.

Carmen put on her best face. She could tell that Kyle was behaving out of guilt. It would be wonderful if all the romance was genuine and heart-felt. All she had to do was figure out the best time to confront him. He was looking especially fine. This was going to be more difficult than she thought.

Shortly after they were seated and placed their order for two mimosas and the brunch buffet, Carmen launched into her subtle interrogation. "So, did you complete your work last night?" she asked.

"Pretty much," he replied.

"So what all did you do last night?" she continued to probe.

"I worked," said Kyle with slight irritation in his voice.

Carmen knew she was going to continue to get these short evasive answers unless she confronted him cold. "So, did you and Amber have a nice time last night?" said Carmen as her angry voice trembled. "Don't lie to me," she ordered before

Kyle could speak.

Kyle tried to conceal his shock. He fidgeted for a moment and then sat back in his chair.

He crossed his arms, placing his right hand to his face with his thumb under his chin and his index finger across his closed lips. He just stared at Carmen for a moment appearing to carefully study her facial expression. He was trying to determine if she were bluffing, if he was being suckered into revealing something that she really *didn't* know or if she really did know what she was talking about. He remembered what a spy Carmen was and figured she had probably driven by his apartment and seen Amber's car. Thus, he concluded he had to at least admit she was there.

"She just dropped by my apartment for a minute," Kyle offered hoping the word "minute" would somehow defuse Carmen who looked like she was prepared to explode.

"For a minute? Did you tell her within that minute that you and I had split up? Did you and her find time to be romantic with each other during that minute? Did you manage to get any work done in that minute? How much time was involved with the two of you planning that minute? Did you think to take a minute to call me last night to see how I was doing? Did you fuck her?" charged Carmen, as she grew more incensed with each sarcastic question. "Who initiated contact with whom?" she demanded.

After calming Carmen down, Kyle went on to explain that it was Amber who contacted him at his office wanting Chris' phone number. He said after he gave her Chris' number, she went on to say that she had some ideas on how he and Langston could drum up business for their firm. She said her dad and a couple of her uncles were attorneys in private practice. He said he had arranged for her to come by the office next week. To his surprise, on last night, she called his apartment and said she was in the neighborhood and offered to bring over some Chinese food. She said she would only stay for a minute, but it was apparent what her motives were once she arrived. Chris' name never came up, Kyle continued to explain. He then told Carmen that he received a page from Langston and promptly asked Amber to leave and that she did.

To Carmen, the story was sounding consistent with what she thought she witnessed.

"Then why does Amber have the impression that we've split up? Did you tell her that?"

"I don't know what you're talking about. I did tell her we were going through some things that we needed to work out. But I did not tell her we had split up."

"Then why did she tell Ava that she understood we had split up?" said Carmen pressing Kyle for answers.

"Perhaps, it's because *you* told her the day you, her and Ava went shopping, that if I didn't hurry up and marry you, that you were going to put my ass out and that we would be through," Kyle retorted.

"Amber told you I said that?"

"That amongst other things," said Kyle.

"Are you interested in her?" said Carmen in an effort to recover from Kyle's accusations for which she was guilty of.

"No, Carmen, I'm not interested in Amber. It's clear she's interested in me, though. What would I want with someone like her ... a woman who would disrespect her friendship with Ava ... a woman who would pretend to be interested in my brother just to get to me ... a woman who would play games with my practice just to get to me ... and a woman who was willing to give up the ass so quickly when she doesn't even know me. Look Carmen, if I were interested in being a player, then Amber fits the profile of an easy target. I don't want her. So can we please enjoy our afternoon together?"

Carmen prayed Kyle was telling her the truth. Her gut still nagged at her for some reason. She wasn't really sure. Perhaps it was because she received his answering machine when she tried to reach him last night, however, *Amber* was able to reach him *and* managed to get him to agree to have dinner with her. And why were there burning candles? As she opened her mouth to challenge that point, the waiter had returned with their mimosas. Besides, Kyle was looking drop-dead gorgeous to her at this moment. She was also elated to know that Kyle didn't have anything going on with Amber. She knew that if she continued to argue, which is what he had stressed he did not like and would not tolerate, he would have a reason to break up with her. If that happened, then he would be free to date Amber or anyone else. She decided she would not make it easy for Amber to get what she thought she already had. Carmen chuckled inwardly at the thought of Amber having egg all over her face once she discovered that she had misread the path that she *claimed* God had put before her. Ava would get a kick out of this, as well.

Chapter 22

Carmen sat at her kitchen table going through her mail envelope by envelope. She stacked the bills by their due dates. She had two piles, bills she would pay now and bills she would pay in the middle of the month. When she looked at her phone bill, she immediately thought she was going to have to curb her spending when it came to Nikki. They were talking to each other almost every other day. Most of the calls she had to pay for because many times when Nikki initiated the call, she would have to call her back because she was busy or not home at the time. Kyle had several calls on the bill as well. Then she remembered ... she was supposed to look for the call he had made to Robbi.

Carmen crossed through each of her calls to make sure all of Kyle's calls stood out. He only had about six. Three of them were to his family in Charlotte. The other three were calls placed to New York on days that didn't coincide with the date she redialed Robbi's number. Now Carmen was confused. She thought she would finally have the evidence she needed to confront Kyle about Robbi. Oh well, she thought. Things had been pretty tranquil lately. Confronting him would have just rocked the boat. Just maybe if she played by his rules she could get what she wanted, marriage and commitment from Kyle. She had devoted the last couple of years of her life to this relationship. A couple of months weren't going to hurt, especially if she got what she wanted in the end.

Her phone rang. She decided to let the answering machine pick it up, since she was trying to complete going through her mail. It was Nikki. She immediately grabbed the phone before Nikki could hang up. After all, she had just complained that all too often she was picking up the tab for the phone calls because of callbacks.

Nikki had been contacted by Lark's mother. Lark's family

was planning a coming home, we-love-you party for Lark. The prayers for Lark to not have cancer were answered, however, she did have an abnormal growth on her larynx that would affect her ability to sing forever. The party for her would be a celebration of life. Cancer would have meant the demise of her voice as well as her existence.

The party was going to be at least a couple of months away. Mother Durham wanted all of Lark's friends to have a chance to plan to attend the event and get decent airfares. She was a classy Lena Horne type. Carmen was not surprised to learn that the big bash was tentatively going to be held at Avery Fisher's Hall at Lincoln Center in New York City.

Mother Durham had put Nikki in charge of gathering all the current addresses of Lark's closest friends. She would be sending out formal invitations, of course.

"Mother Durham is going to be contacting you about designing the cover of the invitation," said Nikki with excitement. "I gave her your home number and your office number. She should be contacting you real soon."

"Wow, I feel so honored. Has anyone spoken to Lark?" asked Carmen.

"Not really. She said that Lark is still very down about the news about her voice, but she's very happy to be alive. Mother Durham said she wants to call everyone to thank them for all the cards, letters, prayers and well wishes, but of course she can't speak that well just yet. I believe that's why Mother Durham is organizing this party ... really on behalf of Lark. It's really kind of two-fold; Lark gets to say thank you and we all get to tell her how much we love her. Ooh, this is wonderful! I'm getting excited and emotional just thinking about it."

"Me, too! I can't wait to hear from Mother Durham. I need to know what she would like. I'm sure she'll want me to paint something. Nik, this is great! I can't wait to get started. I haven't picked up a paintbrush to paint in so long; I've probably forgotten how to. I'm not worried. I'm sure the thought of doing something for Lark will inspire me."

A couple of weeks had passed since the Amber drama. Ava and Amber were no longer friends. In fact, Amber no longer taught aerobics at the gym with Ava. Since it was only part time anyway, it would be no problem for her to teach elsewhere. Besides, she was probably too humiliated to face Ava after what happened. Not only did Amber not have Kyle, she had lost a true friend in Ava. But given that she didn't think she and Ava were that close anyway, perhaps she didn't consider it a loss at all. Ava had reconciled that Amber was not the type of woman she needed around her. How could she ever feel comfortable that J.B. wasn't next on Amber's list the next time she and J.B. were "having problems"?

Carmen had managed to defy spying on Kyle whenever he said he wanted or needed time alone. They seemed to be getting along much better. What nagged Carmen was that everything seemed to be on his terms. He always wanted to spend the nights at her house. While this would appear to be a good thing, she didn't feel quite as welcomed at his home. This was beginning to feel like de'javu. Every time she felt comfortable with Kyle, she felt like something bad was on the horizon.

Ava called Carmen only to find her in a blue funk about Kyle once again. "Follow your gut," Ava told Carmen. She also cautioned Carmen that she was becoming obsessed with Kyle. "Your head is telling you things your heart does not want to confirm. You are not a stupid woman, Carmen. You can give yourself credit for the things you *already know* about Kyle versus the things you are trying to figure out by spying.

Carmen was silent for a moment. Then she said, "What's wrong with me, Ava? Why can't everything be OK?"

"Everything will be OK as soon as you break this awful cycle. Carmen, I'm coming over to your house, we need to talk. I'll stop by Burger King to pick up something to eat. I know you haven't cooked. I think I remember what you like ... a Whopper with cheese, no onions and heavy on the pickles with a small order of fries. I'm sure you already have Coke in your refrigerator. J.B. has the girls. I'm on my way."

Ava arrived to find Carmen in sweats and her hair uncombed. She couldn't believe Carmen was sinking so fast. This relationship with Kyle didn't seem to be healthy at all. Ava knew she had to save Carmen now…later might be too late.

"What are you watching on TV?" asked Ava.

"Nothing really. The television is just on to keep me company," said Carmen as she flipped through the channels. "I'm just really depressed, Ava."

"I know, Carmen…which is why I'm here." Ava didn't want to waste any time. So she announced to Carmen that she was about to get down to the business of why she was there. "I bought you an apple pie, also," said Ava as she began to pull the food out the bag and lay it on the napkins on the coffee table near Carmen. Ava then pulled out her pen and pad. "Carmen, I hope you don't mind, but I'm going to ask you some questions. Please answer them as honestly as you can. I'll write down your answers. Go ahead and eat something. I don't want you to answer these questions on an empty stomach. Are you ready?"

"I guess," said Carmen lazily as she checked for extra pickles on her burger.

"Cool," said Ava. "OK, first question: From a *personal* prospective, what do you <u>have</u>?"

Carmen took a bite of her burger, paused for a brief moment, then answered, "my health, my family, good friends, my job, decent looks, decent personality, talent, a big heart, my own home, my own car, ... hmmm … good taste."

"OK, Now tell me what you <u>want</u>," said Ava as she listened intently.

"Let's see. I want peace of mind, a husband ... a husband with a good job, not a closet gay person, good looking, caring, who loves me, who wants to be my friend and my partner, someone who's not boring, who likes to do things, someone who's good with his hands, you know ...who can fix things, a great lover, I want a couple of kids. I want to have more financial security."

"You don't want much," Ava said with sarcasm as she laughed. "Now, relative to your relationship with Kyle, what do you have?"

Carmen let out a big sigh as she looked upward as if the answers would fall from the ceiling. "Well, I have a man who likes to do things. A man who can fix things, a man who likes to try different things. I have someone who has a great job, is very nice looking, not gay, and who is great in bed.

"I see," said Ava. "Now tell me what you want in your relationship with Kyle?"

Another sigh was released. "I want to be able to trust Kyle. I want Kyle to be proud to have me ... not by just saying it or doing nice things for me. I want him to commit. I want to be able to trust that we will have a better life tomorrow. I don't want him to keep dragging things out and leading me on. I just want to be happy!"

"OK, back to you personally. What would you change about yourself if you could?"

"I would change my willpower ... I would be stronger. I would change my insecurity ... I wouldn't be insecure. I would change my faith in God and the love He has for me ... I would have more faith and I would never ever doubt His love for me, even in bad times. Finally, I would change the confidence I have in myself ... I would have more."

"Final question," said Ava. "What would you change about Kyle if you could?"

Carmen's answer came out like a run-on sentence, "Kyle wouldn't be so private, he would not be such a liar and he would not have so much control over me!"

"OK. Wait while I do something, " said Ava. She studied Carmen's answers while Carmen ate her burger and munched on her fries. Carmen waited patiently. She offered Ava a refill on her Coke while watching her cross through and circle things on her pad. "What the hell is she doing?" Carmen thought to herself.

"OK, are you ready to hear what I have to say?" said Ava as she prepared to share the outcome of her evaluation. "You might not like what I have to say, but I think you should give it some thought."

"I see," said Carmen with a look of skepticism on her face.

Ava let out a big sigh and then cleared her throat. "Let's start with what you <u>want</u> for yourself. Good news, you can have *all* these things. Now let's talk about the things you would <u>change</u> about yourself. More good news, you can change *all* these things. Now, there is a huge gap between what you <u>want</u> from Kyle versus what you <u>have</u> with Kyle. It appears that all the things you <u>have</u> with him are things you can get from a date or a handy man! The things you <u>want</u> from Kyle coincide with the things you would <u>change</u> about him. You *cannot* change anything about another person, you can only change *you*. Now, here's what's interesting… you listed as one of the things you would change about Kyle is the control he has over you. Carmen,. *you* can change the control he has over you without wishing that change in him. The other interesting thing here is that you listed under what you <u>want</u> from Kyle is your desire to be happy. It's interesting that you didn't list this under the <u>wants</u> column for *yourself*. My concern is that you're looking for your happiness in Kyle and not in Carmen! Now because you are not happy, the things you <u>have</u> with yourself are in peril. I'll go down the list; your health: you're not taking care of yourself physically or *mentally*. Your family: you avoid them because you are embarrassed that you allowed Kyle to live with you despite their protest and he still has not married you. Your friends: You become very defensive when your friends try to help you or offer you advise. Your job: You do just enough to get by. You spend most of your time at work worrying about Kyle. Your looks: You aren't looking as vibrant and confident as you used to…look at you right now; and your talent: What have you done with your gift from God? Whatever happened to all those pictures you were going to paint and put on exhibit? God loved you so much that he gave you a gift to share. You should have faith that he will always give you exactly what you need. We've been waiting for your participation in the arts festival for *how* long now?"

"OK, OK, I get it, move on to your next point," Carmen interrupted as the truth stung.

"Carmen, I led off by saying you can have all the things you want. I will conclude by saying that until you take back your control, make yourself happy with *you* , reclaim all the things you have with you, you will never have what you want. You can do it, Carmen. I know you. Yes, it's going to be hard, but you can do it. Removing Kyle from your life as he exists is probably one of the best things you can do for yourself right now. Put your faith and trust in God, not Kyle Sealy.

Carmen's eyes began to well up with tears as she listened to what made so much sense. So much sense that it was scary. She was also slightly embarrassed that Ava now knew things about her that weren't so flattering. Since Ava was a true friend, she didn't worry about Ava telling anyone ... except J.B.. Carmen was well aware of the fact that even though some women swear never to tell a soul, they really mean everyone except their husbands or boyfriends.

For the days to come, Carmen would try to deal with the things she had discussed with Ava. The pain of the truth was so intense, it seemed so much easier to avoid it. Living in a fantasy seemed so much easier than dealing with harsh reality. The last thing she wanted right now was to be caught between everyone's opinion of what she ought to do. Thus, she went out and purchased a journal to keep a log of her thoughts and innermost feelings ... her secrets. The thought of revealing to someone else the things in her head and heart was frightening. She knew that once information exited her lips, it was out there for the recipients to possibly use against her and for them to formulate and render opinions about. She recalled how Amber listened to the information she shared during a "trusting" girl talk and then used it to justify why it was OK for her to pursue Kyle. She knew she could trust her family, however, the problem with family was they had memories like elephants ... they didn't forget ... especially the bad stuff. Even when you would decide to forgive your mate, the family would constantly remind you to be on guard because of what your mate did to hurt you a hundred years ago.

———————

To Carmen's surprise, writing in her journal was more difficult than talking to people.

"'Why was this?" she asked herself. **"To thine own self be true"** came to mind. She realized that whenever she talked to other people, she could put *whatever* spin she wanted on a story. If she wanted people to think Kyle was the scum of the earth, then all she had to do was communicate all the horrible things he may have done or said. She could always be the victim. No one had to know his side of the story. Would people still think he was the scum of the earth if they knew what she had done or said? What if they knew her contribution to a deplorable situation? What if they knew about the times she attacked his manhood, when she told him he had a 'little dick and couldn't fuck.' What if they knew how she attacked his sexuality? ... when she accused him of being gay whenever he refused to give her sex ... she knew in her heart that he only refused her because he was angry at something she had done and that she was trying to use the one tool she thought would lure him back and gain his forgiveness, sex. What about the time she took his car keys and tried to throw them over the balcony into the bushes and then put Vaseline on his windshield to prevent him from leaving her after they had a terrible argument? This would only be the half of it. On the *other* hand, if she wanted everyone to believe she was dating the most incredible human being on the face of the earth, she could pull that off as well. No one had to know the details of her glorious love affair. No one had to know that many times after they dined at fabulous restaurants, she paid her half. No one had to know that whenever she received beautiful flowers at work or at home, they were "doghouse" flowers ... Kyle had been caught doing something wrong and used the flowers to soften her up to forgive him. No one had to know she was suspicious of his whereabouts most of the time. No one had to know that whenever he traveled out of town that he rarely called to say he missed her and couldn't wait to get home. No one had to know that the new necklace or bracelet he had given her paled in comparison to the heavy gold bracelet and Rolex watch she had given him. No one had to know that she had to bitch constantly to get him to finally engage her ... all they needed to know was that he did. When people marveled at the beauty of her ring, no one had to know that during one of her snooping ventures, she found the receipt for her ring only to discover that after taking advantage of a 30% off sale, a promotional coupon, and a trade-in of Robbi's ring, Kyle wrote the jeweler a check for $268.49! She found another receipt where he had paid only $359.00 for her setting! He paid more for the setting than he did for the stone! Not even Kyle knew she knew this. Again, no one had to know. *And* no one had to know her heart had been bleeding pain ever since she saw Amber at Kyle's apartment two nights after he had claimed he didn't want to have anything to do with her!

Carmen meditated on her thoughts for a few minutes. So many emotions clouded her mind ... love, hate, anger, fear, happiness, sadness, rage. Then she decided to be the friend to herself as she had always been to other people. As weird as it sounded, for a moment it felt safe. Her pen kissed the paper of her journal: *As I sit here alone trying to figure out my life and its purpose, I feel like I have the answers, yet I feel frustrated I can't manifest them. I feel stifled and confused. I feel alone and lonely. Everyone always tells me I have so much going for me. If they only knew what I felt inside, they would question my ability to pull it off. What am I so afraid of? Why can't I just be all I can be? I sometimes feel I'm wasting my life away, yet at other times, I feel I need to be more patient. Patient for what? ... what am I waiting for!?*

As she wrote these words, she began to pretend she was listening to one of her friends or co-workers utter the words she had just written. "What would I say to them?" she thought. "How would I advise them?" She decided to write her response as well. She would become Carmen the talker and Carmen the listener and the challenger!

So, Carmen, just what are you waiting for? I'm waiting for happiness. *Can you define happiness?* I want it all. I want a husband, a great lifestyle. *Aren't you going to get that in a few months when Kyle marries you?* I'm not sure. *Why aren't you sure?* Because deep in my heart I don't feel like Kyle is going to marry me. *You don't! Why not?* Because he's doing all the things that someone who's single would do. *Well, he is still single, isn't he?* He's still chasing every skirt tail he can. I have reason to believe he's sleeping with Amber. He is such a liar. *Tell me how that affects you ... knowing or suspecting that he's sleeping with Amber or any other woman?* It hurts me. *Then why are you still dealing with him?* I'm not sure. *Come on, Carmen ... you have to know why you choose to deal with a man who obviously has a problem with commitment, and also sleeps with other women. Aren't you concerned about AIDS?* Well, I know Kyle has condoms. I found them between his mattress. I count them whenever I'm there and the number of them isn't decreasing. So it doesn't appear that he's doing it with anyone else. I mean he and I are together pretty regularly. *OK, lets just say he has another stash of condoms elsewhere that you haven't found. And let's say that he is practicing safe sex, using his condoms. What about the act itself? How does it make you feel when you think of Kyle kissing and caressing some other woman?* I feel that what he's doing is only temporary. He's just taking advantage of the fact that he is still single. He's just trying to get the "dog" out of his system before we get married. *I thought you said you didn't think Kyle was going t o marry you? ... I'm confused.* Well, I only have to wait a few more months, then I won't have to guess. For whatever reason, I can't see giving up on Kyle just because he is being tempted by Amber. I am fairly certain he is just using her because she is stupid enough to think she has a chance to be with him. *Why don't you confront him about Amber?* Well, because I can't produce and confront him with hard evidence without revealing that I have been snooping around and invading his privacy. Besides, I'm still wearing his ring. I am his fiancee'. If Amber wants to be the "other woman" then let her stoop that low. *Is that how you see it?* Yes. *Tell me why you find solace in that.* All Amber is to him is a potential screw. I'm the one who interacts with his family. I'm the one who's wearing his ring. He's mine. I'll just have to spend more time with him to create less time for Amber or anyone else for that matter. *OK, then how are you going to allow him to "get the dog out of his system?"* Well, if I'm nicer to him, he won't want to be with anyone else. *Do you really believe that in your heart, Carmen?* I *want* to believe that. *So, what happens if he continues to cheat despite your overwhelming kindness?* I don't know ... I'll just have to cross that bridge when I get to it.

Carmen paused from writing and then began to read over what she had written. She wanted to do an evaluation of both selves. One self seemed to be level headed enough to ask the right questions ... to be able to challenge silly answers. The other self appeared to be desperate! The question Carmen now had for herself was which self would be the dominant one. Her heart knew what her head was unwilling to confirm. She decided the immediate solution to her situation was to date on the side as well. She figured if Kyle didn't come through by the end of his six-month lease, then she would have ready, 'Plan B'.

Every possible guy she could think of going out with was "too this" or "too that." Kyle Sealy was her benchmark. She decided that it probably didn't matter that they didn't measure up since she thought she would probably end up with Kyle anyway.

--- Chapter 23

Carmen couldn't seem to focus on the invitation design for Lark's party long enough to finish. Her mind would wonder off, as images of her beloved Kyle would consume her imagination. Between brush strokes on her canvas, she would reminisce about all the good times they had shared, all the places they had visited. She could hear echoes of their mutual friends proclaiming how she and Kyle belonged together. She imagined their life together after they would get married. Visions of Kyle coming home everyday showering her with gifts and flowers made her drift deeper into her fantasy. She imagined them holding hands in public and being the enviable couple to onlookers. She imagined them living in a beautiful home with nice furniture and lots of entertainment space for their friends and family. Then she imagined their kids and what they would look like. Their son was sure to look like Kyle and their baby daughter would look like Carmen. All of their friends would think they made a beautiful family. She also imagined herself eventually not having to work because she would be busy raising the kids. She would be the lovely wife of the successful entertainment attorney in Atlanta. _Ebony_ magazine would want to do an article on the magnificent love of these wonderful people. She smiled just thinking about having it all.

As usual, her daydreaming was interrupted by the ringing telephone. It was Nikki calling to provide the most recent update on her situation with Drew. Nikki was in tears because she had called Drew in the early morning hour only to be greeted by the voice of another woman. She explained that she kept her cool by pretending to be unfazed by the unexpected voice of a female. Her first inkling was to hang up because she thought she had received a wrong number, but she settled that issue by asking to speak to Drew. The woman said, "Hold on, he's right here."

A groggy Drew took the phone. "Hello," he said struggling to stay alert.

"Drew, this is Nikki," she said nervously waiting for her worst suspicion to be confirmed. "How are you, Baby?"

"Who is this?" asked Drew.

"This is Nikki."

"I'm sorry but you must have the wrong number," said Drew.

"Drew, it's me, Nikki," she said with hurt and desperation.

"Look, Miss, I told you, you must have the wrong number." Click.

When Nikki called back, no one would answer the phone. Her attempts to reach Drew from that point were futile. She was devastated.

Carmen began to try everything she could to console Nikki. She stopped short of saying, "I told you so." She knew that Nikki needed comforting not criticism. However, as she continued to listen to Nikki, she was convinced Nikki needed counseling.

"I need to see what I can do about moving to Denver so that Drew and I can be together. He is obviously lonely. I'm sure whoever that was who answered the phone was some slut who's trying to manipulate her way into his life. She's probably just like Amber ... trying to take advantage of a man during his weakest moment. I know this woman must know he has a girlfriend. I bet she answered the phone because she knew it was probably me calling."

"Nikki, listen to yourself. Please tell me you're not serious," Carmen said in disbelief.

Nikki was obviously in serious denial. "Nikki, you know that "sluts" don't answer the phone. She is obviously someone who sees herself as more than a screw. How do you explain Drew's behavior with you in the presence of this so-called "slut"?

"Carmen, he was half asleep. I'm sure when he finally realized who I was, he was too embarrassed to deal with the situation at hand."

"Oh, my goodness, Nikki!. . . Snap out of it! Why haven't you heard from him and why isn't he calling begging for forgiveness?"

"I'm sure he thinks I'm going to be angry with him. I know he has needs and I'm sure that woman means nothing. I'll bet he has been chewing her out ever since she picked up that phone. I guarantee you she won't be doing that anymore. He probably won't be seeing her anymore," said Nikki trying to convince herself the situation wasn't as bad as it seemed.

"Nikki, I love you, but you are being incredibly stupid! Remember what you were telling me about Amber ... you felt like she wouldn't have been dealing with Kyle unless he told her we were through. Do you think just maybe Drew did the same thing with this woman. But forget that. Let's just say she was an insignificant warm body for the evening. What about how he disrespected you, someone he is *supposed* to love, in front of this woman? She obviously felt comfortable enough to answer the phone in the first place. I'm sure she's feeling real comfortable now that he dissed you in front of her. I guarantee you she challenged that phone call with him and I guarantee you he told her you were some crazy woman who keeps calling him. And I guarantee you when or if you speak to him again, he is going to downplay that woman's significance."

"Well Carmen, if you're right, then God will show me a sign that Drew is not right for me," said Nikki.

"A sign?!!!" Carmen screamed. "Nikki, God is flashing a blimp-size neon light right in front of you. Open your eyes, girl! ... the sign says RUN!"

"I don't see you running from Kyle," said Nikki in an effort to defend herself.

"Then maybe I'm being stupid, too. When will we women stop being pawns in a man's game? Look at what's going on, you are allowing yourself to believe you need to somehow justify Drew's behavior. You are setting yourself up to accept any ol' explanation as long as it sounds *pretty* good. I bet he's got the other woman more focused on the fact that she answered his phone and how wrong she was to do so…rather than the fact that he obviously pretended not to know a woman (you) who asked for his ass, by name! How could that have been a "wrong" number? ... Now, I bet she's feeling guilty about answering the phone, *but* now her guard is down about him because he has convinced *her* that *she* is special and that *you* are the crazy, fatal attraction, ex-girlfriend. He can tell her *any* ol' thing now and she'll believe it. I'm getting pissed off just thinking about this. I mean, look at me. Kyle has me thinking I need to *prove* myself to him so that he will commit to me. Why the hell is he not *proving* himself to me! Look at how men value themselves...like they are something precious to have!"

Nikki was silent for a few seconds. "You know what, Carmen ... it might not be about how much men value themselves rather than how *little* we as women value ourselves."

"You are so right. Then Nikki, let's promise ourselves from this day forward we will learn to love and value ourselves. I think we are both crippled emotionally, but if we understand the importance of our goal, we will allow ourselves to heal and not get caught up in this type of shit *ever* again!"

"Speaking of healing, I spoke to Mother Durham yesterday. She was telling me that Lark's boyfriend/manager has dumped Lark because she can no longer sing. Can you believe that?" said Nikki.

"Unfortunately, I can. I've always thought he was no good for her. Lark would never branch out because of him. I've always believed she could be so much more if she had a new manager. He has a lot of nerve dumping her in her darkest hour. How is Lark? ... Did Mother Durham say?"

"She said she was pretty bummed out. That's why she wants this celebration for Lark to be extra special. She wants Lark to know that she has people who really do love her. Mother Durham sure does appear to be shelling out a lot of cash for this event. How are you coming with the invitation design?"

Carmen was too embarrassed to admit she had been distracted from finishing because of her consumption with daydreams and fantasies about Kyle. "I'm going to finish it today," she said with a sense of commitment. " Then I'm going to overnight a color image of the painting to Mother Durham in a few days so she can take it to the printers to get the invitations printed and mailed. We have a little over a month to get ready. I can't wait to see Lark.

Carmen had been thinking heavily about the pact she and Nikki had made with each other. Her forgiving spirit made it difficult for her to hold Kyle accountable for what he had done in the past. She only wanted to focus on the future. She decided to have a conversation with her journal.

Hello, Carmen, I knew we'd talk soon. Why is that? *Because I knew you didn't really feel the things you said before. You're afraid to face the truth.* The truth is I'm afraid to be with Kyle and I'm afraid to be without him. *Let's start with why you are afraid to be with him since you said that first.* I'm afraid I will live in a sea of unhappiness. *Wow! That's a powerful statement. Why do you feel that way?* My gut tells me Kyle is not going to change. My gut tells me my fantasies about us being happy is what I want it to be like ... not what I really feel it will *actually* be like. I feel that Kyle will always figure out a way to have another woman on the side. I don't think I will ever be enough woman for him. *So, why do you want to be with him?* Because I don't want to be alone. *Who says you have to be alone if you don't have Kyle. There are other men besides Kyle.* Where? *Depends on what you're looking for.* I'm looking for someone to make me happy. *Then why are you with Kyle, he doesn't make you happy?* I guess I'm with him because I've invested so much time and energy into the relationship. *What does that have to do with being happy?* Well, I just don't feel like starting over. *What does that have to do with being happy?* With Kyle, at least I know what I'm getting. All of the times we've had haven't been bad. He has made me happy on many occasions. *Were you really happy or were you on pins and needles?* I guess I was so happy that I was afraid it was going to end ... that it was somehow too good to be true. *But in most cases it was too good to be true.* Maybe not. *What do you mean?* I mean maybe Kyle was trying to be nice to me and I just wouldn't let him. I always questioned his motives. Maybe if I had just enjoyed the good times I would have gotten more good times and eventually gotten my man. *Carmen, I would agree with you except that whenever you have let your guard down, Kyle has hurt you and you keep going back for more ... Why!? Do you enjoy the abuse.* Abuse, why did you use that word? *Because, isn't what Kyle is doing to you called abuse?* Kyle has never hit me. *That would be called physical abuse. Kyle is emotionally abusing you. He knows you love him and will forgive him for anything. He is taking advantage of your love for him.* Then why am I letting him do this to me? *You tell me ... why are you?* Because I don't want to be alone. *Where is Kyle right now.* I don't know. *Right, most of the time you don't know, Carmen, you are alone <u>with</u> him.* I don't feel like starting over. *Carmen, how many times have you "started over" with Kyle?* What do you mean? *What I mean is, every time you do something that doesn't allow Kyle to have his way, he puts you on trial to prove yourself worthy of him.* This is true. *Of course it is. Carmen, some people don't want to buy a new car because they don't want to "start over" with making payments. So what do they do? ... They keep doing patch maintenance and pray the car doesn't leave them stranded yet once again. The car never gets any better ... if it's not one thing wrong it's another. One day, the car will finally put you down for good. Think about all the time and money you will have wasted for something that was obviously not reliable. In other words Carmen, don't wait for Kyle to put you down, start focusing on getting something more <u>reliable</u>.* So, I need to start working on 'Plan B'. *Exactly!*

--- Chapter 24

A sense of pride and accomplishment described Carmen as she opened her mail to find the invitation she had designed for Lark's Celebration of Life party. The painting she had done of Lark graced the cover of the invitation. It was a picture of Lark with her hands clasped around a microphone with her head bowed in prayer. Carmen was somewhat amazed with her own talent. It was truly a gift from God. Even though she marveled at her own dexterity, she couldn't help but feel sad for Lark. However, the thought of Lark just being alive made her happy again.

Mother Durham was going all out for the party. When Carmen looked inside the invitation she took note of the location. The party was indeed going to be held at Avery Fisher's Hall at Lincoln Center in New York City. Of course, the event was Black Tie. It was less than a month away. Carmen quickly called Kyle to let him know he needed to clear his calendar for the party and that he should buy a plane ticket soon to get the best rates. To her surprise, Kyle was iffy about attending. He said business at the firm had really picked up and he wasn't sure he could afford the time away. She reminded him the party was on the weekend. He still wouldn't commit. She knew then there had to be another reason other than work. All of a sudden Carmen could feel a message from her gut. Drama was on the horizon. Fear described her next emotion. Would she soon be challenged to keep the promises she had made to herself? What could she do to manage the outcome of the anticipated situation? After about five minutes of meditation, she decided she would need hard core proof that she should not trust Kyle or that he was really serious about committing to her. "God, please forgive me. I know you keep giving me signs I should heed. Dear Lord, you know the devil is always busy ... how do I know he isn't trying to break apart what you have put

215

together. Kyle and I have been through a lot. We've managed to stay together despite all the obstacles. In a couple of months Kyle said we can get married. How do I know that I'm not supposed to be patient? If I bail out now, how do I know you won't frown on me because my blessing was just around the corner and I didn't wait? Kyle says he's sincere. Speak to me, Father. Please let me know what I should do. I pray that you will brace me to handle whatever happens. I'm ready to listen. Please speak to me. Amen."

Carmen was elated when Kyle called to ask her to go with him to Lenox Mall to pick out a gift for Lark. He said he wanted to acknowledge his appreciation for all the assistance she had provided to him as he penetrated the entertainment industry. He also said he was doing everything to manage his workload so that he would be able to attend the celebration in New York in two weeks.

It was a beautiful day in Atlanta. The sky was cloudless. Kyle was looking as handsome, as usual, when he came to pick Carmen up. She commented on how sexy he looked and how she couldn't wait to get back home to "take care of a little business."

When they arrived at the mall, they decided to go to *Neiman Marcus* first. They were like little kids playing. They were making fun of all the over-priced merchandise. Kyle toyed with the sales people pretending to be interested in purchasing a twenty-five hundred dollar sports jacket. If the price was not so impractical, Carmen would have purchased it for him ... he looked especially regal in it. "I probably should look at tuxedos while I'm in here," said Kyle. "You did say the event for Lark was Black-Tie, right?"

"Let's go look," encouraged Carmen. She wanted to do everything she could to persuade him to join her in New York.

"Do you have a dress yet?" asked Kyle.

"No, I want something new."

"Of course you do," said Kyle joking her about her spending habits.

"We can go look at the Donna Karan collection after we look at the tuxedos. You can help me pick out something exquisite, OK?" said Carmen.

"You still haven't spoken to Lark?" asked Kyle.

"Not directly. I get all the updates from her mom. She says that speaking strains her voice. I'm sure I will get a chance to talk to her in New York. Did you know that sorry manager/boyfriend of hers has dumped her? I can't believe Lark has wasted all this time with him and he decides to drop her in her darkest hour. I swear, there is just no loyalty. Lark could have been managed by much more connected people and been a superstar by now. But no, she hung in there with that loser to help him with his career. Can you believe the nerve of him? Why do men dog women like that?"

Sensing an argument coming on, Kyle changed the subject gracefully. "She's probably better off without him. Hey, let's go get the tux."

Kyle was unwilling to spend three thousand dollars on the Georgio Armani tuxedo he fell in love with, but Carmen had no problem charging a five hundred and sixty-five dollar Donna Karan dress she had found on sale. It was red and she had the perfect shoes to match. She was feeling quite happy.

As they were about to leave the mall, an unwelcome vision appeared. Amber was just walking in. Oh what a moment! Carmen was dying to see how Kyle would handle the situation. The fact that they were already holding hands made things all the more interesting. Carmen squeezed Kyle's hand tighter.

Amber was obviously shaken when she recognized them. She stopped dead in her tracks. She looked at Kyle, then she looked at Carmen, then back at Kyle. Carmen looked at Kyle.

Kyle looked at Amber. "Hey, what's up?" he said as he motioned his head backward. He then pulled Carmen by the hand to walk around Amber who stood stationary and in apparent shock.

As they walked away, Carmen looked back at Amber. Amber was looking at them walk out. Carmen couldn't resist flashing a vengeful smirk. Even though she felt a small victory with Amber, she sensed a deep loss with Kyle. Why did Amber seem shocked? Where was her shame?

"So why did Amber seem shocked to see us together?" asked Carmen of Kyle.

"How would I know?" he replied. "I can't explain women."

Carmen was on the edge ... should she challenge this ridiculous answer and ruin what had been a great day or should she let it go? Was this the sign she had asked for from God? It couldn't be she thought, because the message wasn't quite clear. She did, however, have one other avenue to explore ... she could determine if Kyle would lie about his interaction with Amber. She knew she had seen Amber at his apartment subsequent to his proclamation of not wanting to have anything to do with her. "So when was the last time you spoke to Amber?" asked Carmen with intense anticipation of the answer.

"She has called the office to try to send us clients," said Kyle with no further explanation.

This was not quite the answer Carmen wanted to hear. It was only half truthful. He was honest about having communicated to her but neglected to offer information about why she was at his apartment. "Has she been trying to come by your house anymore?" probed Carmen.

"Not since the last time," answered Kyle with the craft of evasion. He hoped that Carmen would be satisfied with that answer and drop the subject.

"When was the last time?" Carmen pressed.

"Since the last time I told you she was there," Kyle lied. Carmen wanted so badly to confront him, but she didn't want to admit how she knew he was lying. Once again, she had backed herself into a corner. Once again, she had enough information to know he was lying, but not enough to know to what extent. Yet once again, she knew her heart felt the pain of distrust. Soon her heart would demand a change.

Chapter 25

It was less than a week before they were scheduled to depart for New York when Kyle finally confirmed he would be attending. Carmen was delighted! It had been a while since she and Kyle had been on a vacation. Although this wasn't exactly a vacation, it was nice to get away for a weekend.

She spent most of Thursday making sure she had everything in place before departing the next day. She had called UPS several times to make sure the framed original of the portrait she had done of Lark was going to arrive in time for Mother Durham to have time to set it up. Almost everything was in place. She still needed to go by her seamstress to pick up her dress from being altered. Work had slowed down to a point where she could sneak out without being noticed. She feared if she waited to pick up her dress after work, she wouldn't have time to get further alterations in case the dress didn't fit. There wouldn't be time to do anything on tomorrow, Friday, except get up and get to the airport on time to catch her 10:00am flight to JFK airport. Nikki would kill her if she missed the flight since they had made reservations that would allow them to arrive around the same time.

Kyle wouldn't be flying up until Saturday morning. Carmen and Nikki now had all day Friday to run around Manhattan to do girl stuff like shopping, since Drew wasn't coming at all.

Nikki didn't waste much time being sad about Drew not going to New York. She had recently met a man in investment banking who she convinced to join her in New York for the event. Carmen didn't know much about him except that he was well-off financially, originally from Chicago, had never been married, had no kids, was good-looking and he drove a Porsche. His name was Zachary and he would be taking a limousine from Laguardia to the hotel in Manhattan on Saturday afternoon.

Before Carmen left the cleaners, she sat in her car to make a list of all the things she needed to do for herself and for Kyle since he was very busy trying to rap things up at the office. He had said he would be working very late tonight and wouldn't be able to join her for dinner. So she added taking food to the office for Kyle to her list.

She had tried to reach Kyle at the office after 6:00p.m., but to no avail. She couldn't imagine why he wasn't answering the phone unless he was completely engrossed in work. She thought perhaps he had gone home after all. So she decided to drive by his apartment to see if she saw his car. When she arrived at his complex, she didn't see his car, but she did see a note affixed to his front door. She couldn't resist parking her car and going up to the door to read the note.

The note was folded. Written on the outside was Kyle's name. She casually opened the note and began to read it. Her hands began to tremble as she read the message:

"Hi, Honey!

Came by. Gonna run home real quick to change my shoes. I'll be back in twenty minutes. Be ready! Received the flowers today ... they're gorgeous! I'm in my uncle's Mercedes.

Love ya,

Your Sweety ... (hugs, kisses).

Carmen felt nauseated. Her legs became weak. She could barely think as she stood there paralyzed! "God, help me," she cried out. Somehow, she managed to pull herself together enough to stick the note back to the door and get back into her car before she was noticed. She moved her car to the far end of the parking lot so that she could still have visibility to Kyle's apartment, without him being able to see her car. No sooner than she had reparked her car, she saw Kyle drive up and rush to his apartment. He grabbed the note before he quickly went inside.

Carmen began to pray. "Dear God, am I about to find out why Amber looked shocked to see Kyle with me? Is this the clear message? God, it feels loud and clear. Please give me strength. This is far greater than anything I could have imagined. Amber said she was following the path you put in front of her. I can't understand why her prayers are being answered and not mine. My heart is so full of pain. I know I shouldn't question you, Dear Lord. Please give me understanding. I'm scared. God, Please don't leave me now."

Carmen didn't know whether to leave or to confront Kyle at the scene. A part of her wanted to go into denial to avoid dealing with the pain and suffering. Another part of her felt compelled to take advantage of the opportunity to nail Kyle once and for all.

Soon a car that looked like a Mercedes emerged in front of Kyle's apartment. The driver didn't park in a parking space. They parked in front as if they were only going to be there briefly. Dusk has fallen so it was difficult for Carmen to see clearly. A woman wearing a white dress got out of the car. She did a courtesy knock and then quickly rushed inside the apartment. Carmen decided at that point she would be standing right there when the two of them emerged from the apartment. She didn't care that she was going to be in an awkward situation ... she was operating off pure adrenaline. She didn't know what she would say or what she would do. She figured all was fair in love and war.

She stood in front of the parked Mercedes where Kyle and Amber would have a clear view of her when they came outside. She could hear laughter right before the door opened. When the door opened, everybody was shocked! Kyle's mouth fell open. Carmen's mouth fell open. She was benumbed to see the woman wasn't Amber...the woman was Robbi Gant! Robbi was shocked to see Carmen Layfield! No one could move or speak for what seemed like an eternity.

"What are you doing here?!" snarled Carmen at Robbi.

"Minding my own business." Robbi retorted.

"What are you doing in Atlanta?" Carmen challenged.

"I live here and what I do while I'm here is none of your business. Now if you will excuse us, we're late for dinner," said Robbi with her usual condescending demeanor.

Kyle motioned as if he was going to seek refuge inside his apartment while Carmen and Robbi continued their altercation. "Honey, we don't have to run from this woman," said Robbi. "Carmen, why don't you just get on with your life. You are so desperate. You trying to win Kyle is like you taking a three-point shot at the buzzer and you're down by four points! Can't you see that Kyle doesn't want you?"

"Oh really now? Then why are we engaged to be married?" said Carmen as she held up her hand up to show off her ring.

Robbi looked at Kyle. "What the hell is going on here?" she demanded.

Kyle said nothing. He just walked past Carmen and Robbi to his car, got in and left the two of them standing there.

"He's all yours," Carmen said to Robbi as she turned to leave. Her hands trembled as she put her key into the ignition. If there ever was a time in her life when she needed divine strength, it was now. She felt like her world had just come to an end. Now she knew why Robbi's phone number never appeared on her phone bill ... the call was local!...Robbi had moved to Atlanta! Robbi moving to Atlanta must have been part of the reason why Kyle wouldn't commit and why he had moved out of her home, Carmen concluded. All this time, Carmen had thought *time* and *Amber* were her only obstacles. Her arch nemesis, Robbi Gant, was very much a part of the equation.

Feeling too numb to cry, Carmen returned home where she completed her packing in preparation for her next-day departure to New York. She unplugged all the phones ... everything and everyone would have to wait until she was ready to face the world again. She wasn't even sure if she could ever face the world again. She felt suicidal even though she knew she could never actually go through with it ... or could she? She removed her ring and began to reminisce about the night Kyle proposed. That night was blissful and magical. But it obviously meant nothing more than an evening out. Kyle was reluctant to get engaged in the first place. When he finally did, he skimped on the ring. After that, he couldn't or wouldn't commit to a date to get married. In the midst of all that, he continued to date Robbi.

She was sure now he had dated Amber as well. God only knows who else.

In an effort to save herself, she grabbed her journal: *Talk to me, Carmen. What are you feeling?* I feel like I have nothing to live for. *Of course you do.* What? *Tell me first why don't you feel like you have anything to live for.* I've dedicated a great portion of my life to have the man I love and now he's gone. *Is that a reason to die?* No, but I feel like dying. *Why?* Because I don't want to face the world. I can't take the humiliation. *What humiliation?* Kyle and I didn't get married. I look like a fool. I've made wedding plans. I told everyone I was going to marry the love of my life. *What makes him the love of your life ... he lied to you, he cheated on you and he obviously negated you to Robbi because she didn't regard you as a factor Are those your qualifications for the love of your life?* No. *Then what's the problem?* I bet Robbi still wants him. *And??* They'll end up happy together. I'm supposed to be Mrs. Kyle Sealy. *Why do you want to be Mrs. Kyle Sealy?* Because he's good looking. He's successful. He's intelligent. *Those are "attributes" about Kyle. What do you get out of being Mrs. Kyle Sealy? I thought you said you wanted to be happy. His good looks don't make you any cuter.   His success doesn't make you any more successful and there's no guarantee he'll spend one dime on you. His intelligence will help him figure out every possible way to make sure you don't get half when you inevitably end up in divorce court.* What about Robbi? *What about her?* I don't want her to defeat me. *Defeat you how?* By ending up with Kyle. *Carmen, if Robbi is stupid enough to continue to deal with Kyle after he has obviously lied to and cheated on her, then let her. Let her have the misery you're smart enough to avoid. Don't be ruled by another woman's stupidity and don't chase another person's dream.* What do you mean? *You know what I mean. You somehow believe that Kyle making his dreams come true means success for him and therefore success for you. It doesn't. Make your own dreams come true.* What's wrong with dreaming for a happy relationship? *Nothing, Kyle is a nightmare ... move on!* I just want Kyle to want me. *Damn it,*

Carmen, why? I don't know. I just feel like a nobody without him. *So, you mean Kyle can control your feeling like a nobody as long as he doesn't want you?* Wow, I never thought about it like that. *Then start thinking about it. You don't need Kyle Sealy or anyone else to validate you! As long as you have that mentality, you will always be in bondage.* You are right. I will find the courage. Hopefully soon.

When Carmen put down her pen, she couldn't resist calling directory assistance. She wanted so desperately to believe that Robbi didn't really live Atlanta as she so claimed. She dialed 411. "What City?" said the operator. "Atlanta," she answered. "What Listing?" said the operator. "Robbi Gant," answered Carmen. There was a pause. Then she heard, "Please hold for the number .. .the number is 404-8..." Carmen hung up the phone. She took a deep breath. The next second was the beginning of the rest of her life. "God please help me find the courage," she prayed.

Fleeting images of Kyle and Robbi together haunted Carmen throughout the night before she was to leave for New York City. The devastation she felt had created a pressure on her heart that made it almost unbearable for her to respire. She kept dreaming she heard the phone ringing, thinking it might be Kyle calling to beg for forgiveness. Between dreams, she could hear herself moaning like a wounded animal. Her sorrowful heart yielded tears from the corners of her shut eyes. The beat of her heart was like a thunderous roar. Her head buzzed. She tossed and turned occasionally cradling herself as if she was her only protector. Helplessness and hopelessness was all she could feel. Oh how she wished all that was happening was only a nightmare. Love had never hurt so bad!

Barely coherent, Carmen managed to pack her things and get to the airport on time to make her flight. During her flight to New York, she kept thinking about all the good times she had shared with Kyle. All the glorious possibilities of their relationship overwhelmed her. She felt she had come so close to having a chance at happiness. Deep inside she knew better, but she couldn't help thinking she was somehow responsible for driving Kyle to Robbi. She kept thinking of all the disagreements they had during their relationship. She kept thinking of all the times she had distrusted him and accused him of another woman. If only she had chilled out and been patient like he had asked her to, she thought to herself. She had always been accustomed to hearing Kyle offer a slew of lies whenever his actions were suspect. This time he had offered nothing. Then again, his silence may have been the offering of many words or maybe even just two ... like *"I'm Busted!"*

An explanation from Kyle always gave Carmen a reason to believe he *might* be telling the truth or really gave her a reason to keep hanging on. It allowed her to continue her denial of the unhealthy and unfulfilling relationship she was in. She recalled hearing a lady say once in the beauty salon that "a piece of a man was better than no man at all." Thinking through this, she thought, "Is having a piece of a man worth me giving up something that makes *me* less than whole? What about my self respect? What about *me*?"

--- Chapter 26

Carmen's flight landed safely into JFK airport. When she emerged from the plane she saw Nikki standing there excited and eager to greet her. Of course Nikki had no idea what had occurred between her and Kyle during the last twenty-four hours. "Carmen!" Nikki yelled with open arms. Carmen smiled and tried to hide her grief, "Nikki!" she yelled back. The two of them hugged like long lost friends. They hadn't seen each other since Nikki was in Atlanta for Kyle's kick-off celebration.

"Carmen, you look like shit!" exclaimed Nikki. "What's wrong?"

"I don't want to talk about it, Nik," said Carmen.

"What did Asshole do this time? Did you and Kyle have a fight? Is he still seeing that Amber bitch? What? Tell me!"

"Nikki, let's just go and enjoy the day. I really don't feel like talking about Kyle right now," said Carmen.

"Is he coming up?" asked Nikki trying to obtain any information she could.

"I don't know and don't care."

"So the two of you *did* have a fight?" probed Nikki.

"Worse than that."

"Did the two of you break up?"

Carmen couldn't maintain strength any longer. She began to break down. "Nikki, Kyle is seeing Robbi," she said sobbing.

"Robbi?!" Wait a minute ... first Amber, now Robbi? When did this happen?!"

"I have no idea how long it's been going on. All I know is I saw the two of them together last night and they were headed out on a date."

"A date?!" exclaimed Nikki. She was confused.

"Yes ... a date. Robbi *lives* in Atlanta now and they have been seeing each other. She refers to herself as his sweetheart. I now know why Kyle wasn't coming up until tomorrow ... today

227

is Robbi's birthday. He fed me a pack of lies about having to work. He knew the second I told him about Lark's party that he was going to have a problem with that weekend because of her birthday. I knew he acted funny for some reason. I hate him, Nikki. I hate him! I feel like all my dreams have been shattered!"

"Kyle is no dream ... he is a nightmare," said Nikki. "Carmen you deserve so much better. You see how I kicked Drew's ass to the curb. I've found someone who's much better. All of Zachary's money isn't tied up in divorce court, child support and alimony. Girl, we have got to find you another man. I'm sure there are going to be some fine ones at Lark's party."

"Nikki, I can't think about another man right now. I'm just not looking to meet anyone else."

"That's OK," said Nikki. You don't have to look. We are going to fix you up so they can find *you*. Let's go get checked in and hit the streets. Shopping will help you get your mind off things." Carmen proceeded out of the airport with Nikki. "Has anyone talked to Lark?" she asked.

"I spoke to Mother Durham last night. She said Lark will be getting in late this afternoon. I understand she has appointments lined up with the spa, the salon, the manicurist, the pedicurist, fashion designer ... you name it. So basically she's getting ready to be a knockout at her party tomorrow. Therefore she has no time for chatter right now. I guess we won't see her until tomorrow night," said Nikki.

Carmen was exhausted after running around all day Friday with Nikki. It was now Saturday morning and she had yet to speak to Kyle. She checked her answering machine in Atlanta, however, there were no messages. She didn't know whether or not Kyle would be coming to New York. The thought of Kyle being with Robbi made her ill. The thought of being made a fool of made her crazy. Carmen felt so close to the edge. Anything and everything reminded her of Kyle. Every song on the radio had a meaning she could apply to her situation. Seeing happy couples reminded her of what might have been. The entire world seemed to be painted in Kyle's favorite color. Her yearning for his love seemed to grow stronger by the nanoseconds. "What's so special about Robbi," she thought. "How could Kyle love her and not me?" She began to slip into a deep depression. She than grabbed her pen and began to talk to herself.

Help me. *Help you do what?* Help me stop hurting. *Why are you hurting?* Because I've lost everything. *Have you really?* I've lost a big part of me. *What have you really lost?* I've lost the man I love. *You still love him don't you.* Yes, but I've still lost him. *Again, what have you really lost?* I've lost the opportunity to have him. *You can still have him. Girl, you can take on Robbi. You've moved her out of the way before, right?* Apparently not. *Why do you say that?* Because she's still in the picture. *How do you know she's not the one doing all the chasing. Kyle may not want her.* Give me a break. Kyle has been calling her. He knew she <u>was</u> moving and <u>did</u> move to Atlanta. He is spending her birthday with her. He lied to me to free himself to do so. If she's chasing him, he is encouraging her to do so. *So is this the love you're saying you lost? Well? Why are you silent?* I'm not sure. *Yes you are.* I feel like I was made such a fool of. We could have been happy together. *How Carmen?* I could have made him happier than Robbi can. *How Carmen? You loved the man to the bone. That obviously wasn't enough to make him happy and faithful.* Well, I don't *know* that he was unfaithful. I never caught him having sex with anyone else. *That's true, but let's deal with what you <u>do</u> know. He would not commit and he has tried to make you believe it's all your fault. Meanwhile, he's running around with Amber, Robbi and God only knows who else. You do know that you have been very unhappy in this relationship. And you do know it's highly unlikely that Kyle will change.* What if he does change, then Robbi will have my man. *Is all this about Kyle or Robbi?* I just don't want her to have him. *That's not something you can control. You should try to concentrate on those things you can, and he's obviously not your man. Can't you see, she has "your"* *man even with you in the picture.* There is great potential for us. *Carmen, look how much time and energy you have already put into this relationship. What has it yielded you? A heartache.* What if God takes too long to bless me? *He's blessing you right now ... you just won't recognize it.* Spare me. *Don't even think of being impatient with God (someone you really can trust) when you've been more than patient with Kyle (who you really can't trust). - Remember, God gives us what we need and His word is bond.*

She began to feel better although she still felt sadness. The fact that Nikki was now completely engrossed in her new boyfriend didn't help ... it made her feel that much more lonely.

Not able to resist any longer, She picked up the phone to call Kyle. She wanted to know if he was still coming. She didn't get an answer. She then called the airline to confirm his reservation. "I'd like to confirm reservations for a Mr. Kyle Sealy for flight number 1274 out of Atlanta into New York's JFK please," said Carmen as she waited nervously for the reply. "I'm sorry, I'm not showing a Kyle Sealy on that flight, ma'am."

"Thank you," said Carmen as she hung up feeling like a dagger had just pierced her heart.

The phone rang. It was Nikki calling to invite her to join her and Zachary for lunch. Carmen didn't feel very much like being social. It was enough that she was going to have to muster up enough energy to attend Lark's party at 7:00p.m. She only wanted to sulk. Life couldn't be more miserable, she thought. Nikki wasn't taking no for an answer.

————————

Zachary seemed nice. He seemed to be just what Nikki liked ... a flashy man who desired the best of everything. After they had lunch at a very fancy restaurant, he rode them all around Manhattan sight seeing in his rented limo. Carmen was doing fine until he said, "What lucky gentleman will be escorting you this evening?" She took a deep breath. "I will be going alone," she said with assembled confidence. "As a matter of fact, we should probably be heading back to the hotel. I have a ton of things to do in order to get ready for tonight. Zachary smiled. He admired her sass. "Well all right, Miss Thang. Let's see if we can't get Cinderella home so she can get ready for the ball." Carmen laughed. It was the first time she had laughed all day. It felt rather soothing. "May we have the pleasure of chauffeuring you to the gala tonight Miss Rella?" said Zachary playfully to Carmen. "We can all party all night 'cause this limo won't turn into a pumpkin." Nikki was happy to see Zachary doing his best to cheer Carmen up.

"Oh, Thank you, but I don't want to intrude on you and Nikki's privacy. I can just catch a cab. Lincoln Center is only a couple of blocks away," said Carmen.

"Carmen, don't be silly," said Nikki. "You are not taking a cab when you can ride in a limousine! Besides, we all are going to show up in style and looking fabulous. Mother Durham invited two hundred and fifty people here to have a great time. We're going to have a great time with class. Let's all plan to meet in the lobby of the hotel at around 6:30. And don't be trying to look better than everybody else," Nikki joked.

It was now 6:00p.m. Carmen stood in front of the full-length mirror in her hotel room admiring her own beauty in her astonishing red gown. Her swept-up hair made her look especially elegant. Her shoes and nail polish matched perfectly. Her lips shimmered in sexy red. The only jewelry was long dazzling earrings and a brilliant rhinestone bracelet. To add a final touch, she slowly dabbed perfume behind her ears, on her wrists and in her cleavage. "You look great, Carmen," she said to herself. "I can do this. I can go alone and hold my head up...Princess Diana did it for years. I hope I can look as radiant and confident as she always did." Carmen grabbed her small clutch purse and took a sip of the wine she had ordered before she headed downstairs to meet Nikki and Zachary. "Dear Lord, give me strength," she said as the doors to the elevator opened to receive her.

When Carmen arrived to the reception hall, she was greeted

by Mother Durham who hugged and thanked her for doing a marvelous job with the invitations and with the portrait. Carmen was flattered to see the portrait of Lark displayed next to the sign-in table. Everyone seemed to be awed at the work of art. When she was identified as the artist, she received an abundance of accolades. People raved about her talent. She was overwhelmed by their kindness.

She felt relieved to see that people weren't necessarily coupled off ... they seemed to be mingling in groups. "Where is the guest of honor," asked Carmen of Mother Durham.

"She's here and she is so excited about seeing everyone. She should be out very shortly to join us for dinner. She has a surprise for everyone. I can't tell you what it is. We're going to be moving everyone into Avery Fisher's after dinner. I want everyone to be seated by 9:00p.m."

"OK," said Carmen. "Everything is so lovely. You have really gone all out. I know Lark is thrilled you've done this for her."

"Lark is my baby and I just want to see her happy. I know that seeing all of you is very special to her. I'm just so happy everyone made it. Let's move on in so we can be seated for dinner."

Before dinner was served, Mother Durham took the microphone and thanked everyone for coming. She spoke of Lark's ordeal. She praised God for giving them the strength to make it through victoriously. "...I know all of you have been wanting to speak to Lark. She is now ready to speak to all of you. Family and friends, here she is, my Baby, Linda --Lark--Durham."

Lark emerged looking like a radiant angel. Everyone was so excited to see her ... there was not a dry eye in the house. There was a continuous applause for her as she waved and blew kisses at everyone. There was this sense that everyone just wanted to run up and hug her and tell her how much she was loved and adored. She took hold of the microphone. "Thank you all for the warmth and all the love. May we please bow our heads in prayer." Lark spoke a beautiful prayer, even though her voice was weak. She thanked God repeatedly for his many blessings. When she was done everyone said in unison - "Amen."

It was now a quarter 'til 9:00. Everyone had been seated in Avery Fisher's Hall. Carmen, Nikki and Zachary were amongst the people seated in the front row. They could almost touch the stage. Excitement filled the air. Everyone had enjoyed dinner and were now ready to be entertained.

When the curtain went up, the audience was entertained by a dynamic jazz band. The saxophonist was sexy and fine. Carmen had a clear view of him since she had a front row seat. He was wearing a cobalt blue mock turtleneck muscle shirt and he really did have muscles. He looked like he was about 6'3". He wore a pair of black slacks with a nice belt. He also had on nice shoes...a definite plus! He had on a gold bracelet and no ring!...another apparent plus!...maybe. Nikki, seated beside her, also commented on how fine the saxophonist was. Carmen reminder her that she had Zachary.

As much as Carmen wanted to flirt with the saxophonist, she couldn't help but think about Kyle and how he should have been seated next to her enjoying the magical evening. But instead of feeling sorry for herself, she decided to do her best to enjoy the evening.

The band was excellent! Carmen melted in her seat when the saxophonist took center stage as the band did a rendition of the Kenny Loggin's *Love Will Follow* tune. He made eyes at her as he played the tune while she mouthed the lyrics, "*If you come away with me, I can show you ecstasy. Close your eyes and we will leave and love will follow…*" She smiled with shyness although she loved every minute of the flirtation.

After the band completed their last selection, the bandleader took the microphone.

"We'd like to thank you all for coming out. We're going to be playing live for you after the show at the dance party. We'd love to see you all there. I'd like to take this time to bring on our next act. This act is the headliner for the evening. It has always been her dream to perform here at Avery Fisher's Hall. She's going to be performing the debut tune from her new CD due out in a few months. It's a classic Brenda Russell tune, one of her favorites, it's called *Piano in the Dark.* Ladies and gentlemen, please stand and put your hands together for the ever so incredible, Lark!"

Carmen and Nikki, along with everyone else was shocked and amazed when the curtain opened to reveal Lark seated before dimmed lights with a harp! Everyone just continued to applaud and cheer. Lark seemed genuinely touched. She smiled and kept mouthing, "Thank you, Thank you." She winked at Carmen and Nikki as they waved at her and blew her kisses.

Lark walked up to the microphone. "Before I begin, I would just like to say… *Surprise!!!*" Everyone began to applaud again as they remained standing. "Thank you so much! It's so wonderful to see everyone here. My heart is truly touched." Lark cleared her throat. "As you all can imagine, the road I have recently traveled has been rough. In the beginning when I learned of my illness, I thought my life was over. I felt that God had taken away the gift he had given me, my voice. How was I to go on? What was I supposed to do? I didn't understand why I was being tested. I felt angry and abandoned. But I remembered that God would *never* abandon me. He's always with me to guide me … to lead me. I've always prayed that God would provide me the opportunity to always share my gift. I thought my voice was my only gift. Well, God is a generous God. He gives us everything we need. He's given me another gift … the gift of life. Life isn't easy. There is always a challenge on the horizon. But, I've found that life is about choices. We can choose to be victims or victorious. There is always a path of victory for those who know and love the Lord. Because of His loving kindness, I'm able to make my dream come true tonight. I have chosen victory. I'm going to finally perform at Avery Fisher's Hall. Praise God." The audience very softly said Amen in response to Lark's testimonial. Then there was a stillness and look of anticipation from every tear-filled eye in the audience. Lark closed her eyes and began to play. Then the rest of the band joined in. The image of her on stage with such conviction and courage would leave an indelible image in everyone's mind.

Carmen found a sense of courage by just watching Lark. She was inspired by Lark's unwillingness to be the victim. The fact that her manager/boyfriend didn't believe in her didn't prevent her from believing in herself. She didn't depend on his validation.

As Carmen continued to listen to Lark, she decided that she would chase her dreams. She decided she would complete and showcase her art in the next arts festival in Atlanta. She vowed that she would never let another person's dream overshadow her own. She knew she had somehow made Kyle's dreams her target. She had made Kyle and everyone else responsible for her happiness. All the times she had lied to herself was her way of not having to challenge herself to be all she could be. Her plan now was to be happy and to understand what really makes her happy. No more *pretending* to be happy just to create the *facade* that she really is. "I'm happy with *me* and anything else is gravy," she thought to herself as she felt peace flow through her body.

Later that evening at the reception, Carmen mingled with the guest trying desperately to look happy despite the bottomless pit she felt in her heart. She eventually found a spot beside the table with the colossal fruit tray where she felt comfortable nibbling on strawberries while she people watched. She could see that Nikki and Zachary were having a delightful time dancing and being social. The two of them appeared to be made for each other. He was an investment banker, she was a CPA, and they both were interested in mingling with people who they thought had money. Carmen chuckled to herself when she remembered when Nikki said, referring to the financial arrangement between men and women, "Girl, forget that ol'

saying 'you put in five, I put in five, and together we have ten.'
I say to the man, *you* put in ten and together we have ten...*I'll* do
the counting and spending."

The music was sounding very nice. The crowd applauded as
the band concluded the last selection. The bandleader
announced that they would be taking a break and invited the
guest to enjoy the sounds of music delivered by the disc jockey.
People began to head for the punch and champagne table for a
refreshing drink after heating up the dance floor. Carmen
hurried to beat the crowd to get a refill on her drink. She hadn't
been dancing, but needed the drink to help rinse the strawberry
fragments from between her teeth. She hoped no one watched as
she swished the champagne around in her mouth. This wasn't a
very classy sight, she thought to herself. She was happy when
the disc jockey slowed the music down and dimmed the lights.

Carmen braced herself as she saw the saxophonist from the
band approaching her from across the room. She began to suck
her front teeth really hard to make sure there were no remnants
of fruit lodged between them to ruin her smile. "Oh my God, he
is so fine," she said to herself as she tried to act composed,
watching him in all his sexiness grow closer to her.

"Hello. Would you like to dance?" the man said in a smooth
and sexy tone reaching for her hand with the confidence that her
answer would be yes.

"I'd love to," said Carmen. She placed the glass of
champagne she was drinking on the table and allowed the man to
take her by the hand to lead her to the dance floor.

The man handled Carmen very carefully as he positioned her
for the dance. He was careful not to turn her off by being overly
aggressive. He was trying to be the perfect gentleman.

Carmen was very nervous and she didn't do a very good job
of camouflaging it. "Just follow my lead, pretty lady" he
gingerly instructed. They began to dance. "What's your
name?" he asked.

"Carmen. Carmen Layfield. And yours?"

"Lance, Lance Underwood. It's a pleasure to meet you."
He slowly pulled her closer to him as they danced slowly to a

Kenny G tune. She could feel herself dissolving. "You are absolutely beautiful. I can sense you doubt that somehow," he said.

Carmen was slightly appalled that he would make such an observation and be bold enough to say it. She didn't want to admit to him that he was right. "Actually you're wrong. I feel very beautiful ... inside and out," she said bravely.

"I like that. I stand corrected. Are you here with someone?" he asked.

"I might be," she said with sass.

"Well, I know you're not. Because if you were, you wouldn't be slow dancing with me. A man would be a fool to let you out of his sight."

Carmen smiled. "Then you must be alone, too."

"No, I'm not," he said.

Carmen stopped dancing. Lance looked at her and laughed, "I'm not alone because I have the most beautiful woman in the world right here in my arms."

"Another smooth talker," she thought. "Do you live here in New York?" she asked.

"I do right now, but I'm thinking of moving to Atlanta to open another recording studio.

"What about you. Do you live here in New York?" he asked.

Carmen paused. "No. I live in Atlanta right now. If I don't decide to stay to open up my own art studio and advertising company, I might be moving to New York with my next assignment. I work for an advertising firm." She continued to dance thinking that it was funny that they each might be moving to the city where the other would be leaving! Relationships are never easy, she thought. Then she said to herself, *"Self, put on the breaks. Who says this man is even interested in a relationship with you? There you go again assuming."* "When are you thinking of moving to Atlanta?" she asked.

"When are you moving to New York?" he flirted.

"I asked you first," she said followed by a giddy chuckle."

He laughed. "Somehow I have this feeling that you and I

will end up in the same place.

"Oh really now," she said.

"If you'll let me, I'd like to get to know you better," he said sincerely as he looked down directly into her gazing eyes.

Carmen inhaled and exhaled slowly, "We'll see," she said as she placed her face cheek-to-cheek with his. They continued to dance. She closed her eyes and allowed the chemistry to flow.

--- *Chapter 27*
Closure

When Carmen returned to her hotel from the gala, she saw that her message light was on.   Before she could check the message, her phone rang. It was Nikki. "Hey, I was just calling to make sure you made it to your room OK?

"Nikki, did you have too much to drink? You and Zachary walked me to my room about two minutes ago," said Carmen.

"I know, but I need to tell you something."

"What?"

"Have you checked your messages yet?" asked Nikki.

"No. Why? What's up?"

Nikki hesitated for a moment. "Weeelll , before we went to the gala tonight, I got a call from you-know-who.

"Who? Drew?"

"No. Kyle!

"Kyle!" shouted Carmen. "What the hell did he want and why was he calling you?"

"Carmen, I feel so bad. I should have known better. But you were so sad.

"Nikki Vaughn! Spit it out!" Carmen demanded.

"Well, like I said, Kyle called me and he sounded like he was crying. He was begging me to tell him how he could get you back. He was telling me how much he loved you and how sorry he was and that he would do anything to have you. I told him he could start by setting a date and stop bullshitting you. I told him that he had to buy you a bigger ring, two and a half carats...minimum! I told him he had to send you one hundred long stem roses representing his 100% commitment to you. I told him to deliver them to the hotel so that they would be waiting for you when you got back to the room. Have you been in the bedroom yet?"

Carmen didn't say anything. She turned with the phone in

her hand and walked to the door of the bedroom. There were red roses everywhere!

"Carmen, are you still there?" asked Nikki. Carmen still just held the phone. She was dumbfounded. "I can hear you breathing...so I know you're still there," said Nikki. "I take it the roses were delivered. Otherwise, you would be asking me why I asked if you had been in the bedroom yet. So anyway," Nikki continued, "Kyle wants me to help him pick out a ring for you. I told him I would. But now that you have met Lance, I feel like a fool."

Carmen broke her silence. "Nikki, you should feel like a fool anyway. I told you what Kyle did to me with Robbi. How could you encourage him? Why would you do this to me? I'm trying to move on from Kyle. And another thing, there's nothing going on between Lance and me."

"Well, not yet. Now you have options. If Kyle doesn't work out, then you can make something go on between you and Lance...with his fine self. Lance can be 'Plan B'. Girl, you don't *have to* be manless," said Nikki. "Look, get that two and a half carat ring from Kyle. If it doesn't work out, at least you will have something to show for all the pain and agony you had to go through with him. No offense, but don't you feel kinda silly when you look at that ring he gave you and compare it to all the pain he caused you. Girl, you let him off the hook with that little ring. You should make him pay! Think about it Carmen, if Kyle is not sincere, then he loses.

"You certainly have changed your tune," said Carmen.

"No I haven't," Nikki said defensively. "Girl, all the men in Atlanta are gay or married...or both!...and the single ones are still running around like they will be young forever, meanwhile getting older, uglier and filling prescriptions for Viagra by the nanosecond! Lance lives here in New York. You, on the other hand, live in Atlanta and so does Kyle."

"Let's not forget that Robbi lives there, too," said Carmen. "I can't believe I'm having this conversation with you. Where's Zachary?"

"Snoring!" said Nikki. "Carmen, what kind of idiot would

she be to continue to hang around Kyle with you walking around with a two and a half carat ring from him on your finger? Robbi wasn't threatened by that carat he gave you...she knew that was her ring in reincarnation. As far as she was concerned, you were wearing her shit. Girl, here's your chance to let Robbi know who the woman of choice is. Remember how that bitch snubbed you and tried to make you feel like you couldn't possibly think you were Kyle's woman. Let that bitch be manless in Atlanta, not you!"

"Thanks for the advice, Nikki. But it seems to me that anybody can have a man and still be manless. For all that a non-committed relationship is worth, you can just call anybody your man just so that you can say that you have one. I don't mean to pick on you, but when you were dating Drew, was he your man or Tracy's? By the same token, I could be married to Kyle and Robbi could still think of him as her man. She didn't seem to have a problem thinking of him as her man when he was engaged to me. Why should I think things will be any different if Kyle and I were married?"

"Well, if you were married, then you would have a commitment," said Nikki.

"Excuse me, isn't that what an engagement is supposed to be?" said Carmen sarcastically. "A man can give you all the diamonds in the world, but if you don't have his heart, you have nothing."

"Well, not exactly...at least you'd have all the diamonds in the world," joked Nikki. "I'm just kidding. I get your point. I just want you to be happy. How old is Lance? Is he seeing anyone?"

"He's thirty-two. He dates. He's never been married. He has no kids. He is a Christian. He lives in New York, I live in Atlanta," Carmen rattled. "Don't you want to know how much money he makes or what kind of car he drives?

"I already know he's loaded and he drives a Lexus coupe, a Benz, and a Porsche Boxster!" said Nikki proudly and with approval. "Zachary had a conversation with him. He's fresh out of a relationship with a girlfriend of a year and a half. He caught her cheating…with a woman! Can you believe that?"

"How do you know all this?" asked Carmen.

"Zachary told me. He talked to Lance. Lance knew we were all together. He told Zachary he couldn't figure out why someone as gorgeous as you wasn't with a man. He was interested in meeting you but didn't want to go down the same road twice. Zachary assured him that you weren't chasing cat. Zachary also told him that you had just broken up with your man in Atlanta. So, basically you guys have something in common…both your mates were cheating with other women," Nikki joked.

"So, Lance already knew things about me before he asked me to dance," said Carmen. "He was carrying on like he was so intuitive. I can't believe him."

"Don't blame the man for doing a little homework. The point is that he was and is interested in you. Only time will tell just *how* interested. In the meantime, you can have a two and a half carat diamond ring!…Oh, and Kyle."

Carmen yawned. "Oh well, I need to get off this phone. I need to pack so I can check out on time tomorrow. I'll see you downstairs for breakfast. Call me when you get up. Bye."

When Carmen hung up with Nikki, she hit the button on the phone to retrieve her messages. There was a message from Kyle. "Hi, Baby. This is Kyle. Please call me no matter what time you get in," the message said. Carmen looked at the clock. It was already 2:00am.

The sound of Kyle's voice made Carmen weak. As much as she despised him, she couldn't just turn off the love she had for him. She debated with herself about whether she should call him back or not. "God, if I grow weak at the sound of his voice, what will I do when I see him," she said to herself. She knew she would have to face him someday. Now was as good a time as any to speak to him, she thought. Curiosity got the best of her. She dialed his number.

Kyle picked up on the first ring as if he was waiting by the phone for her call. "Carmen?" he said.

She started to say, "No, it's Robbi." But she didn't. "Yeah, it's me," she said.

"How was the party?" he asked.

"It was nice."

"Do you miss me?"

Carmen wanted to slam the phone down. "No, I don't as a matter of fact," she said with an attitude of disgust.

"Carmen, this has all been a big misunderstanding. I love you and I don't want to lose you. Can't we work things out?"

"What arc you saying is a big misunderstanding?" she asked.

"This whole thing with Robbi. I'm not seeing her. She was just trying to hurt you when she said those things."

"So what did you tell Nikki you were sorry about?"

"Um, I told Nikki I was sorry I didn't tell you Robbi was moving to Atlanta. And I was sorry I didn't handle the situation like a man, I just freaked out when I saw you at my door."

"Why was she at your apartment?" asked Carmen, as if she didn't know the answer.

"Carmen, let's not dwell on the past. Robbi is history and I know who I belong to. I want you, Baby," said Kyle in pleading expression . "I'll give you anything you want... Anything!. Did you get the roses I sent you?"

"Yeah, they're beautiful. Thanks."

"So can we work things out?" Kyle appealed.

Carmen paused. Let me think about it and call you back tomorrow, OK? I'm tired. I'm really tired. I'm going to bed now."

"So you're going to call me tomorrow?"

"Yclp. I'm gonna go now."

"Carmen, wait!" said Kyle. Are you still scheduled to get back to Atlanta tomorrow evening? I was thinking you could change your flight reservations and come back early. I'd like to spend the day with you...just the two of us. We can spend the entire day planning our future together."

Carmen took a deep breath. She felt like she needed a glass of wine. "Kyle, I'm really tired. I need time to think. Let me call you tomorrow. I really need to go now. I'll talk to you later, OK?" Click.

Carmen could feel nothing but stress. She grabbed her temples and buried her face in her hands as she bowed her head forward. The silence in the room was overwhelming. All she could hear in her head was Kyle's hypnotic voice. She poured a glass of wine and turned on the radio to comfort her in her loneliness and state of confusion. She could hear the Vanessa Williams and Brian McKnight song, _Love Is_. The song was very beautiful and Vanessa sang like an angel. Carmen thought of Lark and how she used to sing just as beautifully. She recalled Lark's memorable rhythmic serenade to the crowd, despite her "loss". What a blessing,...talk about a serious 'Plan B', Carmen thought. She then walked over to the mirror where she stood just before she left to go to Lark's gala. She stared at herself from head to toe for a couple of minutes. _So Carmen, here's your chance to have the man you love. Kyle wants to work things out. He says he love you and will do anything to have you.. What are you going to do?_

Carmen continued to stare at herself. Listening to the lyrics of _Love Is_ made her eyes well up. She felt herself weakening. She took a large gulp of her wine, spilling some of it onto her chin. She thought of Lark again. Then she thought of the conversations she had earlier with Nikki..._two and a half carats and Kyle._ She thought of all the things that she had told herself she would and would never do again. She thought of all the highs and lows, the peaks and valleys of her relationship with Kyle. She remembered all the tears and all the laughter. There was a cinema playing in her head of all the memories...good and bad. The tears from her eyes spilled over onto her face. "Oh God, give me strength," she cried. She continued to stare at herself in the mirror. _Tough one, huh? What are you going to do? You can now have it all. All you have to do is pick up that phone, call the airline, change your flight to return to Atlanta earlier, meet Kyle tomorrow and plan the rest of your life with the man of your dreams. You don't have to settle for less now._ I need a drink. _No, you need guidance. Good guidance. Drinking makes you stupid._ I need help. I'm going crazy. _What do you need help with?_ My decision. _Your decision to do_ *what?* To give Kyle another chance or not. *Haven't we traveled this road before? This seems like awfully familiar territory. What are you going to do?*

Carmen closed her eyes and absorbed only good thoughts about herself. She wanted to rid herself of the demons of low self-esteem. Then she looked at herself again. She stared at herself as if she were face to face with here greatest challenger. She felt defenseless against herself and her emotional dependencies. *Well Carmen, think this through. Give yourself some good advice. What are you going to do?*

Carmen walked into the bedroom. Greeted by the site and scent of roses, she was reminded of Kyle's undying romantic quality. She quickly grabbed the Bible from the nightstand and retreated to the living room, shutting the bedroom door behind her. She finally took off her dress and pantyhose so that she could be more comfortable. She didn't bother to hang the dress up since it was already pretty wrinkled and smelled like the wine she had spilled on it. She placed it across the back of the chair. She felt a little chilly, so she put on a robe and turned the thermostat up a few notches before she sat on the sofa. "God, I need you. I'm afraid to face Kyle. I'm afraid the very site of him will overwhelm my better judgment. I don't trust myself. Please let me trust you. Please tell me what to do. Please help me to find the courage to do whatever it is you would have me to do. Speak to my heart and my head. I'm holding this Bible. It is my strength. Please guide me through the passages so that I may know the voice I hear is from heaven."

Carmen turned immediately to the passage she had read before in the book of *Isaiah*:

The voice says, "shout!"

"What shall I shout?" I asked.

"Shout that man is like the grass that dies away, and all his beauty fades like dying flowers.

The grass withers, the flowers fade beneath the breath of God, and so it is with fragile man.

The grass withers, the flowers fade, but the Word of our God shall stand forever."

Then she turned to the book of *Joshua*. She just kept reading and praying. Then she found a passage that spoke to her powerfully, *Joshua 1:9*,

Yes, be bold and strong! Banish fear and doubt!

For remember the Lord your God is with you wherever you go.

Carmen, this is the voice from heaven. How do you feel?. I feel moved. I feel God is truly with me. *Do you feel any less confused?* I'm getting there. I have so much going on inside my head. *Like what?* Like my whole life…what it has been like. I think about my life before I met Kyle. I think about my life during Kyle. And quite frankly, I'm trying to imagine my life without Kyle. *What are you thinking?* I'm thinking that everything has happened to me for a reason. I'm supposed to grow from my experiences, not regret them. When I think about it, Kyle really taught me a lot…mostly about myself. *Do you think God put Kyle in your life?* Sure, I think God puts most, if not all, people in your life. It is your relationship with him that determines how you interact with the people you encounter. *Are you sorry God put Kyle in your life?* No. Like I said, Kyle really taught me a lot… a lot about love and what it is supposed to be. *You really loved him, huh?* Yes. With all my heart. I'm just praying for the courage to deal with the love I *still* have for him. It's pretty intense. *What are you going to do?* Continue to pray over it.

Carmen clinched the Bible as she held it next to her heart. With her eyes closed, she meditated for about ten minutes without interruption. Then she opened her eyes and breathed a sigh of relief. "I feel courageous now. I know what I'm going to do," she said. "I don't care what people think. I don't care what they say. I don't care if they think I'm a fool. I'm going to do what's right for me." She began packing her things. She didn't quite fill up the extra suitcase she had brought along, since she and Nikki never really got to power shop as they had originally planned.

After her packing was complete, Carmen took a quick

shower. When she dried off, she slipped on a T-shirt and a pair of red satin panties. She then picked up the phone and called her boss in Atlanta, leaving her a message letting her know that she would be taking at least the following Monday and Tuesday off as personal days. She felt the rest of her life was about to change and she needed a couple of days to get used to the idea of moving forward and being happy. She then picked up her purse and unzipped the side to locate her ticket for going back to Atlanta. Without much hesitation, she picked up the phone to call the airline. "Hi, My name is Carmen Layfield. I'm currently scheduled to return to Atlanta later this evening from New York/JFK on Flight #149, departing at 5:30p.m. and arriving at 7:55p.m. I need to change that reservation please..."

After Carmen concluded her call with the reservations agent, she walked into the bedroom and looked at all the roses Kyle had sent her. They were so beautiful. She knew she could not take them with her, so she begin comprising a note to the maid to take one dozen roses for herself and to please have the hotel send the remainder of the flowers to the local hospitals. The roses would certainly brighten someone's day.

Carmen was wide-awake now. She felt rejuvenated. She thought of turning on the television, but decided to continue reading the Bible instead. She was startled when her phone rang. "Nikki, must be having trouble sleeping," she thought. "Hello, Nicolette" she said with assumption.

"Hey, Baby. It's me, Kyle. I couldn't sleep. You sound like you're up, too. What are you doing?"

"Hello, Kyle. I'm just sitting here reading the Bible and counting my blessings," she said.

"Oh, that's nice," said Kyle. "I should be counting my blessings, too...you being one of them. What are you reading in the Bible?" he continued.

"I'm reading in the book of Matthew about forgiving and forgetting," said Carmen.

"That's wonderful, Baby. So did you change your flight?" he asked.

"Oh, absolutely! I just hung up with the airlines a couple of minutes ago," she said. "I bet you thought I would not forgive you, huh?" she continued. "But, ya' know, Babe... I thought about all the things you and I have been through over the past three years. I have no choice but to forgive and forget. You know, put the past where it belongs and get on with being happy."

"Carmen, I feel so relieved to hear you say that. I was so afraid you were going to let Robbi come between us. So, Baby, you forgive me? I'm so happy," Kyle beamed with relief.

Carmen cleared her throat and took a deep breath. She placed the Bible down on the table near the phone. "Good, Baby. That means now we're *both* happy. Whew, I was so afraid I was going to have to settle. I made a promise to myself that I'm never going to settle for anyone who makes me less than happy. Ya' know, so many times we think that by giving up the material things in a relationship means that we are "settling". When in actuality, we are so frequently willing to settle with being *mistreated* by the people we say we love... just to be able to be associated with their material possessions or superficial attributes. Funny, huh? Ya' know what else, Sweetheart?... I never really took the time to just reflect and realize just what I have in you. But now I know. Sometimes I'm a little slow. And you know me, *I'm always late.* But hey, better late than never, right? So, yes, Kyle, Honey, my darling, I *do* forgive you. I really do. And most importantly, more than *anything*, anything in this world, I forgive myself. I forgive myself for being such a *damn* fool for you for so long! *So*, in the spirit of forgiving *and* forgetting...All is forgiven and one more thing, Kyle... YOUR ASS IS FORGOTTEN!" CLICK!!!

Carmen leaped over to the mirror with a big smile on her face. *Praise the Lord. We did it!* "Yelp, we did it! We are loosed! Girlfriend, we have released the wedding funds, the flight reservations are all set, and we're all packed. When the morning comes, we are going power shopping at *Harrods*...in London!"

THE END!

About the Author

Photo by John Howard: Avelco's Photo & Video

Lawanda Howard is a new and emerging novelist. *"Raggedy Panties"* is her first composition. It is a composition that captures the many years of her observations and experiences with life, love and relationships.

She believes her purpose in life is to help others. Her first novel is just one of her methods for reaching out and giving back.

She received a Bachelor of Science degree from the world-renowned Tuskegee University in Tuskegee, Alabama. She currently works as a sales executive for one of the largest companies in the world.

Lawanda is a member of Alpha Kappa Alpha Sorority, Inc. She is also a member of Black Women in Publishing. She currently resides in Atlanta, Georgia, where she is working on here second novel.